VICTORIA

LT. KATE GAZZARA NOVELS BOOK 5

BLAIR HOWARD

DEDICATION

This one is for my friends, Ron Akers, firearms instructor; Gene Flowers, firearms and close combat instructor; and David Young, firearms and shotgun expert.

OCTOBER 2018

"Honey, I'm driving," Marcie Cox said as she clenched her phone between her shoulder and her ear. "Well, we'll see if Alex can stay overnight on Friday. I'll check with his mom. Later, okay? I've got to go. Yes, you can have the last blueberry bagel. I love you, too."

She quickly took her phone in her left hand and hit the tiny red circle to disconnect. Of course her twelve-year-old son Gary had to call while she was trying to get to work, especially when she'd told him to call only if it were an emergency. Such an emergency would, of course, include him wanting to know if Alex could spend the night on Friday.

She took a deep breath and dropped the phone on the empty passenger seat. Normally, she wouldn't be so aggravated, but an accident, a jack-knifed semi on I-75, had caused a traffic backup almost to Ooltewah, well, Bonny Oaks, anyway.

"Mrs. Randolph," Marcie said to herself, out loud, rehearsing her excuse, "I'm sorry I'm a little late, but there was an accident on I-75. It was sooo bad, you wouldn't believe it. I'm sure if you turn on the radio, you'll hear all about it."

Victoria Randolph was the worst of her clients. Anyone else would say that being fifteen minutes late due to a traffic accident was not a big deal. Especially when it rarely happened inside the city limits. Maybe in the winter when the streets were covered with black ice, or if a springtime rainstorm hit early in the morning, would Marcie run a little late. Oh yeah, normal people would understand, but not the Randolphs.

Marcie shook her head as she turned north onto Shallowford Road, heading in the opposite direction of her destination in order to avoid the train of cars. Marcie decided to take the roundabout route and so, of course, did everyone else in the southbound lanes.

At North Terrace she rejoined the interstate, I-25, at Market Street, and from there to Scenic Highway and Lookout Mountain.

"If she starts anything with you, Marcie, just quit. Tell her to shove it," she said to herself, ignoring the stunning views to her left. "Just quit, okay? And find another client or two to replace her."

That was easier said than done. The Randolph family was her wealthiest client. What Marcie made cleaning their home alone paid for her son's tennis lessons. Tennis lessons were expensive. But Gary was exceptionally good at it; his coach said so.

And Marcie also knew it burned Victoria Randolph that her son got private lessons from the same coach to whom she sent her two daughters. It wasn't very Christian, but Marcie didn't think the Lord would banish her to the fiery pit for this one small indulgence. Besides, He knew what kind of woman Victoria Randolph was.

"Where does your son go to school?" Victoria had asked when she interviewed Marcie for the weekly housekeeping job.

"He attends Whitewater Preparatory School," Marcie had replied proudly.

"I see," Victoria had said, wrinkling her nose slightly. "How nice. And what does your husband do?"

Marcie had cleared her throat. "He's in construction."

She hadn't liked the line of questioning, but she needed the job. One job on Lookout Mountain might lead to more if she could impress the Randolphs. Little did she know that nothing impressed Victoria Randolph.

"Construction? Oh how nice." She didn't actually roll her eyes, but she might as well have with that condescending tone she used. Oh well!

Marcie shivered at the recollection of that interview. At the time, she'd wanted to work for the Randolph family, confident that her happy personality and reliability might crack through their hard shell. She'd never been so wrong, and every Thursday she found herself considering the same thing. Quitting.

The thought of quitting the Randolph family was a tempting one. But Victoria was well-connected. For a

woman who had come from even more humble beginnings than Marcie did, she had climbed the social ladder
with impressive speed. Of course, being tall with an hour-
glass figure and long blond hair hadn't hurt.

Marcie looked in the rearview mirror, smoothing her
plain brown hair that she'd pulled back into a ponytail.
She was wearing black yoga pants and a white T-shirt—
her standard uniform when she arrived to clean a client's
home.

"Just remember the money, Marcie," she muttered to
herself as she pulled into the long cobblestone driveway.

When she'd interviewed with Victoria and her
husband Darby, Marcie remembered thinking how the
trickling, natural stone fountain in the front yard was the
most beautiful thing she'd ever seen. Now, it made her
insides recoil as she dreaded setting foot inside the house.

Victoria, after seeing that Marcie drove an old Dodge
Neon, had her park behind the guest house and walk to
the back entrance. Normally, that wouldn't bother her.
But on days when it was raining or cold, or when she was
running late, it added another five minutes to her trek just
to get inside the house. She'd been going through this
routine for six months now. It wasn't getting any easier.

"Lord, keep one hand on my shoulder and the other
over my mouth," she muttered as she parked, grabbed her
caddy of cleaning supplies, and locked up her car before
heading to the main house.

Marcie knew that as soon as Victoria realized she was
there, she'd give her that look. Her lips would be pinched
together, and she'd look at Marcie as if she had shown up

on a day she wasn't scheduled. She'd have something sarcastic to say like "Oh, you *are* working today then," or "Oh, I see you managed to make it after all."

She felt like Sisyphus, but instead of pushing a boulder up a hill only to have it roll back down, she was carrying cleaning supplies that kept getting heavier and heavier with every step. She was sure that Victoria didn't know who Sisyphus was. A woman didn't have to be smart if she looked like Victoria did.

As she reached the back door and pulled out her keys, Marcie seriously thought about turning around and leaving. But she didn't. She opened the door, steeled her nerves and went inside, locking the door behind her. Normally, there would be the pounding of footsteps as Victoria came running down the stairs to confront her. But this time, as Marcie stood there listening and holding her breath, she didn't hear anything. She let her breath out slowly... relieved.

"I better buy a lottery ticket because today might just be my lucky day." She smiled as she headed across the mudroom and up the stairs to the middle level of the house.

Not quite convinced that this wasn't some kind of setup, a new game Victoria might be playing, Marcie entered the kitchen slowly and carefully and looked around.

The girls were at school already, she knew, and by then Darby would have left for the office. He thought he was a big-shot lawyer, but everyone knew he rode on his grandfather's coattails.

Hmm, Marcie thought, *Victoria must have a social engagement, or maybe something's going on at the church... No, she would have left a note.*

That was something else that always agitated Marcie. Victoria had wrangled herself a part-time job at the church. You'd think that Jesus Christ Himself had come down in all His glory and pointed to Victoria anointing her as His holy secretary.

"I don't *need* to work," Victoria had made sure to tell Marcie. "But I just feel like I'm being called. And Pastor Ed was kind enough to offer me a position in the church office." She then followed it up with a lecture on how Marcie would be responsible for her duties at times when Victoria wasn't there to check up on her.

Marcie had not had a single complaint from any of her clients in her more than a decade-long career as a housekeeper. She enjoyed the work. She knew how to do it. And without being too prideful, she had to admit she was good at it. But if she was fired from this job, she could kiss goodbye any future employment possibilities at the residences of the movers and shakers on Lookout Mountain. Her goal was to find one more client in the neighborhood and then drop the Randolph family.

"Pastor Ed has no idea what he's getting himself into," Marcie mumbled to herself, shaking her head as she began her chores.

In the old Southern tradition, Victoria designated Thursday as silver polishing day for Marcie, in addition to her regular duties of changing the sheets and pillowcases, mopping the kitchen floor and counters, clearing cobwebs from the corners of the ceiling, and the weekly laundry that included ironing. That was what she decided to do first. While the laundry tumbled in the machine in the basement, she'd polish the silver. By the time all the laundry was washed and dried, the silver would be spotless and sparkling. Well, that was the plan.

The laundry basket was in a closet upstairs, on the same level as the four bedrooms. She climbed the hardwood stairs, dragged the basket out into the hallway, then went to the girls' room to grab whatever they'd left lying around. Of course the room was pink with their names, Taylor and Courtney, emblazoned on the walls in giant letters. The bedroom was as big as Marcie's living room. She shook her head at the extravagance of it all: luxury on a scale she'd never know, and that was just the kids' room.

She picked up the stray socks and T-shirts that were on the floor, opened the hamper in the corner of the room, and grabbed the rest of their laundry. She stood for a moment and looked around the room. Every flat surface was covered with girlie things: nail polish, dozens of hair ribbons and barrettes, teen magazines and popular books for young adults. Marcie sighed, looked at the unmade beds and shook her head. She'd strip them and make them up with clean sheets and pillowcases after she'd finished doing the laundry.

She dumped the kids' dirties into the basket and went to the master bedroom. For the umpteenth time, she admired the beautiful décor, the California king four-poster bed, antique dresser, chairs, hope chest, and a down comforter that would have made Scarlett O'Hara pea green with envy, as it did her.

She finished grabbing laundry upstairs, grasped the heavy laundry basket, and headed downstairs to the basement. Her arms aching from the weight of the basket, she had to set it down on the kitchen counter for a moment. With any luck she'd be done and out of the house by three o'clock, just in time to welcome Gary home from school.

"Okay, let's get this done as quickly as possible," Marcie said to herself as she hoisted the heavy basket onto her shoulder. Carefully, she negotiated the stairs to the basement, the mudroom, turned right and with her foot pushed open the door to the laundry room. To the left of the laundry room was a beautifully furnished basement—an apartment with a kitchen, full bathroom, and guestroom. It was rarely used so Marcie had no reason to go in there.

Her usual routine was to walk into the laundry room, set the basket on the washing machine, then turn and flip on the light. Today was no different. When the light came on, she blinked and rubbed her eyes. She turned to the laundry basket, grabbed it, and then banged it down on the long table set against the far wall.

She dumped its contents on the table, picked up a piece of clothing and... something not quite right, something out of place caught her eye.

Victoria Randolph was very particular about there being a place for everything and everything being in its place, which is why she noticed it.

What on earth? she thought. *Who dumped that there, I wonder? And what's with all the red paint on the wall?* Those were the thoughts that went through Marcie's mind as she looked toward what looked like a heap of clothing flung into the corner of the room. Her eyes saw the body, but Marcie's brain didn't register what her eyes were seeing.

Must be a trick of the light, she thought. *A pile of clothing, that's what it is. Nothing more.* Her mind was racing, trying to find a rational explanation for what she was seeing. *But the paint... it's not... paint. It's blood.*

Marcie stood stock still, staring into the corner, and she began to tremble. With one of Darby's button-down shirts clenched tightly in both hands against her chest, she stepped slowly away from the table toward the heap. What she'd thought to be a pile of clothes morphed into a crumpled-up body. What she'd thought was a shadow on the floor next to the body was blood, darker in places where it had pooled in the folds of skin and fabric. One leg was extended, the other twisted unnaturally beneath the body. A woman's body.

"Oh, my God! Victoria?" Marcie whispered, and jumped at the sound of her own voice. Not that the thing on the floor was going to answer her, because the entire left side of what had been her face was shattered, unrecognizable.

From where she was standing, Marcie had the incongruous thought that someone had taken a pound of ground sirloin and slapped it on her boss's pretty face, leaving it to hang and drip there. If only that was true, but it wasn't. Victoria's face had been smashed, mangled, almost beyond recognition. But that wasn't all. Her body had been beaten bloody.

And then Marcie had a horrible thought, *Oh, my God... Somebody killed her. I'm here all by myself. What if the murderer is still in the house?*

She put her hands, still clutching Darby's shirt, to her mouth, staggered backward against the table, still staring at what once had been her employer, looked wildly toward the door, then dropped the shirt and ran to the door, out and up the stairs to the kitchen, grabbed the phone from its cradle, ran outside, down the steps, and didn't stop until she was at the end of the driveway where, shaking uncontrollably, she dialed 911.

It was less than five minutes later when the first police cruiser screeched to a stop beside Marcie Cox, now calm, but red-eyed and cooperative. Had they arrived only one minute earlier, they would have seen her violently retching into the hydrangeas.

2

I hated going into McDonald's for a coffee to go. It was just across the street from the Police Services Center on Amnicola, and that meant every cop in the building was in there at one time or another throughout the day. Yes, I know, I could go through the drive-through, but that was an even worse nightmare. No matter the time of day, the line was always all the way out to the street. It was quicker to run inside and... well, I'm sure you've done it yourself.

Anyway, unfortunately, that also meant the likelihood of me running into someone I know and getting sidetracked was more than a possibility. Talking shop in a fast-foody wasn't really a break; it was an off-sight meeting.

There were days when I didn't mind such meetings, but that day I just didn't want to talk at all. I was waiting on results from the lab, hoping for a match on some DNA. The case was over three months old, and it was the one thread I had that I hoped would sew it up for me. It was a bit of a Hail Mary, but stranger things had happened. But I'd learned the hard way, a long time ago, that when all your eggs are in just one basket, rarely does it turn out the way you want it to.

So, instead of McDonald's, I decided to drive to Hamilton Place and stand in line at Starbucks, ready to fork over too much money for a black large. So there I was, drink already ordered, waiting, happily dreaming about nothing at all when my cell phone rang. *Tracy*, I thought when I looked at the screen. *Damn!*

"Look, Tracy," I grumbled into the phone, "you begged me for this one, and I was happy to hand it over. Now you want me to help you with it? If you think I want to be up to my eyeballs in semen and spit, you're crazy."

As the words left my mouth, I happened to glance at a barista on the other side of the counter from me. He had a beard, was wearing a knit cap, his forearms were covered with tattoos, and he stared at me wide-eyed as I continued to speak.

"Yes," I said into the phone. "Yes... No... Okay, go check with Collins. I think he has a CI over there. If so, he—or she—might be able to help. But don't tell him I told you. And I can't promise anything will come of it, but it's what I would do. Now, can I get back to work?"

Detective John Tracy was not my favorite person. Not by a long shot, but boy did I ever owe him.

To his face we called him either John or Tracy.

Behind his back he was Dick Tracy, or just Dick, which he was, and is.

Back in the day, for just a few weeks, he was my partner. It didn't work out and I... well, we won't go into that. It's a long story and not a pretty one. It was ironic then, that not too long ago, the man saved my life—literally. And I have to say that for a vice cop, at that moment when I was sure I was going to become the next day's headlines, he came through like a pro.

But for me... well, there was no way I could repay him for saving my ass, so I handed him a juicy case that had all the makings of a Quentin Tarantino movie. Drugs, sex, a seedy gambling house: it was like his birthday, Christmas, and New Year's Eve at five to midnight all wrapped up in one neat package.

I won't lie. I would have loved to have kept the case for myself, but Tracy played the puppy-dog-eyes ploy and like I said, I owed him.

"You think? Well, okay. Good luck, John," I said before tapping the red button on my phone to disconnect the call.

"Kate! Black grande!" a different barista shouted at the other end of the counter. What a production. I grabbed the paper cup, made sure that it was my name scribbled on the side, with a smiley face, and I left the coffee shop.

I'm Lieutenant Catherine Gazzara, by the way; Kate to my friends and just about everyone else, so it seems, even my superiors. I'm a homicide detective assigned to the Major Crimes Unit of the Chattanooga PD. I'm thirty-six years old, and I've been a cop since I graduated from college in 2002. For six years I was partnered with Harry Starke—you've heard of him, right? If you haven't, you're not living on this planet. Anyway, he quit the force in 2008 and I became a lead detective, which is when Henry Finkle foisted Tracy on me as my partner.

Harry? He and I had been something more than just partners. There was a time when I thought we'd be even more still. But, never mind about that. Harry went into business for himself: Harry Starke Investigations. He... Oh hell, I don't know why I'm telling you all this. It's not really relevant to this story—not at this point anyway.

So I grabbed my coffee and left the coffee shop—the hairy barista unashamedly watching my ass. Of course, the stuff was too hot to drink so, as I walked back to my car with my purse hooked over my shoulder and my phone still in my right hand, I checked the time. The lab didn't like getting calls before eleven o'clock; it was ten thirty-three. Damn!

And then my phone rang again.

"I don't like getting calls before eleven o'clock either, but that doesn't stop anyone," I muttered before answering it.

"Hey, LT." It was the very chipper, newly appointed Detective Janet Toliver. My new partner of just ten days when Lonnie Guest retired, much to my dismay. "I got some news for you this morning. You ready?"

"Lay it on me." I shook my head as I took a sip of coffee, knowing it was hot but unwilling to wait any longer.

"First, I was called detective this morning by one of the uniforms," she said.

I waited for the rest like they'd catcalled or maybe made some derogatory remark.

"And?"

"And? Isn't that great? They all know I'm Detective Toliver now."

I could almost hear her smiling like a lunatic on the other end of the phone and couldn't help joining her. I remember how I felt the first time I was called detective. There is something about it, that first time. Like when the first rays of sun come up after a girl's wedding night. Everything has changed.

"It is. What is the second, Toliver?"

"Ah, yes. We got a call. A homicide at 400 Laurel Lane, Lookout Mountain. Female. Found by the house-keeper. We're to get up there ASAP."

"Lookout Mountain?" I yawned. "They've got their own police chief. I think he's also the fire chief."

Lookout Mountain is a small but very exclusive community set high atop the mountain of the same name. It's where the elite of Chattanooga live. Just the address bestows a level of prestige that most of us peons would never know. Harry and Mrs. Starke live up there on East Brow Road. *It doesn't come more prestigious than that.* I thought. *Good for you, Harry.*

"Yeah," Janet said, "Chief Wilbur. He responded to Miss Cox's call. The situation requires they bring in the big guns, I guess."

I smiled at that. Janet was enjoying her new status,

perhaps a little too much. Maybe I should take her down a little? Nah. She's fun. Can't dampen that youthful enthusiasm.

"If we are the big guns, that's kind of pitiful." I chuckled. "Okay, Janet, talk to me. Is it a residence or business?"

"Residence."

"I'll meet you at Amnicola in..." I checked my watch. "Let's say fifteen minutes. Call Mike Willis and tell him I said to stand by."

"You got it, LT."

"Fifteen minutes," I said. "Be at the door, Janet. We'll leave right away."

"Yes, ma'am," she replied and hung up.

Ma'am? What am I, the queen? Geez.

I took another gulp of the hot coffee that was just the perfect temperature now, climbed into my unmarked cruiser, turned on the blue lights and the siren, and swung the big vehicle out of the Starbucks lot. I weaved my way through the traffic onto Shallowford, swerved left onto I-75 then right onto Highway 153 to Amnicola Highway and the police department; I made it in thirteen minutes.

Janet, bless her heart, was standing out front. She saw me and ran out to meet me, jumped into the passenger side, and away we went.

I glanced sideways as Janet took out her little notepad and smiled to myself when I saw the CPD sticker she'd applied to the front cover. She flipped it open and began to fill me in on the few details she had already gathered.

Her handwriting was loopy and neat, and I wouldn't have been surprised to see she dotted her "I's" with tiny hearts or smiley faces, but she didn't.

"Okay," she said. "The address is 400 Laurel Lane. The initial call to LMPD came in from the family's housekeeper, a Marcie Cox. She's worked for the family for several months. Chief Wilbur said that the woman is in shock. It sounded like he was, too."

"I can't say that I blame him," I said.

"Wow. Do you believe these houses?" Janet asked as we drove through the Lookout Mountain neighborhood. "The lawns look like they are covered in carpet, not grass."

I nodded but didn't say anything. The houses were beautiful. Added together, I'd say the inhabitants of Lookout Mountain here in Tennessee had some of the oldest money in the country. I doubt a new family had moved into this part of town since Lincoln was president. Okay, that might be an exaggeration. But to some people, marrying into the right families was more important than being in love, not that I was an expert in such things.

I parked on the street outside the home, noting the brass plaque that informed me and any other interested party that we had arrived at the Randolph Estate, Established 1854. There was one black-and-white cruiser and an ambulance already there. We exited the vehicle, and I immediately spotted a woman who was sitting with a blanket around her in the back of the ambulance staring at the wall, unblinking, with the EMT taking her blood pressure.

"That must be the housekeeper who found the body," I said to Janet. "Go talk to her. I'll see what's happening inside. Be gentle, okay?"

Janet nodded, strutted the few steps toward the ambulance, her badge in one hand and her notebook in the other. I saw her extend her hand to the woman who was looking terribly shaken up. *The girl will make a good detective once the green has worn off.*

Me? I strolled along the short driveway to the house. The rear door was open. I entered, flashed my badge at the uniformed officer, told him who I was, and he showed me to the door that led to the basement. I thanked him, watched him go back to his post at the rear entrance, then I turned in the opposite direction and walked into what I took to be the living room. I wanted to get a feel for the place before I did anything else.

The house was even more beautiful on the inside than it was on the outside. It was an extravagant world of fancy crown moldings against high ceilings, stark white walls with hardwood accents, banisters, doors, and trim. I'm no interior designer, but I know expensive when I see it. The Randolph residence was top-notch, spotless, a place for everything and... you get the idea. The furniture looked new, untouched by human hand or butt. It was an old-world parlor intended for only entertaining and pre-dinner cocktails; no television and, as far as I could tell, no signs of a struggle.

There were family photos on the mantle over the natural stone fireplace, and on the bookcases, and on the... Is that a harpsichord, for Pete's sake? Victoria

Randolph was featured in almost every one of them. I was especially surprised to see the wedding pictures. Umm, not the pictures exactly, but the wedding dress.

It was crystal clear that it was not the image of a blushing Southern bride she was going for. I'd never had a problem with a well-endowed woman using the gifts the good Lord had bestowed upon her, but among Tennessee's high society you didn't show 'em off at church, and you sure as hell didn't display them for all to see at your own church wedding.

Wow, and I thought I was lucky in that area, not so much, I thought gazing at her stunning figure. *No wonder Darby Randolph is smiling,* I thought, as I moved on out of there.

The kitchen was all white, everything, walls, counter-tops, cupboards, even the floors. I wondered if she hired Jo and Chip to design the interior. It sure looked like it. Not that I spent much time watching HGTV, but enough to recognize the style. My kitchenette was beige, an easy-on-the-eye baby-poop beige I found almost impossible to keep clean. Bubbling spaghetti sauce is not conducive to clean walls, or floor, or backsplash or anything and, try as I might, I couldn't imagine cooking anything at all in an all-white kitchen. *Who am I kidding? They probably have a cook as well as the house-keeper.* Even so—

"Detective?"

Startled, I turned quickly and was relieved to recognize Chief Wilbur, who I assumed had just come up from the basement. Poor guy. He didn't look at all well... No, he looked like he'd just come up from below decks on a boat heading out of a perfect storm.

"Chief Wilbur," I said, holding out my hand to greet him. "Lieutenant Gazzara, Homicide." I flashed my badge and creds.

He shook my hand, weakly, and I continued, "By the look on your face, I have a feeling I'm not ready for this."

He nodded and wiped his brow with the back of his hand.

"That bad, huh?" I asked, still making a mental note that there were no signs of a forced entry and, so far as I could tell, nothing in the kitchen seemed to have been disturbed.

"Detective Gazzara," he said in a low voice. "Thank you for helping us out. Yes, it's bad. More than we can handle, that's for sure."

Chief Wilbur was, to put it politely, a robust man who hadn't had to chase a suspect on foot in many a long year, if ever. He was about five-ten, an inch shorter than me in bare feet, gray, balding, impeccably dressed in a fitted blue uniform with two stars on each collar. He wore a gold band on his left ring finger and... well, it was a smart look spoiled by the cheap, gold-plated watch on his right wrist: the plating was worn to the point where dull gray metal showed through.

"I understand," I said.

"You'll need to get your ME up here," he said. "And forensic team. We don't have anyone to assist and no place to put her, what's left of her." Wilbur looked down at the glistening floor, shook his head, and said, "Frankly,

Detective, I don't mind passing this one off. I've got two years left until I retire. I've seen enough. When I took this job here in Lookout Mountain, I was sure I'd be able to skate through with nothing worse than a burglary to handle, the occasional domestic, but nothing like this."

"You should know better than that, Chief." I smiled at him, sympathetically. "When did police work ever go without a hitch? It's like, well, expecting a politician to be honest."

"You've got me there, Lieutenant. Listen, I've got to get some air. Go on down and take a look. It's a freakin' abattoir down there, a hell hole. We'll talk when... when you come up for air." He stepped past me and headed outside.

I pulled out my phone and called Mike Willis and asked him to get moving, and then I called Doc Sheddon. It went to voice mail.

I sighed, silently to myself, then left him a message, "Doc, when you get this message call me back. Need your help on Lookout Mountain. Thanks."

Doc Sheddon, Hamilton County's chief medical examiner, knew my voice even if he didn't know my number by heart. We'd worked on lots of cases together. I'd hear from him soon.

As I carefully made my way down the stairs to the basement, I had a bad feeling in my gut. I'd seen some horrific crime scenes during years as a homicide detective, but very few that were so bad I could sense it before I even saw the body. This... was one of those occasions.

3

I reached the bottom of the steps to find the entire floor flooded with bright sunlight from the wall-to-ceiling windows, something I wasn't expecting because, from the street view, the house had only two stories.

At first glance, the white tiled floor appeared to be spotless. It wasn't. I spotted what looked like two small bloody smudges on the wall and two scuff marks on the floor.

"A white mudroom? That's just over-the-top," I muttered, trying to imagine what it would look like after a midwinter rainstorm.

I shook my head and made my way across the mudroom and turned right into a short passageway. A uniformed officer stood outside the door to what I assumed must be the laundry room.

I held up my badge.

He nodded, stepped to one side, grabbed the doorknob, pushed open the door and, without turning to look inside, said, "She's in there." Like Chief Wilbur, the officer was visibly shaken.

"Thank you, Officer... Quinn," I said, squinting at his name tag, then taking a pair of latex gloves and a pair of Tyvek shoe covers from my jacket pocket, put them on and entered the room, closing the door behind me.

"Holy cow," I muttered to myself when I saw what was left of her head. "Whose cat did you kick?"

The left side of her head from just above the ear to the jaw was practically caved in. She was wearing a burgundy skirt with a white blouse. I stood beside the body, not wanting to disturb anything, and observed some anomalous blood stains. At first, I thought they were tears in the fabric of the blouse. I crouched down and inspected them closely, and I realized they were stab wounds, but unlike any I'd ever seen before. The fabric had been rammed deep into the flesh.

I shook my head, leaned in closely. "How in the world?"

From what little I could see without moving her, I could tell that Mrs. Randolph hadn't put up much of a fight. There were no defensive wounds.

I stood up, took a step back, looked around the room once more, then turned and walked to the door, opened it, and stepped out into the passageway.

"Do you know if the rest of the house has been searched?" I asked the officer.

"I don't think so, well, just the basics, Detective. Chief Wilbur said to leave it to the experts."

"Who was in the house when you all arrived?"

"Just the housekeeper. Except, really, she wasn't in the house. She was outside. She was the only one here. The two girls had left for school, and Mr. Randolph had left for work, so the housekeeper said."

I nodded. "Stay here. Don't come in," I said as I turned and went back inside the laundry room, leaving the door open.

"So that doesn't leave a lot of time," I said, loud enough for the officer to hear. "Yet the place is almost spotless."

I took out my iPhone, turned on the flashlight and shined it across the spatter on the white cement wall and then on the tiled floor. Other than the small amount of spatter, there wasn't much else, just a few tiny smudges, including those I'd spotted when I first entered the room.

I turned to face the officer who was standing at the door watching me.

"The place had been cleaned," I said.

He shook his head and said, "I don't see how. There wasn't no one here except the housekeeper. We didn't find no signs of forced entry. No signs of a struggle. Nothing missing as far as we can tell. The Chief called the husband, told him there was a problem but didn't tell him what it was. He's on his way here now."

"How did you get his number?" I asked.

"Darby Randolph? Wasn't hard. The guy's known all over Chattanooga, Detective," the officer offered.

"He is?" I asked.

"Yeah. He's the grandson of Alexander Randolph."

Quinn must have seen the stupor on my face. "Governor Randolph?"

"Oh, I remember; the guy who had the Little League scandal a few years ago?"

"That's the guy," Quinn replied. He didn't look at me when he spoke. Instead, he turned his head like I was changing my clothes and he was trying to be a gentleman.

Many years ago—I don't remember exactly how many—the then Governor Randolph had been accused of taking kickbacks... free luxury vacations, to be precise. Nothing was ever proved and the investigation, if it could be called that, was eventually dropped and, with time, all was forgotten. Ha, not really. It still comes up now and again, as it did then.

"Great," I said, rolling my eyes. "A politician's grandson. Please tell me you've been able to keep a lid on things. The press will be salivating all over every little detail as soon as this gets out."

Quinn shrugged, then said, "As far as I know, the only call that went out was to you."

I nodded, walked across the laundry room still shining my flashlight. Compared to the rest of the house, this room was like a dungeon. There was only one small window that was at ground level with the yard and it was glazed with glass block, the kind you can't see through.

"Okay," I said. "Nobody in; nobody out until Doc Sheddon or Lieutenant Mike Willis and his CSI team get here. Got it?"

"Got it," Quinn said.

I walked to the door and turned again to look back

into the room. I didn't feel good about it. There was... something. I shook my head. I was frustrated, but there was little I could do but wait.

"I have a feeling we are overlooking something, Quinn," I said. "It's just too clean."

"I thought the same thing," he said, "and the chief commented on it, too."

I sighed and headed back upstairs just in time for the ruckus.

"Victoria? Victoria!" a male voice shouted, obviously that of Mr. Darby Randolph. He was in the kitchen. As soon as he saw me, he charged at me.

"Whoa!" I said loudly and put my left hand up and my right hand on my pepper spray. "Mr. Randolph—"

"Where's my wife!" he shouted, interrupting me.

"Mr. Randolph, you need to calm down," I said, holding up my badge. "I'm Lieutenant Catherine Gazzara, and I need you to take a step back. Now, sir!"

And he did exactly that. He stopped dead in his tracks, then took a single step back.

"Where is she? Where's Victoria?"

"I'm afraid your wife has suffered a severe injury to the head. Mr. Randolph, your wife is dead, sir."

Yes, I know. It was cold of me to lay it on him like that, but the man was hysterical. I couldn't let him go charging down to the basement to be confronted by Quinn, who wouldn't hesitate to restrain him by any means necessary. Fortunately, it didn't come to that.

"What?" he whispered.

I saw the color drain from his face.

"I'm sorry, Mr. Randolph," I said quietly. "Your wife... is dead."

He stared at me, his mouth wide open, slowly shaking his head.

"No," he said. "Nooooo."

Darby Randolph was a tall man, impeccably dressed in a dark blue business suit, white shirt, light blue tie, and tan Oxford shoes. I looked at his hands. There were no cuts or scratches that I could see, no blood on his hands, clothes, or shoes.

"Are you all right, Mr. Randolph?" I asked, taking a step toward him.

He looked like he was about to fall.

"She's dead?" He blinked then shook his head. "She can't be. You're wrong. She was here this morning. She was sleeping when I left for work. I had to go to the office early. I had work to do; important work... I had to get some work done that I should have done yesterday." He was almost babbling. The enormity of it was slowly sinking in. He swayed.

"Please, Mr. Randolph. Sit down." I motioned for him to take a seat on one of the stools at the kitchen island. Before I could ask any questions, my phone went off... and then my phone rang. It was Doc Sheddon's number.

I told Randolph that I had to take the call and that I'd be just a minute, then I went out into the living room and took the call.

"Hey, Doc."

"We're starting rather early this morning, aren't we Detective?"

"Sorry, Doc. We have a bad one. I need you, ASAP."

I heard him sigh. "You'll be the death of me, young lady. Fine. Tell me where."

I smirked and gave him the address.

"Lookout Mountain? Hmm, most peculiar. All right. I'll be there shortly."

I returned to the kitchen and Darby Randolph.

4

M ike Willis and his team arrived just as I was ending my call with Doc Sheddon, and they quickly locked down the crime scene. There was no room for me down there, but I knew Mike would come and get me if he needed to, so I continued my conversation with Darby Randolph.

I opened my iPad, tapped the icon to activate the record app, informed him I'd be recording the conversation, and then, as gently as I could, I gave him a very limited version of what I thought might have happened, leaving out the gory details.

"Can I see her?" he asked, subdued. "Oh, Lord, please let me see her."

"Not yet, Mr. Randolph," I replied. "Lieutenant Willis has secured the scene, and Dr. Sheddon, the medical examiner, is on his way. You really don't want to see her just now."

I watched his reaction as I said it. His face was pale,

his look stoic. He'd slipped into that weird state of calm that people in his situation often do as the magnitude of what has happened sinks in. It isn't acceptance or understanding. It is usually the calm before the storm.

"Mr. Randolph, I'd like you to tell me about the events of this morning."

Darby stared at the kitchen counter, then at his hands. They were meticulously clean, the fingernails impeccably manicured and... clear-polished.

"I..." he began hesitantly. "I had billing to do. It has to be done by the fifteenth of every month. Today's the seventeenth. I was late because I had depositions all day for the past two days." He folded his hands in front of him and looked up at the ceiling. "If I'd stayed late on Monday and did my work like I was supposed to, maybe—"

"But you didn't," I said, interrupting him. "And you left this morning before the rest of the family arose? What time would that have been?"

"No, the girls were already up, ready for school. I gave them cereal for breakfast, and we left the house at around seven. I dropped the girls off at school, and from there I went to the office. Victoria was still in bed, asleep. She's not... wasn't an early riser."

"Can you think of anyone who might want to hurt your wife, anyone who might have a grudge?"

"No!" He looked sharply at me, then continued, "My wife was an angel, a saint, Detective, a living saint. Oh, I know what you're thinking. Everyone says that about their loved one."

I tilted my head to the right and stared at him, quizzically.

"But it's true," he continued. "You can ask anyone who knows her." He paused for a second or two, then continued, staring down at his hands. "My wife came from very humble beginnings," he said very quietly. "She never forgot that. She never forgot her roots."

He sat up straight and cleared his throat. "She was a wonderful wife, thought only of helping others. She volunteered at the food pantry at our church. In fact, Pastor Ed at our church just hired her as his new assistant. She was a friend to everyone she met. And our daughters, she..." And then he lost it, he broke down, tears streaming down his cheeks. He lowered his head into his hands, and he sobbed, blubbered. "How am I going to tell our daughters? What will they do without their mother? And what am I going to do without her?"

"Excuse me, Detective?"

Was I ever grateful for the interruption. I twisted around in my seat.

"Yes, Chief Wilbur?" I said as I rose and joined him just inside the kitchen door

"Doctor Sheddon's here. He's gone around the back. Coming in the same way the housekeeper did. By the way, I had my officers do a search of the outside of the house. They found no sign of a break in; nothing appeared to be disturbed, but I... I dunno, Detective, something doesn't seem right." He shrugged.

"Okay, and thank you, Chief, but I imagine Mike

Willis will want to search the grounds in detail," I said. "How's the housekeeper doing?"

"Still talking with Detective Toliver."

I nodded and decided I needed some air before I went downstairs to join Doc and Mike, but just as I was about to head downstairs, Janet appeared in the kitchen doorway. For such a young woman, her poker face was perfection.

"Chief," I said quietly. "Would you mind asking one of your officers to watch Mr. Randolph? The last thing I need is for him to go charging downstairs. He's in shock, and I think a familiar face might help."

"Sure, Detective. Just give me a holler if you need anything else."

He tapped his radio and asked officer Quinn to join him. Randolph was still seated beside the kitchen island, his head in his hands, weeping silently.

I put a hand to Janet's elbow and steered her out of the kitchen.

"What did you find?" I asked her quietly.

She consulted her notebook.

I really must get the girl an iPad.

"The housekeeper's name is Marcie Cox," she began. "She's worked here for six months, well a week shy of six months, actually."

I couldn't help but roll my eyes; thankfully, she didn't catch it.

"She's not a shy woman. Didn't hesitate to inform me that it's the worst job on her route," Janet said quietly, her lips barely moving as she looked up and around the foyer in which we were standing, probably trying to gauge the cost of the furnishings, just as I had.

"Really?" I said.

She nodded. "That's what she said. She also said she'd never pray for harm to come to anyone but, and I quote, "That Mrs. Randolph is not a nice lady. Mean-spirited, always bragging, nothing is ever right for her."

Hmm, I thought. *That doesn't quite gel with what her husband just told me.*

"Okay, Janet. Right now, I need to go talk to Doc. So we'll talk later, in the car."

I turned and peered into the kitchen at Randolph. He had his arms crossed on top of the island, his face hidden in the crook of his elbow. His shoulders were shaking; the man was still crying... *If he's faking it, he's one hell of an actor.*

I turned again to Janet and said, "Why don't you look around upstairs while I go check in with Doc. I'll come and find you when I'm done down there, okay?"

Janet nodded before slowly and carefully going up the winding staircase to the upper level. She pulled out her flashlight even though the entire house was bright and, dare I say, cheery? She shined it along the floor-boards and in the corners. I smiled: for a rookie, she was doing just fine.

I descended the stairs to the basement and the laundry room with Marcie Cox's words echoing in my head: "Worst job on her route." *What did that mean?* I wondered. *Hardest? Most boring? Worst pay?*

I needed answers, but I didn't want to ask Darby, give

him the heads-up that the "angelic" Victoria Randolph might not be quite the saint he thought she was. Darby was her husband and that, by definition, made him my prime suspect. That was a given, and it also meant he was about to come into serious, in-depth scrutiny.

Will his alibi hold up, or did he simply drop off the kids then come on back home and beat his wife to death? Did anyone see him at his office, I wonder? If not...

Even without any physical evidence, in situations like this, the spouse is always at the top of the list of suspects.

I stepped off the stairs into the mudroom. Mike Willis and his team were working in the basement apartment. If I could, if he could make time, I'd talk to him a little later, when I'd consulted with the medical examiner.

5

"Hey, Doc," I said, taking a tentative step into the laundry room.

He was down on one knee beside the body, head covered, a surgical mask over his mouth and nose, latex gloves on his hands.

"Hello, Kate. Give me just one moment, will you, please, and I'll be with you," he said, without looking up as he delicately touched Victoria's head.

Doctor Richard Sheddon was a small man in his late fifties, five-eight, overweight, almost totally bald, with a round face that usually sported a jovial expression, but not today.

Finally, he turned his head, looked up at me, and stood. "You were right, Kate. This is a bad one; one of the worst I've seen in quite a while."

"Indeed," I said. "I hope I didn't ruin your breakfast."

Doc's incongruously large black bag was open, close at hand, but his hands were empty.

"Ah, my dear Kate. It would take a lot more than this to ruin my breakfast." He glanced down at the body.

"We have something of an anomaly," he said thoughtfully. "She's been dead for a while."

"What do you mean for a while?"

"Since last night. Judging by the liver temperature, the state of rigor, at least ten hours, give or take an hour. I'd say she died sometime around midnight. Here, take a look."

I stepped closer.

"Closer, young lady," he said and crouched down again beside the body. "See... come closer, look here."

Victoria was lying partially on her left hip, facing us, her legs one atop the other; her torso flat on its back, her head twisted to the right. He pointed round to the back of her thighs. I had to lean right over her to see what he was pointing at. The bluish gray of her skin at the backs of her legs was interrupted by the dark purple of livor mortis; the blood had pooled beneath the skin.

"That means whoever did this had to be in the house, which explains why there were no signs of a break-in."

I looked up at the ceiling, below the kitchen, thinking about Darby Randolph's response to the news of his wife's death. My training told me he was our man; he was the only person in the house that could have done it. Not the kids, that's for sure. Marcie Cox? Nah. So I knew it had to be Randolph... But my gut was telling me, *not so fast*.

"Actually, it means the body's been moved, rolled over onto its side. But yes, someone in the house, and it's personal. Whoever did this to this poor woman was extremely upset," Doc said, pointing at the strange punctures I observed earlier. "Look at these stab wounds."

"Upset? Ya think?" I paused, staring at the ragged holes, then said, "I was right, then. The punctures are stab wounds. She was stabbed as well as bludgeoned. So the cause of death?"

"Oh please, Catherine, you know better than that. I won't be able to tell you that until I've completed the autopsy. I will say this, though. What we have here is a textbook case of overkill," Doc said. "I'll need to get her under the lights to find out what else was done to her."

"Sexual assault?" I asked.

"Again, I won't know until I've finished the autopsy, but somehow I doubt it. Her clothes don't seem to have been disturbed."

"Well, that's something, I suppose. When will you do the autopsy?"

He stood up; so did I.

"I'll try to get it done later today. I already have a client, a six-year-old girl—"

"Whoa, Doc. That's enough. More bad news I can't handle. Just give me a little notice, okay?"

He nodded. "I'll call you when I'm ready, but it could be late?" He raised his eyebrows, questioningly.

"Sounds like a plan," I said. "You know how I love our late nights together, Doc." I winked and patted his arm.

He chuckled softly. "Do me a favor, Kate, if you

wouldn't mind. Send the boys down here with the gurney?"

"Has the scene been photographed and videoed?" I asked.

"Yes, Mike did it himself, just before I arrived, so she's good to go. Then he can get back in here and work his magic. And I do hope he can conjure up a little physical evidence." He laughed at his own joke, though I could see little humor in it, but that's Doc for you.

It was then that I realized I'd missed something. *Didn't Darby say that he'd seen her this morning? I need to talk to him, right now.*

I ran up the stairs to the kitchen and found Randolph still sitting at the island with his head in his hands. Officer Quinn was standing stoically beside the kitchen door, chest out, hands locked together behind his back. He nodded at me as I entered the room.

"Mr. Randolph," I said as I sat down at the island opposite him and opened my iPad. "There are a couple of things I need to clarify, if you don't mind."

He looked up at me, his head still in hands. He nodded, his finger pushing his cheeks this way and that; it would have been funny in any other situation.

"You said that you left your wife in bed, asleep, when you left to take the children to school," I said gently.

He nodded again.

"But that's not true, is it?"

He sat upright with a jolt, grasped the edge of the worktop, and stuttered, "I... But... No, yes, it is true. Her door was closed. She was asleep."

"What you're telling me is that you didn't sleep with your wife last night?"

He stared at me for a long moment, then resignedly shook his head and said, "No, I don't sleep with her anymore; haven't for... well, more than a year. She says... said I snore. I use the guest room at the end of the hall."

"So when did you last see her?"

"I'm not sure. I'm usually in bed by nine. I was last night. I get up early you see, and..." He trailed off, staring down at the pattern in the granite top.

"So you last saw her where? Doing what?"

"Downstairs. Watching TV, but she was also looking at Pinterest on her iPhone."

I nodded. "And the girls?"

"They were in their room when I went up. I looked in on them, said goodnight, and I went to my own room."

"And you didn't go down into the basement?"

"No. Why do you ask?"

That wasn't a question I wanted to answer, not then anyway, so I changed the subject. "Why didn't you tell me all of this when we talked earlier?"

He shrugged. "I didn't think it was important. No, that's not true. I didn't think of it at all. All I could think about was my wife. When can I see her?"

That one I was ready for. "I'll talk to Doc Sheddon and let you know." But I didn't.

I stood and headed toward the basement stairs. I told Quinn to keep an eye on Randolph. He nodded.

So, I thought as I made my way down the stairs, *if*

Darby didn't go down there, he couldn't have moved her. So who the hell did?

By the time I reached the basement, Victoria Randolph was already on the gurney.

It didn't take them long to load her into the back of Doc's converted Chevy Suburban. Unfortunately, they weren't quite quick enough. Just as he closed the vehicle's rear doors, a crazed Darby Randolph came running out of the mudroom door.

"Where are you taking her?" he shouted, his eyes red and wild.

"Damn it, Chief," I shouted as Wilbur and Quinn came running out after him. "How did he get down here?"

"I want to see her!" Randolph yelled as Quinn grabbed him from behind. "Let me see my wife!"

The two officers hung onto him as he struggled like a fish on the end of a line.

"Let me see my wife!" he wailed, his voice echoing across the yard.

I was taught a long time ago to be prepared for such situations and to subdue the crazy quickly, before he could hurt anyone, or himself.

Randolph was indeed crazy, out of his mind.

"Mr. Randolph. You are not helping her right now," I shouted. "Please, sir, I need you to calm down."

"Don't tell me to calm down," he screeched. "You come in here and tell me my wife, the mother of my daughters is dead. And then you tell me I should calm down! What the hell is wrong with you, woman? Let me see my wife!"

Smack! "Calm DOWN, young man."

Doc Sheddon said with emphasis as he smacked him across his cheek, leaving a deep red handprint.

Darby froze, stood still, stiff from head to toe, shocked. Chief Wilbur and Officer Quinn stood like a pair of bookends holding his arms.

And then it happened, Darby's legs gave way and he sank to his knees, hanging by his arms as the two police officers tried unsuccessfully to hold him upright. And then he began to wail again, long shuddering howls.

I shook my head. I'd had enough. I could take no more. I turned away, left them to it, and headed back into the house. I could still hear him as I climbed the stairs.

I met Janet in the kitchen. She was sitting at the island paging through her notebook.

"Well," I said, somewhat impatiently and immediately regretting it. "Did you find anything?"

"This house is amazing. What does a girl have to do to get a set-up like this?"

"Marry an ex-governor's grandson," I replied almost bitterly. "So, did you? Find anything?"

She shook her head and said, "No. I didn't see anything out of place, anywhere. Even the girls' room was all neat and tidy, and you know how they are... worse than boys. The victim must have been a neat freak."

"What about the guest rooms? No, forget it. I need to see for myself," I said. "Let's do it again. No, dang it. Mike Willis will probably have the place locked down for a week. I hope Darby and the kids have somewhere they can go. Why don't you go and ask him? Just to make sure." You've no idea how glad I was to pass that buck.

Finally, maybe thirty minutes later, we left, drove away down Scenic Highway back to Amnicola and sanity... Yah think? Not hardly!

It was not quite noon and my head was pounding, so I made Janet drive. She eased the big car onto the road, and I swear I could still hear Darby Randolph's pitiful cries as we drove away. *Yeah, if he's faking it, he's one hell of an actor.*

6

"So, what's Marcie Cox's story?" I said as Janet merged with the traffic on Highway 41.

"Well, she didn't hold back, that's for sure," Janet said. "She didn't like the Randolphs, not one bit. She liked their money, though, but she said that Victoria Randolph was a rabid snob. And she didn't know how a woman who claimed to have a direct line to Jesus in Heaven could be so uppity and conceited."

"Okay," I said, "so our Vicky is not the saint her husband claims she was. So what?"

I reached for the Starbucks cup in my cupholder, happy I hadn't thrown out my morning coffee. It was cold, but it was wet, and bitter, and surely better than nothing.

"Right," Janet nodded, staring ahead at the traffic on Broad. "Anyway, Marcie said she was at home all night, with her husband, Michael, and kid, Gary who's twelve. They also had a neighbor over. Apparently, the neighbor's kid plays with Gary. I have her name, the neighbor, so I can talk to her, check the alibi. Anyway, Marcie was in a state of shock, I suppose. She kept rabbiting on about quitting the Randolphs. She said she did that every Tuesday night, dreading that she had to go the next day but, like always, the money talked: she had to pay for her son's tennis lessons."

I opened my mouth to speak, but Janet was on a roll.

"She was late getting to work this morning, due to that wreck on I-75. So even that worked for her, because Gary, her son, called her this morning while she was driving to the Randolph's place. Wanted to get her permission for the other kid to sleep over, on Friday, I think. Cell towers can verify that easy enough."

"Yeah, I heard about that truck accident," I said, thankful for the opportunity to break up Janet's enthusiastic diatribe. Yes, I know; I'd asked for it. I took another sip of coffee, and then she was off again.

"Mrs. Cox is a straight shooter, LT. She didn't hold anything back. She said she only hated working for the Randolphs because of Victoria. Said she normally wouldn't speak ill of the dead and would pray for the woman's soul, but she really didn't like her."

"That's interesting," I said. "Victoria's husband called her a saint. Kind to everyone. Loved by all."

"Yes, that *is* interesting," Janet said. "He doesn't know her very well, does he?"

I didn't answer, so she continued.

"Mrs. Cox said she didn't see anyone or hear anything when she got to work. She assumed that

Victoria was either at some coffee klatch or at her new
part-time job at the Church of the Savior. According to
Mrs. Cox, Victoria never tired of telling her that she
didn't need to work but that she was called to work. That
she was the preacher's right hand."

"So Victoria saw herself as a saint, too?"

"Sounds like it, doesn't it?" Janet said, merging with
traffic on Riverside Drive. "I asked Mrs. Cox if Victoria
had any enemies, or if she and Darby got along. But
Marcie said she didn't know about any of that. Claimed
that as far as she could tell, Victoria had Darby wrapped
around her finger, and he seemed to like it that way, and
that's about all I could get out of her."

"Huh! That's a blast. Doesn't give us much to go on.
Nothing, in fact." I chewed my lower lip, and then my
phone rang.

"Where are you, Lieutenant?"

Oh hell; it's Finkle.

"On Riverside. We just left the Randolph residence.
It's definitely a homicide. Toliver and I were just—"

"Well, you need to quick screwing around and get
back to the office, *now!*"

I clenched my teeth. Although Assistant Chief
Henry Finkle and I had come to an understanding about
where my boundaries lay, it didn't stop him from being a
misogynistic, rude little turd. But he was still my boss.

"We'll be there in—" I started to say, but he'd already
hung up.

The creep was an expert at playing head games, and
now he had me wondering what the hell he wanted. I'd

tried to get along with him, treat him with respect. Not that he deserved it. The guy was married, but that didn't stop him trying to get into my pants. *As if I'd ever be that desperate.* It reached a point where I had to do something about it, so I played him. I agreed to have a drink with him at a bar called the Sorbonne.

I plied him with drinks and an unspoken promise... Hey, it was a harmless prank. Just a couple of drinks and a few selfies, although no one can tell who is in the selfies except Finkle... with pants around his ankles. No one knows about it except for Laura and Bennie who run the Sorbonne. It was my little secret, a little security to keep him off my back, and it worked, so far anyway. I couldn't keep his eyes off my chest and ass, or his crass remarks, but I had stopped the constant innuendos.

So, I was diligent in my efforts to keep our relation-ship professional, but Finkle was having none of it. He was out to get me. If I made a mistake, he couldn't be reasoned with. He'd get revenge eventually. There wasn't going to be an explosion or huge temper tantrum. He was more subtle than that. He'd get back at me. I just didn't know when or where. So, in the meantime, I was going to do my job.

"Here we are," Janet said, easing the big car into my parking space.

"Yeah, here we are," I said dispiritedly. "So, I need you to do a background check on Victoria Randolph, Darby Randolph and, oh hell, you may as well go ahead and get the information on Marcie Cox, too. We'll need to cross her off the list sooner rather than later."

"You got it, LT."

"Let me know what you find," I said to Janet as she headed off to her desk.

I walked past my previous partner Lonnie Guest's old cubicle. He'd been gone for a couple of months, and his desk was still unassigned. Not gone as in dead. Gone retired. The SOB became a barber; opened a little shop in Harrison, would you believe? So, the Chief, in his wisdom, assigned Janet Toliver to be my new partner and promoted her to detective, the youngest on the force.

It wasn't that Janet wasn't a good detective. She really was. But I wasn't all that comfortable with her. Not yet. She'd spent her formative years in Chief Johnston's office where she'd been little more than a file clerk. She earned her stripes on our last case together, but that didn't change the fact that she had been in close quarters with the chief for almost two years. I'm not saying she was a mole or anything. But you never know, do you?

Yes, Finkle had me going again, just like always. I couldn't imagine what the flap could be about, and I wasn't going to go out of my way to find out. I'd already had my clock cleaned by Internal Affairs, and I couldn't imagine that there'd been another complaint; I'd been a model police officer ever since... not. Okay, so I could be tough; I was trained to be. But that wasn't it. It had been my language and tone that had gotten me in trouble. Can you believe that?

So when I got to my office, I closed the door, flopped down behind my desk, sipped my cold coffee, and stared up at the ceiling, trying to organize my thoughts.

The message light on my desk was blinking. *Screw 'em.* I opened my laptop. *Emails, oh how I hate thee.* There were more than I could count... Okay, maybe twenty, and half of them had those annoying little red tags that flagged them as "urgent." *Urgent my rear end. I've played that silly game myself. Still, I'd better... Nah, I'll look at 'em later.*

There was also a stack of files on my desk, but only a half dozen of them that I hadn't updated to my lord and master, the aforementioned Henry "Tiny" Finkle, assistant chief, responsible only to the mighty Wayne Johnston, the Dark Lord of Amnicola. Anyway, those half dozen cases were in a state of limbo, awaiting lab reports or witness interviews, so I couldn't see them being the issue. But hey, what did I know about how the man's mind worked? Then again, maybe it didn't... work, that is. I always figured him for a dumbass.

I went back to the emails and tapped the first of the day that had arrived in my inbox at five-oh-three that morning. *Who the hell's at work that early in the morning?* It was a request for some info on an old case I'd solved years ago. Some dude in prison had claimed he was responsible for the crime, and my guy was trying for a new trial. Those guys sitting out their lives at the Riverbend Maximum Security Institute in Nashville would cop to anything if it provided them with a diversion, or a thrill, while they waited for the inevitable.

As crazy as it seemed, once I got started, I managed to knock out all the flagged emails, put out a couple fires, make a few deals, and before I knew, it was almost four o'clock.

I just had one small errand to run, to pick up some paperwork from the County Clerk's office, before heading home for the day. That being so, I was just about to head out when there was a knock on the door. It opened and a shock of red hair appeared.

"I got something, LT. Got a minute?" Janet asked.

I waved her in, and she sat down in front of my desk. Little did I know that what she was about to tell me would keep us there until almost seven o'clock... and my nemesis Finkle made nary an appearance.

7

"It's quite a story," Janet said, smiling and shaking her head as she dumped a pile of paperwork and notes, "so you might want to grab some popcorn."

I sat back in my chair, laced my fingers together in front of me and stared at her. I didn't find it at all funny. I wanted out of there, and from the size of the pile of crap she had in front of her, I knew that wasn't going to happen.

Come on, Kate. Go easy on the kid. She's thorough, and she's just trying to please. She can't help it that Lonnie retired.

She stopped smiling, looked a little chastened, and said, "Okay, ready?"

I nodded.

"Darby Randolph is the grandson of Alexander Randolph. I'm sure you've heard of him." She looked up at me.

I nodded again.

"Darby met Victoria Tate at a frat party his senior year at UTC—he'd applied for several of the Ivy League schools but wasn't accepted. It was love at first sight. She graduated from Francis M. Paul High School, but she didn't go to college."

"Really?" I asked politely, not at all intrigued.

"Yep. They were married six weeks later, just before he graduated. It was a small affair, considering Darby's family, just fifty guests according to the Times Free Press, which is really weird. The Randolphs are high society. You would think the wedding would have been a block-buster; it wasn't. And that leads me to believe that the wedding might not have been blessed by certain members of his family. For the honeymoon, they spent a month in St. Kitts and Nevis, in the Caribbean."

She was right. Darby's parents' wedding is still talked about today... at least by those who care about such things. *Maybe Victoria wasn't the family's first choice.*

"What about *her* family?"

"She doesn't have one. Victoria's an only child. Her mother passed away when she was three. She didn't know her father; he disappeared before she was born. But her stepfather, Harvey Tate, appears to have been a steady influence in her life; he adopted her shortly after he married her mother. Harvey had a couple of minor brushes with the law. Driving under the influence. Public intoxication. He died a couple years ago. If he was abusive, it was never reported. He gave her away, and he's in some of the wedding photos. So, I think they must have gotten along okay."

"He's in some of the wedding photos?" I said, a little surprised. "I didn't see any at the house with him in them, and there were plenty. Plenty of Victoria by herself and with Darby and his family, but not with anyone that looked like a father of the bride. Where did you see them?"

"I pulled up the Times Free Press coverage of the wedding during my research. See?" She handed me several print outs.

I looked at them, one after the other. Tate was a good-looking man.

"So," I said, laying the printouts down on my desk, "A girl from the wrong side of the tracks, so to speak, makes good by marrying into a prominent family. Happens all the time." I'd heard it all before, many times. Totally bored, I sipped the last drops of my cold coffee.

"It does. But most don't end up dead." Janet looked down at her notes. "So, Victoria and Darby married. They had two girls. They were living the dream until all this. She had recently been hired at the Church of the Savior as the pastor's personal assistant."

"Hah, living the dream, you say?" I said. "If that's the way the Real Housewives of Lookout Mountain live the dream, I'll pass. It all sounds rather boring to me... Any financial issues? What about insurance?"

"Nothing out of the ordinary there, either." Janet flipped a couple of pages in her notebook. "Darby's doing very well for a dumb—" She didn't finish the sentence. "He's a senior partner in the prestigious law practice of Hirsch, O'Shea and Randolph which, considering that he was no better than an average student in college, would ordinarily be unthinkable, but... Well, I think we know how he landed that gig. It's not what you know, or don't know—it's who granddaddy knows, right?"

I nodded and made a circling motion with my forefinger, indicating for her to get on with it. I was getting antsy, impatient.

"She did have an insurance policy for just a couple hundred thousand dollars, but so did he. Both of them signed the forms. To me it doesn't look like their relationship was anything out of the ordinary." She shrugged.

"So, no financial issues?" I said. "How about visits to the doctor, plastic surgeon, Botox, tucks? Lavish hotel and restaurant charges? Shopping sprees? Rumors of affairs? Alcohol? Drugs? Rehab? Anything at all that you would consider out of the ordinary?"

"Nope."

I took a deep breath and folded my arms behind my head, closed my eyes and tried to think.

Someone undoubtedly had a real problem with Victoria. The level of violence inflicted upon her indicated rage out of control, and in my experience, only one thing ever caused such rage: jealousy. And that meant she must have pissed someone off big time: either her husband or a boyfriend which, as far as we know, she didn't have.

So that brings us back to Darby. But I've had enough. I wanna go home, take a nice hot bath and enjoy a large glass of red... Huh, not hardly. God only knows when Doc will call.

"I've had it, Janet," I said. "I don't think we can do much more tonight. I'm going home to wait for Doc to call. I'd suggest you do the same. We'll get an early start in the morning, okay?"

"Sounds good, LT. You got any big plans for this evening?"

"After I get finished with Doc Sheddon, yeah. A bottle of wine and a hot bath," I said. "See you tomorrow."

Janet nodded, rose to her feet, gathered up her papers, and left the office.

After she'd gone, I thought maybe I'd been a little rude to her. I didn't mean to be. It niggled at me all the way home. I decided I'd apologize to her the next day.

By nine o'clock, I'd had enough of the waiting, and I called Doc. He told me to stand down. Seems he'd developed a headache and had decided to go home. *Gee, thanks for letting me know.*

I hung up, poured myself a glass of the good stuff, took a shower, and went to bed only to be awaked at three o'clock by the sweet sounds of my phone. Reluctantly, I dragged myself out of one of those peaceful, but heavy dreams; you know what I mean, right?

"Gazzara," I grumbled as I fought to stay awake and out of dreamland.

"It's me, LT," Janet said breathlessly. "We've got another one."

8

"What?" I squeaked, suddenly wide awake.

"Yeah, another one," Janet said. "The address is 612 Lincoln Avenue. Lookout Mountain."

I closed my eyes, trying to figure out exactly where it was.

"That's just a mile south from where the Randolph's live," I said as I dragged myself out of bed. "612, you said?" *Better put that in my phone right now before I forget.* "Okay. I'll meet you there as soon as I can. Make sure the scene is secured. Have you called Mike Willis? No? Okay, do it now! And call Doc Sheddon. Good, that was smart. You go on up there. I'll be there soon."

I staggered into the kitchen, punched the button on the coffee maker, and headed for the bathroom. I took a quick, scalding-hot shower, then back to the bedroom where I quickly dressed in jeans, white blouse, and a black leather jacket, twisting my hair into a ponytail.

Then I grabbed a tumbler of coffee and ran out of the apartment to where my car was parked on the road, slopping the coffee as I ran down the steps. *I'll need to get one that's spill-proof if this keeps up.* I all but fell into the driver's seat, set the coffee in the cupholder, and then lay my head back against the rest, closed my eyes, and breathed deeply for several minutes.

Finally, somewhat more relaxed than I'd thought possible, I inserted the key and started the car.

When I pulled up in front of the home on Lincoln Avenue, all was quiet, just a single cruiser—its lights flashing red and blue—and Janet's car, no gawkers, no one on the sidewalk. Janet and Chief Wilbur were standing together on the porch. Next to them sat a man on the steps with his elbows on his knees and his head in his hands.

I sighed, shook my head, and exited the car, just as Doc Sheddon's black Suburban pulled up behind me.

"Morning, Kate," he said as he climbed down from the big vehicle. "I was just about to call you when Janet called. I don't think we've had a homicide up here in more than ten years. Now we have two in less than 24 hours. What the hell's going on?"

I watched as he circled around the front of the SUV and then dragged his big black bag out from the passenger side and placed it on the ground beside him.

"It's a full moon, Doc," I said then yawned.

"Isn't it always?" he replied.

"You were going to call me? I wouldn't have answered, not at four o'clock in the morning."

He grinned at me. "Yes, you would. You can't help yourself. Meet you inside."

I nodded and headed up to the house where Janet was waiting for me.

"Hey, Chief," I said. "Janet, Mister..."

The man looked up at me and said, "Dilly, Connor Dilly." His eyes were red. He let his head sink back into his hands.

Wilbur looked tired. No, he looked worn out.

"It's good to see you, Lieutenant," he said wearily. "What can I do to help?"

"Right now, I need you to secure the scene. Have you been inside? Are you all there is?"

"Yes, unfortunately, I've been inside, and I wish to hell I hadn't. Don't even ask. I'll let you see for yourself. And no, I'm not all there is. Quinn and Jones are on their way. I had to get 'em out of bed. Should be here anytime now. I'll get them on it as soon as they arrive. I'll go wait for them. Can you take care of..." He pointed down at Dilly and mouthed silently, "Him?"

I rolled my eyes and nodded, then said, "Where is she, Chief?"

"Living room. First on the right. You can't miss it." He walked down the steps and headed down the drive to the road.

"I'll be with you shortly, Mr. Dilly. I'm sorry for your loss. Are you okay?"

He mumbled something through his fingers I took to be in the affirmative. I turned to Janet, took her arm, and steered her to the far end of the porch.

"Talk to me," I said.

Janet consulted her pocket notebook. "I haven't been inside yet. I just got here. But Chief Wilbur—he was first on the scene as you can see—said they got a 911 call from the husband, Mr. Connor Dilly. Mr. Dilly told the dispatcher that he'd arrived home from a business trip and had found his wife dead."

"How did he know she was dead? Did he touch her? Did he touch anything?"

"Oh she's dead all right, but no, I don't think he touched anything, but I haven't talked to him yet."

"What do you mean by that, that she's dead all right?"

I looked back along the porch at Dilly. He hadn't moved.

"According to Chief Wilbur," Janet said, "she was killed in exactly the same way as Victoria Randolph. And —you're gonna hate this—she's been dead for days. Well, at least two." Janet wrinkled her nose.

"What?"

"That's right. She was killed before Victoria Randolph."

"Sheesh, is this a bad day or what?" I said under my breath as I checked my watch. "It's only frickin' four o'clock," I grumbled. "Come on. We have a lot to do."

I walked back to Dilly; Janet followed me like a puppy that had lost its mother.

"Mr. Dilly," I said. "I'm sorry, sir, but I need to check the—" I was going to say body, but thought better of it and said instead, "I need to secure the scene. I'd like to talk to you when I'm finished so please, I'd like you to stay here. I'll be but a few minutes. Is that okay?"

"Where am I going to go?" he whispered, without looking up.

At that, Janet and I stepped inside the house, into a large open foyer. It took just a couple of seconds to figure out which was the living room. We could have simply followed our noses. The smell of a corpse that has been left out in the open for thirty-six hours, or more, is one that will never leave you: a thick, sweet smell that settles over everything and can't be scrubbed away.

I pulled a pair of Tyvek shoe covers out of my bag and put them on. Janet looked at me like a kid who hadn't brought a pencil to class, so I handed her a pair too. *I'll have to remind her to get some of those from supply.*

Doc Sheddon was already at work when we stepped into the living room.

"Ah, Kate, Janet," he said, looking up at us. "Do come in. I'm almost done. Another nasty one, I'm afraid. I don't envy you, Kate. I'd say this poor woman died sometime around mid to late afternoon on Tuesday. Come take a look."

And we did, at least I did. Janet stayed two steps back and put her hand over her nose. *I'll have to remind her to get some face masks from supply also.*

I joined him, crouched down opposite him on the left side of the body. He was correct, it was indeed a nasty one. The left side of the victim's head had literally been crushed. Even I could see that the left side of the skull, including most of the eye socket, had been smashed, caved in, by several heavy blows: five, maybe six. Obviously, I didn't know for sure, but judging by the shape of the indentations, the weapon was similar to the one used to kill Victoria Randolph.

"Looks like the same weapon," I said. "Cause of death?"

"Really, Catherine?" he said, smiling. "One, you know I can't say for sure. Two, ain't it freaking obvious? Blunt force trauma."

"Silly question," I said. "Sorry, force of habit."

He nodded, smiling; he always was, smiling. Nothing ever seemed to phase him. Wish I was like that.

The body was fully dressed in jeans and a button-down shirt, lying flat on its back, arms and legs spread wide, head turned to the right. And yes, there were puncture wounds through the clothing.

"Are those what I think they are, Doc?"

He nodded. "Looks like it. Can't say for sure, not yet."

I sighed, stood up, and looked around. *Holy shit! What a frickin' mess.*

There was blood spatter everywhere: on the carpet, the furniture, the ceiling and when I took out my iPhone and shone the flashlight on the wall, I could easily make out the droplets there, too.

How the hell hard did he hit her to send it that far?

"Doc," I said, "I'm going to have to leave you to it. I have the victim's husband on the porch and need to talk to him. You'll call me, right?"

"I will. Please answer the phone when I do."

"I promise. I will."

The house was huge—five to six thousand square feet, maybe more, and it screamed wealth: white walls and dark furniture, paintings—original oils—that depicted the Antebellum South. They depicted pre-Civil War Southern living in all its glory, and I was certain they must have cost a pretty penny; there was dried blood on at least two of them.

"Check the upstairs, Janet. I'm going to talk to the husband."

Janet nodded and left, still covering her nose.

I took another quick glance around the living room, taking in the family photographs on bookshelves. Mrs. Dilly wasn't anything like Victoria Randolph. She was a rather plain-looking woman, not exactly pretty, but somehow attractive. In most of the photos, she was wearing casual clothes, jeans, sweaters, laughing with a wide, toothy smile, making faces with her children. Had I seen her at the grocery store, I'd never have guessed she lived as she did on Lookout Mountain.

The epitome of the modern Southern lady, I thought. *What a waste; what a damn shame!*

"Later, Doc," I said, finally.

"Later," he replied. "Wait, I need to move the body. Where's Willis?"

"On his way, as far as I know."

"I can't wait for him. I'll photograph the body for him. Tell him to call me when he has a minute."

I nodded, stepped carefully backward out of the room, and headed toward the front porch.

9

I stepped out onto the porch and breathed in deeply the sweet, clean, early morning mountain air. *Wow, did I ever need that?*

Connor Dilly was seated on the porch swing staring into space, his hands on either side of him grasping the edge of the seat.

"Mr. Dilly?" I said.

He nodded and sniffled, stood quickly, and extended his hand to me. "Connor Dilly, ma'am."

I shook his hand and said, "I'm Lieutenant Catherine Gazzara. I know how difficult this must be, sir, but I do need to talk to you. Can you please tell me why she was here by herself and... how you found her?" I was trying to be gentle with him, but how the hell could I?

"I was out of town, at my other office in Memphis. I go twice a month. I left early on Tuesday morning. I don't usually stay more than two or three days. My return flight was delayed. I called my wife at about seven last night, to let her know, but she didn't answer. I thought nothing of it. It was after midnight when I arrived back in Chattanooga. I drove home and... I found her."

"You drove home? I didn't see your car."

"It's in the garage."

I nodded.

"When did you last talk to your wife?" I asked.

"That was on Tuesday morning," he said, his eyes filling with tears.

"It didn't worry you that your wife didn't answer last night?" I asked, shifting from one foot to the other.

"Please, Detective. Let's sit down. The swing will hold both of us."

We sat down together, and I repeated my question.

Connor Dilly slowly shook his head. "We're not that kind of couple. We don't worry about each other, where we are, what we're doing. We love each other, trust each other. Meryl was my whole life. The good Lord saw fit to bring us together. Let no man put asunder. I just assumed she was busy, in the shower, perhaps."

"Mr. Dilly, can you think of anyone who would want to hurt your wife... or you?"

I watched his reaction. His eyes were red, bruised where he'd been rubbing them. He shrugged, and I prepared myself for another diatribe such as Mr. Randolph had given me about his wife being a saint, walking on water, working for world peace, climate change, helping orphans and puppies, but that's not what I got.

"My wife wasn't perfect," he said. "She was a plain

speaker, pulled no punches. Whatever she said, no matter who to, she always told the truth, sometimes to her detriment. Some people don't like hearin' the truth," he said, working his jaw. "But no, I can't think of anyone who'd want to hurt her. This is the work of the devil. Plain and simple... Oh, my beautiful Meryl. What will I do without you?"

Behind me, I could hear the rattling sound of the ME's gurney.

"Mr. Dilly," I said, trying to divert his attention, "did your wife ever mention seeing anyone suspicious loitering around the house, or the neighborhood, currently or in the past?"

He shook his head, leaned forward, put his head in his hands. His shoulders were shaking. I gave it up, told him I'd talk to him later and to call me if he thought of anything. He was a suspect, of course, but his grief seemed genuine.

I stood, placed a business card on a small side table, and was about to leave when he looked up and reached for the card. He stared at it, then said, "Lord, please give me the strength to deliver this news to my children."

Dilly looked at me. "Our son Joseph just moved to Virginia. Landed a government job. My daughter, Elsie, is finishing college at Alabama... Yes, Detective, I'll call you."

"I'm very sorry, Mr. Dilly."

"The Lord will see me through this. I'll weather this storm with His hand to steady me." He stood, stiff and proud, obviously holding himself together.

I suddenly felt unnaturally sad, something that didn't happen to me very often. I wished I could offer him some words of comfort, but I couldn't. I'd long ago learned to keep my distance. If I didn't, I'd lose my mind. Yet, there was no denying that this was a bad one.

Who the hell could have done this? I thought. *What kind of animal hammers a woman's head to a pulp? Why? Why did he do it? What was his motive? Two harmless, defenseless women. There has to be a connection. What the hell is it?*

Back in the living room, I watched as they carefully lifted Meryl Dilly onto the gurney, covered her with a fresh white sheet, and rolled her out to Doc's SUV. I was about to take a look around the area where the body had been when Janet appeared at the door.

"Anything?" I asked as I waved a hand goodbye to Doc Sheddon.

She looked around as if to make sure no one could hear her, and then jerked her head toward an empty, dark hallway that led to the family room and the back of the house.

"There was no sign of a break-in," she said," just like at the Randolph house." She put her hands on her hips and continued, "Other than the religious pictures and statues in every room, the place is unremarkable, clean, tidy, lived-in. I peeked in some of the drawers and closets, nothing; no fancy underwear, just the opposite in fact." She shrugged.

I nodded, not really listening to her; my mind was

elsewhere. "Where the hell is Mike Willis?" I muttered. "You did call him, didn't you?"

"Yes, of course. He said to make sure Chief Wilbur keeps the scene secure and he'd be here as soon as he could. His team is still working the Randolph place. He said he had all eight of his techs there, and that he'd have to split them into two teams."

"Geez, good thing Doc had the foresight to photograph the body before he took it."

Janet scrunched up her face.

She's probably remembering the sight and smell of the body. I was like that too, the first time, I remembered.

I continued, "Well, it looks like we're getting to the office early today. Oh, I was going to ask: did you find out anything more about the Randolphs?"

"Yeah. I was going to bring you up to speed when we got back to Amnicola. LT, I know I don't have much experience, but it seems to me that we... that we..." She paused, looking helpless.

"Come on, Janet, spit it out."

She pinched her lips together and shook her head, obviously frustrated. I could see her mind working to put the pieces together. *That's what I like to see.*

"It's just that we don't seem to have anything to work with... I can't see how either Mr. Randolph or Mr. Dilly could have done this, and so far, we have nothing—"

"You're right," I said, interrupting her. "We don't, but we will. I promise. You just have to be patient, Janet. It's here, we have to find it. Mike's the best. He'll find something for us to work with."

My new partner stood looking at me, soaking up my words.

"Janet, the one certainty about a murder is that the killer always leaves something at the crime scene, and always takes something away from it. So, for the moment, all we can do is leave the searching to Mike and his team while we talk to people, dig into the past, ask questions, find the inconsistencies. Look, I'm almost done here. Why don't you head on back to the office and run the Dillys through the wringer? I'll pick up coffee and bagels. Then we can talk over breakfast. I'll buzz you when I get in."

Janet smiled at me, sheepishly, nodded and left. Me? I hung around for a while longer and roamed the house looking, for what I don't know. I would have been grateful to find anything right then, but Janet was right: the place was pristine, virtually undisturbed, except for the bloody mess in the living room.

There was a basement, mostly devoted to a home gym and a family room—no bar, or course.

At the far end of the family room, I found what I assumed was Connor Dilly's office. Beautiful, something I'd always wanted for myself: floor to ceiling bookshelves filled with books, and two desks, pushed together facing each other.

"His and hers," I mumbled out loud.

Janet was right about the religious iconography. Religious paintings adorned every wall. I peeked at the papers on the desk: nothing there that grabbed my attention, just a bunch of bills, all marked paid, two church magazines, and several pamphlets for The Church of the Savior beneath a paperweight that read "Jesus is my Lord and Savior."

That's where the lovely Mrs. Randolph was working, I mused, not getting overly excited about it. *Hmm, they both belonged to the same church. Well, they would, wouldn't they?*

The Church of the Savior wasn't the only church on Lookout Mountain, but it was well attended; I knew that from what little research I'd already done. Pastor Ed packed the seats every Sunday and on Wednesday evenings.

Okay, so I've got nothing else, I thought as I picked up one of the flyers, folded it, and stuffed it in my pocket.

I returned to the living room and took one last careful look around the spot where the body had been... and I saw something I hadn't noticed before. There were two bloody indentations in the carpet like it had been pierced. Whoever killed Mrs. Dilly stabbed her so hard, the weapon went right through her body and to the carpet. I took out my iPhone and photographed the indentations. Yes, I knew Mike would do it, but I wanted copies of my own to study.

"This kind of rage can't easily be hidden," I mumbled to myself.

"What's that Detective?" Chief Wilbur asked.

"Nothing. I'm just talking to myself."

"You know what they say about people that talk to themselves?" He smirked.

I tilted my head and smirked back.

"Yeah. That it's the only way to have an intelligent conversation."

Chief Wilbur chuckled, nodding. "A neighbor dropped by, a Mrs. Courtland, attracted by the lights. She's sitting with Mr. Dilly. I don't know what to say about all this, Detective. I've never seen anything like it before. I'm not trying to sound like a jackass, but things like this don't happen on Lookout Mountain. That's why people live here."

"Mrs. Courtland, you say?" I asked as I made a note of the name. "Yes, I hear you about the neighborhood, but you know, Chief, that's why criminals eventually come here," I said. "They know how lax homeowner security in a community like this can be. But we aren't dealing with your average criminal, are we? What can you tell me about the Dillys? How well do you know them?"

"I know them pretty well. Like the Randolphs, they're in church every Sunday. I see them there myself." He cleared his throat and hitched up his pants. "They're close with the pastor and half the congregation. Darby Randolph, coming from the family he does, has to maintain a good rapport with the community, you know."

"Politics, right?" I asked.

"Right! Connor Dilly runs a successful carpet business, here and with outlets in Nashville, Memphis, and Birmingham. He donates generously to the church, and the school. He's a member of the Fairyland Club, and the golf club, as is Randolph. I mean, the guy gives back, Detective. He didn't deserve this. Neither did Meryl."

"No one deserves it," I replied. "You say you all go to the same church?"

"Yeah, everyone here on Lookout Mountain goes to one church or the other. Savior is a little highbrow for me personally, but my wife happens to like Pastor Ed. He's good people, right enough but... well, she'll be the first to tell you that as far as the Church of the Savior is concerned, I'm a square peg in a round hole."

I chuckled and nodded my head. "I hear you, Chief."

"How can you joke?" Connor Dilly shouted at us from the doorway. "My wife is dead and all you're doing is standing around joking? What's wrong with you? Don't you have any sense of compassion?"

"You've got it wrong, Mr. Dilly. I can assure you."

"I know your name, Detective," Dilly shouted, pointing at me. "I'll file an official complaint. You bet I will! And you, too." He pointed at the uniformed Chief. "I have donned the armor of God. I shall fight to my last breath to find who did this! Even if you don't." He continued to rant, calling upon Jesus to give him strength and assuring us that the good Lord would smite his enemies down.

"I think it's time for me to go, Chief," I said. "I don't need another official complaint on my record."

Wilbur smiled and told me not to worry, that he'd handle Dilly.

And then, just at the right moment, Mike Willis arrived with his CSI team. I told Dilly that we had the situation in hand and asked him if he had anywhere to go while the forensics team was at work in the house. He said he didn't, but that he would get a hotel room.

That's awful, I thought. *All alone in a hotel room after this. I feel for the guy, I really do.*

He disappeared into the house, I assumed to pack a few things. Willis checked in with me and also headed into the house, followed by four members of his team.

Lord, I hope we don't get another one. Willis is already stretched to the limit.

I turned again to Wilbur and said, "If we don't get something soon, and Dilly carries through on his threat, his accusations will stick, even if they aren't true. I'm sure you know how IA can be."

"That I do," he concurred. "That's why we do what we have to do, in order to stay safe and sane."

I nodded, somewhat dejected. "As I said, Chief, it's time for me to go." I clapped him on the back and headed to my car.

As I drove down the mountain into the city, I thought about the similarities between the two murdered women. Or lack thereof. They were as different as chalk and cheese. As far as I could tell, the only thing they had in common was they both went to the same church.

So much rage. So much violence. Whatever could they have done to generate so much hate?

So far, I had only two suspects, and neither of them seemed likely. And now I had to go face my nemesis, Henry Frickin' Finkle. Just thinking about it gave me a headache.

When I walked into our reception area at the Police Services Center on Amnicola that morning, I was more than a little surprised to be told by the duty officer that someone was waiting to talk to me.

I checked my watch. It was six-fifteen. *What the hell? Who would be here at this hour? Hah, I might have known.*

"Clemont Rhodes," I said, not offering my hand, walking straight past him to the elevators, "of the Chattanooga Gurgle." Yes, I was pulling his chain. It's the Bugle, not Gurgle.

He smiled a row of perfectly even teeth that must have cost the equivalent of a year of my salary: they almost blinded me with their whiteness.

"Nice to see you too, Lieutenant."

"Oh, yes, and why would that be, and what the hell

are you doing here at this time in the morning?" I said, not waiting to hear the answer. I hated reporters.

I reached for the elevator button, but what he said next made me stop and turn to look at him.

"What can you tell me about the murder on Lookout Mountain, Kate?"

He blinked and continued to grin. It was creeping me out.

"What murder?" I asked. "And don't call me Kate."

"Please, *Lieutenant* Gazzara. I know that Mrs. Victoria Randolph was found dead in the family home early yesterday morning, murdered. Do you have any leads? Is the husband, Darby Randolph, cooperating with the investigation? Is he a suspect?"

"I don't know what you're talking about," I replied.

"Come now, Detective, the people of Chattanooga have a right to know. Victoria Randolph is a mother and wife, an active member of her church, a saint, so I hear. A regular Mother Teresa. What are you doing to bring her killer to a swift and final justice? Do you have any persons of interest?"

Geez, 'a swift and final justice'? What the hell has he been reading?

When I heard the word "saint," I squinted at the reporter.

"Who have you been talking to?" I asked. Stupid question. I already knew the answer.

"You know I can't reveal my sources, Detective," he sneered.

"What can you tell me, Detective? Or do you intend

to keep secrets, as usual? If there's a killer on the loose, the people of this city need to be aware of the danger."

"Piss off, Clemont. I have no comment for the press. If you're looking for a juicy story, go talk to Detective John Tracy. He's about to break open something big. But take a little advice, don't just show up on his doorstep like you did to me." I cleared my throat. "He's Vice, and he has some nasty habits. Then again, if you play nice, he might have something for you."

"I'm not sure I'm interested in a drug case," Rhodes said. "Not when there's murder afoot on Lookout Mountain. Hmm, I like the sound of that," he said, more to himself than to me. "And you know," he continued, "how much the people love to hear about scandals among the rich and famous, how they love to see the elite one-percent get their comeuppance."

"Comeuppance?" I rolled my eyes. "Wow, where did that come from, Clemmo? And since when is a snoopy son of a bitch like you not interested in a story about drugs? Drugs mean sex, right?" I looked him up and down. "And you *do* look like a guy who enjoys—what should we call it—the seedy side of life. Didn't I see you out at Summit a couple of weeks ago, poking around the... Oh, never mind. I don't have time for this crap. Go talk to Tracy."

I reached for the elevator button.

"You can't rattle me, Detective, with your... innuendo."

"Wow, another big word. Who are you trying to impress, Clemmy?"

I looked behind him.

"I can't rattle you?" I smirked. "Maybe not, but she can."

I jerked my head at Janet, who was standing behind the reporter with a notebook in her hand. To her credit, she instantly slipped into character.

"You're a reporter?" she squawked, loud enough to gain the attention of every uniform on the floor as well as several secretaries. "Y'all know who this is, right? He's the media. Who the hell invited him in here anyway? Get him the hell out of here. We've got work to do!"

The press is never kind to any police department and, over the past several years, Rhodes had been particularly vocal in his criticisms of our department and of several unfortunate individuals. So, as soon as they realized who and what he was, a half-dozen uniforms advanced on him like zombies on a fat man. One had a Taser in his hand. It was almost comical to watch the cocky smirk fall from Rhodes' face.

"What the hell?" he howled at Janet. "Why did you do that? If I get hurt, you're gonna..." He didn't finish the sentence. Instead, he turned and hurried toward the exit.

"That was fun," Janet said as we rode the elevator. "Should we go and make sure he leaves?" Janet asked, her face morphing from angry scowl to cute young lady.

"No," I said. "Let him go. He was here because someone leaked the Randolph killing to him, and I want to know who it was."

"Wha-at?" Janet said. "That's not possible... is it? Unless it was Chief Wilbur, and I just don't see that. One of his officers, do you think, maybe? I hear tell that some of those reporters will pay big bucks for an exclusive."

I shook my head. "I don't think so... I need to think. Let's both go to my office."

I hung my jacket on the back of a chair beside my desk, flopped into my seat, set my phone and iPad on the desk, and opened my laptop, and that's as far as I got. I heaved a sigh, leaned back in my chair, closed my eyes, and nothing. I guess I'd been awake far too long, and then I realized I needed coffee, real coffee, not the paint-stripper from the incident room. Then I remembered something; I was supposed to get bagels on the way back to the precinct. I'd promised Janet.

I opened my eyes, looked at Janet and said, "Hey, I forgot the coffee. I can't drink the crap from the incident room. You want to run over to McDonald's and get us some decent coffee and bagels? My treat."

She grinned at me and literally jumped to her feet. "No," she said. "*My* treat," and off she went.

Wow, where the hell does she get her energy?

Then I got to thinking again, *No. I don't think any of Wilbur's guys are responsible for the leak. It's a small department in a high-value community. They get paid well enough... No, I think I know who it was that tipped Rhodes off.*

I must have sat there daydreaming for some fifteen minutes, or so, until Janet returned loaded up with a tray of four large coffees—two each—and a paper sack with four sausage and egg bagels therein—two each. *Good thinking, sister.*

She dumped the lot on my desk and sat down across from me.

"Did you figure it out?" she asked, grabbing a bagel. "Who's the leaker?"

"Maybe," I said, taking a sip of the strong, dark, life-restoring liquid. "But first things first. Tell me about Meryl Dilly."

She wriggled her backside in the chair, got comfortable, and began flipping through the pages of her first notepad; oh yes, she was now on her third. *I really must get the kid an iPad.*

"This is rather sad, LT—" Janet began.

"Hold that thought," I said, interrupting her and reaching for my desk phone.

"Hey, Jimmy," I said when the quartermaster picked up. "How are you, buddy? Great, that's good to hear... Yes, not bad, busy, but that's better than the alternative, right? Jimmy, I need a favor. My new partner, Detective Janet Toliver, needs an iPad. She's still scribbling in paper notebooks... You do? Oh yeah, used is good... An iPad Pro. Yes, sir. That will do fine. Thanks, Jimmy."

"You didn't need to do that," Janet said reproachfully. "I like my notebook."

"Tough," I said. "I need for you to get with the program. You can't record an interview with a friggin' notebook, and you can't share your notes, read and send emails, Google stuff. It's the way we do things, Janet."

"Well, okay, then. If you insist." She really did seem a little put out, but she'd get over it.

I nodded and said, "Meryl Dilly?"

"Yes, of course. Well, it seems that Mrs. Dilly is a cancer survivor—ovarian. She went into remission about nine months ago, after radical surgery."

"Lots of doctor bills?" I asked.

"Yes, but they had insurance. They're all paid up. Nothing in default. Not much debt, either. He makes good money. The company is sound, making a profit, and they're wealthy, as you might imagine, and that huge house is paid for—no mortgage. They'll be good to go when they retire."

"Well, *he* will be," I said after clearing my throat. "She's awaiting the good offices of Dr. Richard Sheddon."

Janet's face lost a little of its color. I figured she must have been contemplating her first autopsy, and I didn't blame her.

"So there's nothing out of the ordinary in their financials?" I asked.

"No, they're clean."

"That's about what I expected," I grumbled.

"But I did find something," she said. "It's not much, but it is, well, interesting."

She flipped the page of her notebook and looked at me from the corner of her eye.

"I like interesting," I replied.

"The two families, they both belong to the same church, the big one, the one where Marcie Cox said Victoria was working, the Church of the Savior."

"Yes," I said, "I know. Chief Wilbur goes there too. I think just about everyone on the Mountain belongs to that church."

"Right, but what you don't know is that Darby Randolph is listed as the church's attorney, and that both victims worked there, and that Connor Dilly donated the floor coverings. That must have cost him a fortune. Have you ever been inside that church?"

I shook my head.

"Well, I have. I went to a wedding up there last year. Would you believe the sanctuary can seat fifteen hundred people? Carpeting that space would have been a huge donation. And there's more: it seems like there might have been a little quid pro quo, because less than a week after the carpet was installed, Meryl Dilly was appointed the church's hospitality coordinator. What kind of a BS made-up job is that?" She looked at me. "Seems to me that both Mrs. Randolph and Mrs. Dilly were... well, I dunno. Bit of a coincidence, don't you think?"

"You mean maybe we need to talk to some of the congregation?" I said, smiling. "Is that what you're hinting at?"

It wasn't much of a lead, but hell, any lead is a good lead when you have nothing else.

"Yes, exactly," she said enthusiastically. "People who attend church talk to each other, open up to their friends, their pastor." She leaned forward in her seat. "Maybe someone knows something." And then she ran out of steam and slumped back in her seat.

"Yes, they might at that," I said thoughtfully.

11

I stood up, yawned, stretched, walked over to the window and looked out. The sun was up, and for a short while there were blue patches in an otherwise overcast sky, but it didn't last long. The blue soon disappeared, engulfed in a roiling mass of dark clouds that matched my mood perfectly. I was tired, cranky, and having a hard time staying focused. And, of course, it was at that moment that Assistant Chief Henry Finkle barged into my office, without knocking, as always.

"You," he said, pointing at Janet. "Out!"

She jumped to her feet, startled, and was gone before I had time to blink.

"What the hell—" I said, turning away from the window.

"Shut up and sit down," he snarled, interrupting me.

"And good morning to you too, Chief," I snapped. "I'll stand, thank you," I said, as I stepped forward, knowing that my extra four inches in height intimidated the hell out of him. It was a mistake, as I found out less than a minute later.

"Have it your way. You've been talking to the press, Lieutenant. Explain."

He stood there looking at me, smirking, staring at my chest. I was instantly embarrassed. I was wearing only a T-shirt, and I was sure he was checking to see if I was wearing a bra.

"Yes, I spoke to a reporter, Clemont Rhodes. I think you two know each other," I said snidely. "I told him to leave, and I had a couple uniforms escort him out of the building. Why? Has he made a complaint? Did they rough him up? If they did, he provoked them."

"Rough him up?" he replied, just as snidely. "From what I remember that's your forte, Lieutenant, at least according to Internal Affairs."

I rolled my eyes and said, "I've never laid a hand on anyone, ever, and you know it."

It wasn't the first time he'd provoked me by referring to my one run-in with Internal Affairs, and it wouldn't be the last; of that I was sure.

Some months ago, I arrested a creepy little shit with a record that filled a file folder six inches thick. He lodged a formal complaint against me, claimed that he didn't like "my tone," and that I'd used excessive force and verbally abused him. It wasn't true, and I denied it, of course, but it earned me an IA investigation which came down to my word against his. I lost, and it earned me a mandatory week off and a black mark on my permanent record, much to Finkle's delight.

"I'm disappointed in you, Lieutenant. Even a raw rookie knows not to talk to the press. He's another one you're sleeping with, I suppose. How many more are there... besides Starke? By the way, does his wife know you're screwing him?"

Finkle sniffled, put his hands on his hips, and straightened himself up, all five-feet-nine-inches of him.

"Perhaps someone should let her know..."

That did it. I felt my blood boil. How the hell I didn't slap his stupid face, I don't know. Good thing I didn't, because it would have totally screwed up what I was about to do next.

"Screw you, Henry," I said, not backing down this time. "I've taken all of the bullshit from you I can stand. You know damn well I didn't talk to that reporter. It was Victoria Randolph's husband, Darby, that tipped him off. No, I'm not sleeping with him, and I'm not sleeping with Harry Starke either—"

"That's enough, Lieutenant," he snapped, interrupting me.

"Damn right, it is," I said, picking up the desk phone.

"What are you doing? Put that phone down."

I ignored him, punched in the number and waited, staring at him, defiantly.

"Cathy, it's me, Kate Gazzara. I need to make an appointment to see Chief Johnston. Yes... No... As soon as possible."

I saw the color drain from Finkle's face. He turned and strode out of the office, slamming the door behind him.

"Three o'clock this afternoon is fine, Cathy, and thank you."

I ended the call and slowly returned the phone to its cradle, thinking, wondering... *Okay, Kate. You just crossed the line. You better have your damn ducks in a row.*

I smiled at the thought, nodded to myself, closed my eyes, and enjoyed the moment; it had been coming a long time.

12

"Yikes," Janet said when she returned to my office after my meeting with Finkle. "What was that all about?"

"That, Janet, was a typical review of my caseload." I yawned. "You ready to go take a peek at The Church of the Savior?"

"You betcha," she said enthusiastically.

Inwardly, I shook my head. The kid was as perky as a parrot. *Was I ever that excited about this job? I think I was... I must have been... when I was a rookie and partners with Harry. Before "Tiny" Finkle started bothering me.*

"Good. You drive."

We arrived at The Church of the Savior, an imposing structure, typical of the Southern Evangelical movement, half ancient Greek temple, half modern American courthouse. Think Supreme Court of the United States, but with a tall spire with a gleaming white cross at the tip. Huge windows lined the building, not the delicate stained-glass variety one associates with most Catholic churches, but crystal clear, sparkling behemoths, that on a sunny day, must have bathed the inside of the church with sunlight.

A pair of vast oak doors with a massive cross carved into the surface graced the front entrance. Not quite a cathedral, but it was indeed a church in the grand manner. I decided whoever designed the church wanted to be sure that both God and man took notice.

To the side, a two-story building attached to the main structure housed, I assumed, the church offices. A second building, as indicated by the sign out front, housed the primary school run by the church.

Janet parked the car, and we ascended the steps to the church doors. I grabbed one of the handles and tugged, then tugged again, but they were locked.

"Are they only open on Sunday, then?" Janet asked.

"I guess so, let's check around the back. Come on."

At the bottom of the steps, I noticed a tiny sign pointing the way to the church offices where we were confronted by a video doorbell. I thumbed the push and a tinny female voice I could barely hear asked how she could help us.

I introduced myself. Less than a minute later, an imposing woman, with an amazing bust that seemed to be at odds with the sweatshirt she was wearing, opened the door and smiled condescendingly at us.

"The po-lice?" she said, drawing the word out for emphasis. "And how may I help you?"

"We are hoping to talk to the pastor. Is he available?"

The woman stepped back, looked us up and down, then drew the door open for us to enter.

"This is about Victoria Randolph, isn't it?" she asked.

She was unremarkable yet kind of attractive, with a round face, tan complexion, and wire-rimmed glasses that made her look older than she really was. I estimated she was about forty years old, tall, almost as tall as me, and looked to be in good physical shape. Her heart-shaped face was accentuated by a pair of rosy cheeks surrounded by a wreath of lustrous brown hair that hung in gentle waves to her shoulders.

"What do you know about Victoria Randolph, Miss..." I asked.

"Karen Silver. Call me Karen, please. Miss Silver sounds so... formal, don't you think? I'm the church administrator. Mr. Randolph called yesterday and told us the terrible news. Pastor Ed was devastated. He rushed right over, of course. I made the family a casserole. Who could possibly cook after such a traumatic event?"

Or eat? I thought but didn't say.

"Is the pastor available?" I asked. "We have a few questions."

"He is. If you'll wait here, I'll announce you."

The waiting area looked more like the lobby of a law firm than a church office.

"Look at these seats," Janet said. "They're leather."

She ran her hand over the loveseat and then the side chair.

"You sure they aren't fake?" I asked skeptically.

"I'm sure. My sister-in-law loves leather furniture,"

Janet said as she pressed the cushion of a seat with her index finger. "See how it wrinkles? That indentation will stay there. That's one way to tell if it's real leather." She leaned down and sniffed the armrest. "Yup. You can tell by the smell."

"I didn't know you had a brother," I said, wrinkling my nose as I watched her inspect the material. "Is he older or younger?"

"He's three years older than me," Janet said as she continued taking mental pictures. "He and Sarah have been married for almost five years. They live in Memphis."

I nodded, not really listening to her, and stepped out into a reception area even more luxurious than the waiting area. A pair of double doors stood wide open, so inviting to an inquisitive mind like mine, so I stepped into what was obviously the main office. Lined with shelves stocked with enough office supplies to keep the Pentagon in business for a month, I had to wonder what it was all used for. Filing cabinets flanked the bookshelves. Paintings of Jesus in various poses hung wherever there was a space: some of them traditional depictions that reminded me of Catholic school when I was young, others were more modern: bolder colors and geometric shapes reminiscent of works by Picasso.

There were two desks. One was covered with stacks of papers and a laptop adorned with colored sticky notes, and three framed photographs of the same two cats: a tabby and one with black and white fur. That desk, no doubt, was where the erstwhile Ms. Silver served her masters, one in his office, the other in Heaven.

The other desk was vacant, the fifteen-inch MacBook Pro laptop thereon was closed.

"Hmm, that's an expensive piece," I mumbled to myself. *I wonder if that's where Mrs. Randolph worked?*

I turned around slowly, taking in the furnishings and the expensive books.

"No expense spared, is there?" Janet asked.

Before I could answer, Karen came hurrying in.

"Ah, there you are," she said, smiling brightly. "Taking in the sights, were you? Lovely, isn't it, the church? I do so enjoy working here."

She stretched out her hand, touched the empty desktop with the tips of her fingers.

"This is where Vicky worked. I put everything away when I heard... well, you know." She stared pensively at the MacBook, then said, "So, if you'd like to follow me, Pastor Ed is waiting for you. Can I get you anything: coffee, tea, bottled water perhaps?"

We both declined and thanked her.

She guided us along a wide, expensively furnished corridor to another huge oak door whereupon was a large brass plaque with the words "Pastor Edward Pieczeck" engraved in ornate letters.

Karen nocked three times, opened the door, and announced us as if we were entering His Majesty's royal chamber.

"Lieutenant Catherine Gazzara and Sergeant Janet Toliver."

I half expected her to complete the introduction with the words, "My Lord."

Pastor Ed rose to his feet beaming, his arms open wide, welcoming us into his sanctuary as if he was the Pope himself, only I was sure the Pope's office, if he had one, was nowhere as luxurious.

"Ladies, do come in. I'm Pastor Ed. What can I do for you?"

His voice was deep, resonant, and I could imagine him in the pulpit, pounding the podium with his fists, shouting halleluiahs and about hellfire and the Lord's wrath. He was around forty, fit—ripped, I think, would properly describe him. The cuff of his short-sleeved shirt hugged his biceps and stretched snuggly across his chest. He wasn't exactly in Arnold's league, but I mean, the man obviously worked out.

"Thank you for seeing us, Pastor. We'd like to ask you a few questions about—"

"About Victoria. Such a terrible thing, poor, poor woman," Pastor Ed interrupted.

"About Victoria Randolph and Meryl Dilly," I said, and watched as the color drained from his face.

"Meryl Dilly?" He swallowed and licked his lips. "What about her?"

"She's dead, murdered. Her husband found her early this morning," I said as I pulled my iPad from my bag. "Do you mind, Pastor? I'd like to record our conversation," I said while holding up the device and tapping the green icon to start it recording.

I smiled to myself as, out of the corner of my eye, I saw Janet opening her notebook.

"Yes, yes, of course, please do," he said, "and please... sit down."

We did, and I watched as he sank slowly back into the leather monstrosity that could only have been called a throne. *Hell, even Harry's chair is not that big,* I thought.

Harry? I hadn't seen him since that altercation, if you could call it that, with Nick Christmas and his private army. My hearing will never be what it was... But that's another story.

"Pastor, what can you tell me about Victoria Randolph? I understand you recently hired her to work in your office, is that right?"

The pastor sat, his hands clasped together on top of the desk, stared at me, said nothing, then seemed to come together with a start.

"I'm sorry, Detective." He blinked. "I had no idea about Meryl Dilly. Oh dear, what is this world coming to? I have a feeling we're quickly approaching the end of days."

He took a deep breath and looked up at the ceiling, mumbling something I couldn't understand: a prayer maybe, whispering in tongues? Who knows?

"And yes. Victoria Randolph expressed an interest in working part-time in the office. She came in twice a week."

"What was her job?" I asked.

"She would just do a few things to help Karen. Filing. Stuffing envelopes or maintaining my schedule, that sort of thing. The congregation has grown so much over the past few years, thank the Lord, Karen needed the help."

"Was Victoria happy? Did she ever mention any problems at home?" I asked.

"Oh yes, she was very happy, and no, she never mentioned any problems at all. She was a devoted wife and mother." He placed his hands flat on the desk and spread his fingers. "She really was salt of the earth."

I was feeling myself cringe as the pastor said that. Everyone said it except the housekeeper.

"Would she come to you if she were having a problem?"

"Yes... well, I would hope so," Pastor Ed replied. "But now that you mention it, there was something I noticed when she first started working here. I don't think it means anything but..."

He spoke so quietly I had to lean forward to hear him.

"Victoria Randolph was a beautiful woman," he continued. "Some of the ladies in the congregation were envious of her."

"Really?" I looked at Janet who was listening and scribbling in her notebook.

"You know how women can be, Detective. You're a *beautiful* woman, yourself."

Are you freaking hitting on me?

He continued, "You no doubt have experienced the judgmental gaze from women who wonder how you attained the position you now hold. There is a reason the serpent approached the woman in the garden first."

He gave me a sad expression like "Oh, you poor woman."

Holy shit! What the hell?

"No, pastor, I didn't sleep with the chief, if that's what you're implying. I earned my promotion by working hard and closing cases," I replied quickly.

"Oh, please, Lieutenant. I wasn't implying anything. I wasn't suggesting that at all. Please forgive me if I've offended you. I certainly didn't mean to."

I looked hard at him. He stared right back at me. There was something about that stare that was unnerving.

"Who was it that had a problem with Victoria?"

"Oh, I don't want to name names." He smiled sheepishly. "Gossip is one of the devil's favorite tools."

"You brought it up, Pastor. I need the names, please."

"I'm sorry, Lieutenant. In all confidence I...well, I can't."

"You do realize we are investigating the homicides of two members of your church?" Janet interrupted. "Murder is one of the devil's tools, too."

"Yes, Detective, that's so true." He'd recovered his composure, leaned back in his chair and steepled his fingers together.

"The Randolph family," he said, smiling benignly, "has been an important part of this congregation since our inception. Victoria, however, joined us only after she married Darby. It was only recently that she approached me, stating that she was looking for a way to serve. I suggested she come work in the office, and she seemed happy with the idea. For the short while we had her, she was an absolute joy."

"Salt of the earth, yes," I said dryly, "so I've heard, many times over the last forty-eight hours. You said it yourself." I cleared my throat. "Tell me about the Randolph family, Pastor. Did they accept Victoria?"

Pastor Ed took a deep breath and laid his palms flat on the desk again. "Eventually, yes, I do believe they accepted her, although it was rather rough sailing at first."

"How so?"

"Well, Victoria wasn't from around here, you know. She didn't come from—well, let's just say her family wasn't as affluent as was the Randolph family."

He smiled, showing his teeth, and then I got it: his smile reminded me of a prominent politician.

"You know how these Southern families are, Detective." He grinned innocently. "Lineage is very important. The Randolph family is proud of theirs."

"So you don't think they were pleased that Darby married Victoria then?" I asked.

"I think they believed she was after the family name and... the money," he admitted. "But you know, I can't say I ever saw anything in Victoria that wasn't absolutely genuine. Unfortunately, jealousy and envy can cloud a person's judgment. And I do believe that several members of the Randolph family, and indeed some of my flock, are victims of the green-eyed monster. It's really a shame."

"Did you ever see anything strange while she was working at the office? Any strangers dropping her off or picking her up. Anyone you didn't recognize lurking around? You know how a pretty girl can become the object of unwanted attention." I smirked.

"As I'm sure you well know," he said slyly. "But no, not that I know of. Well," he said, rising to his feet, "I believe I've answered all of your questions."

"Not yet, Pastor. What can you tell me about Meryl Dilly? She was also a member of your church."

I watched Pastor Ed as he appeared to re-center himself. He took a quiet, deep breath, squared his shoulders and sank slowly back onto his throne.

"Meryl was a very fine woman. I am so sorry to hear of her passing. She was a lovely woman... and had been the hospitality coordinator here at the church for years." He swallowed hard, and his eyes darted around the top of his desk like he was searching for something.

"Are you all right, Pastor?" I asked.

"I'm afraid I have to close this interview," he said. "This is all so very shocking. I feel I must consult with the Lord. He will show me the way, guide me, and Mr. Dilly must need me now."

"Of course," I replied, somewhat taken aback. "But you will make yourself available, I'm assuming. Either Sergeant Toliver or I will be in touch. Or perhaps it would be easier for you to come down to the Police Service Center on Amnicola to talk to us?"

"Whatever is easiest," Pastor Ed stuttered. "I really must ask you to leave now. I will be happy to answer any questions you may have, but not now. Not now."

He rose again, looked first at Janet, then me, and then

the door. As if on cue, it opened to reveal Karen Silver. She looked happy and accommodating. But I have to admit that the hairs on the back of my neck stood up.

How the hell did he do that? There must be a button under his desk.

I grabbed my iPad, closed the cover, stood, and said, "Thank you for your time, Pastor. We'll talk again soon."

I extended my hand. He took it, weakly. The power was completely gone from his grip; his hand was moist with sweat.

We stepped out of the office, and Karen pulled the door closed behind us.

"This is such a terrible turn of events," Karen said in a whisper. "I don't know if this is any help to you. I'm sure Pastor Ed didn't mention it, but we've been having a problem with our groundskeeper."

"No. He didn't," I replied, looking at Janet.

She quickly retrieved her notebook and began to write.

Karen led us to the front door, looking over her shoulder at Pastor Ed's closed office door.

"God forgive me for breaking the pastor's trust, but Marty Butterworth, he's been our groundskeeper for several years," Karen said quietly, conspiratorially. "He does good work when he's sober, but the Lord sees fit to test him. And he really doesn't always cope well, and there's been some talk. He watches... the ladies."

I stared at her, inwardly shaking my head. "This Mr. Butterworth, did he know Victoria?" I asked, skeptically.

"He knew her husband, and he knew Mr. and Mrs.

Dilly, but..." Again, she turned her head and looked back toward the office. "I can't say anymore. I really can't. I need this job. I live alone, you see. But I thought you should know." She pulled the front door open and held it for us. "God bless you both and keep you safe."

"Thank you, Karen." I handed her one of my business cards. "If you think of anything else that might help us, please give me a call."

She nodded but looked down at the ground as she shut the door behind us. We headed back to the car and climbed in.

"That was one weird interview," Janet said. "Did you notice how the pastor acted when you brought up Meryl Dilly? That was a strange response."

"Yes, I noticed, and it was, especially since he seemed so comfortable talking about Victoria... You know," I continued thoughtfully, "there was a moment when I had a feeling he was hitting on me."

"You did? Well he did get a little personal about how you got your job, but hitting on you? Can't say I noticed."

I buckled my seat belt, and Janet pulled the cruiser out of the parking lot. Thoughts swirled in my head about the case and my upcoming meeting.

"We need to head back to Amnicola. I have an appointment with Chief Johnston at three, and I need to prepare." I looked at her, "Aren't you tired? We've been up almost the entire night. I'm frickin' exhausted. How come you have so much energy?"

She laughed. "I don't know. I'm excited, I guess. I'm sure I'll fall over as soon as I get home tonight. Okay, so when we get back to Amnicola, I'll run a background on Marty Butterworth and see what I can find out. And I have a funny feeling about... well, I thought I might run one on the pastor too. What do you think?"

"You read my mind." I yawned and closed my eyes.

13

I t didn't take long for me to gather together what I needed for my interview with Chief Johnston. I was done and ready an hour after we arrived back at Amnicola, a little after one o'clock that afternoon.

Janet went to lunch and then to work on her background checks. Me? I didn't want another run-in with Finkle before my meeting, so I left the building and spent a pleasant forty-five minutes on the deck of the Boathouse, drinking coffee, enjoying the view, and thinking... and that was a mistake. Suddenly, I was filled with doubt and the enormity of what I was about to do... and I almost didn't, do it. But the more I thought about it, the more I knew I had to.

So, reluctantly, I went ahead with the next part of the plan. I called Sheriff White. He'd mentioned more than once that he'd love to have me on his team. That was the back-up plan if what I was about to do went wrong and I had to walk away from the Chattanooga PD. That done, I drank what was left of my coffee and drove back to the Police Service Center.

It was ten minutes to three when I parked my car at the rear of the building. I grabbed my laptop from the seat beside me and walked confidently, so I thought, into the building. The Chief's suite of offices was two doors down the corridor and on the left. I opened the outer door and walked inside.

"Good afternoon, Cathy."

She had the phone to her ear, but she nodded, smiled, and pointed to a chair. I sat down, feeling like a schoolgirl awaiting an interview with the school principal which, in a way, I suppose I was.

Cathy finished her call, disconnected, tapped a button on her console, and said, "Lieutenant Gazzara is here, Chief."

She nodded, though of course the Chief couldn't see her, and set the phone back in its cradle.

"He's waiting for you, Kate. You can go on in."

I'd known Police Chief Wesley Johnston for many years. I can't say he was a friend, or even a sympathetic boss, but he was a fair administrator. I knew he would listen to what I had to say. Yes, he would listen; how much good it would do me I wasn't sure. Well, I was prepared for the worst, hence my call to Sheriff White.

Johnston was seated at his desk but stood when I entered.

"Please sit down, Lieutenant," he said, indicating a chair in front of his desk. "Now, tell me, what can I do for you?"

He was in uniform: the blue shirt pressed to perfection, the four silver stars in each of his collar tabs glinting under the artificial lighting. He was a big man... No, he was larger than life with a large head, bald, shaved, polished. The Hulk Hogan mustache was pure white and perfectly trimmed, and the man had an air about him, not quite arrogance... no, he was confident, supremely confident. I never, ever felt really comfortable in his presence, something I think he actively cultivated.

So I sat down, my laptop on my knee, and I took a deep breath and began.

By then, he was seated too, leaning back in his chair, elbows on the armrests.

"I wish to lodge a formal complaint against Assistant Chief Henry Finkle."

I paused, looked at him. He didn't even blink, just looked stoically back at me.

"Go on," he said.

This is not going to be easy, I thought. *Ah, screw it.*

And, quite suddenly, the heavy weight lifted, and I relaxed.

"I've had it, Chief. I can't take his crap anymore. I don't deserve it, and I won't stand for it. I'm done. Either you get me out from under him, or you can have my gun and my badge, right now."

"Take it easy, Kate. Keep your weapon and badge. I don't want them. Talk to me."

"Sir, I'll let Finkle talk for me," I said.

I placed my laptop on the edge of his desk, opened it, took a thumb drive from my jacket pocket, inserted it, opened the file, and tapped play. Henry Finkle's voice sounded from my computer.

"I'm disappointed in you, Lieutenant. Even a raw rookie knows not to talk to the press. He's another one you're sleeping with, I suppose. How many more are there... besides Starke? By the way, does his wife know you're screwing him? Perhaps someone should let her know."

I tapped the icon and halted the recording.

"That, sir, is just the latest. I have more, many more, going back more than a year. The man has been trying to get me into bed with him even longer than that. I have it all recorded." I had to struggle to stop myself from tearing up.

"So, finally," I continued, "I... It's... over. Either he goes or I do. And I suppose that will be me. He is, after all, an assistant chief—"

"Stop it, Kate, before you say something you'll regret. How did you get those recordings?"

I looked down at my wrist, shrugged, took off my watch, and laid it on his desk.

"I tried the usual methods—iPhone, iPad, laptop, but he was too smart. Made me turn them off, so I used that." I nodded at the rather plain-looking man's watch lying on the desktop.

"It belongs to Harry Starke, a gift from the Secret Service. I borrowed it from him, more than a year ago. The recording equipment is in the trunk of my car."

"It was that bad, huh?" He looked at me.

Is that sympathy I see in his eyes?

He picked up the desk phone, tapped an icon on the screen and said, "Henry. Come in here, will you?"

Two minutes later, the door opened and Finkle sauntered in.

"Yes, Chief. What can I do for you?'

"You can sit down. No, not there," Chief Johnston said as Finkle moved toward the couch by the wall, "There." He indicated the seat next to me, in front of the desk.

That's a first, I thought.

The Chief tapped another icon on the console and said, "Chief Finkle, I must inform you that this conversation is being recorded. Lieutenant Catherine Gazzara has indicated that she wishes to lodge a formal complaint of sexual and workplace harassment against you. Do you have anything to say before I accept her complaint?"

"Say? Hell, yes, I have something to say. It's bullshit. She's a lunatic. I've never—"

"*Stop!*" Johnston said loudly. "Lieutenant, please play for the assistant chief what you just played for me."

I tapped the play icon.

"I'm disappointed in you, Lieutenant..." Finkle's voice seemed to echo around the room, at least to me it did.

I turned my head to look at him. His face was white, the muscles of his jaw rigid. I didn't know if he was angry or scared and, frankly, I didn't care.

"That's... that's just..."

"Just the tip of the iceberg," Johnston finished the

sentence for him. "She has more, Henry, much more, going back many months."

He swung around in his seat. "How, did, you—"

"That doesn't matter," the Chief interrupted him. "It's what you did that matters. What do you have to say for yourself?"

"I want my FOP representative present before I say another word."

Johnston nodded. "That, of course, is your right." He leaned forward and placed his hands on the edge of his desk, then reached out and tapped the off icon on the console, and said, "But before we do that, I should warn you that if you turn this into a formal IA inquiry, and should the outcome not be in your favor, it will result in your dismissal from this department for cause. And I can assure you, from what I've heard, that's exactly how it will end. She's got you by the balls, Henry, so is that really what you want?"

He tapped the on icon and started recording again.

"We can handle this situation one of two ways, Chief Finkle," Johnston continued. "Lieutenant Gazzara no longer wishes to work for you, and I can't say I blame her. I, personally, no longer have confidence in you as a leader in this department. That being so, I offer two options. You can either take a demotion or early retirement. Which is it to be? I suggest you leave now. Go home and think about it. I'll see you in this office at nine o'clock sharp tomorrow morning."

Holy crap! That, I didn't expect.

Finkle sat still, stiff, his jaw working, eyes blinking.

Then he stood, turned on his heel, and walked out the door, slamming it behind him.

"That work for you, Kate?"

I didn't know what to say, so I didn't, say anything.

He smiled benignly at me and said, "Do you think I didn't know what was going on? I did. Let's just say there's someone else in the department that's got your back, kept me up to speed. The problem was, there was little I could do about it, other than chew Henry's ass, not until you made a complaint, gave me something to work with." He chuckled, then said, "Go on, get out of here, Kate. Go back to work. I need results on the Lookout Mountain cases."

And I did.

14

"Are you all right?" Janet said as we took the elevator down to the ground floor. "You look really tired. Would you like me to drive you home?"

"No. I'll be fine. Go get some rest. I'll see you tomorrow."

"How did your interview with the Chief go?"

"Fine," I said, not wanting to talk about it. "He said he needed results, and quickly." It wasn't a lie, and I wasn't prepared to talk about what had just happened— with Janet, or anyone else. In fact, I was still overwhelmed by the outcome. My problem was solved... or was it?

Surely, he wouldn't accept a demotion... Oh, dear God, I hope not.

Janet left and, as I watched her go, I half regretted not taking her up on her offer; I could barely keep my eyes open. So I sat behind the wheel of my car for several minutes, the engine running, wondering if I shouldn't get one of the uniforms to drive me home.

Nope, right now the only company I need is my own.

I rubbed my eyes, rolled down all the windows, turned on the AC, and pulled out of the lot onto Amnicola.

Ten minutes later, I was parked out front of my apartment wondering how the hell I'd managed to get from point A to point B. Have you driven from one place to another and when you arrived, had literally no memory of the drive? That was me that evening. I sat in my car, freaked out because I didn't remember a damn thing.

Wow, Kate, that's freakin' scary.

"Hey, baby," I said as I opened the door to my apartment and scooped Sadie Mae into my arms. "Were you waiting for me?"

The little chocolate-colored wiener dog was my attempt at having a semblance of a normal life. And who doesn't appreciate some unconditional love when you arrive home? I certainly didn't have time for a man in my life, even though that would be nice, someday.

Sadie Mae came to live with me after her owner ended up in jail, put there by me. At the time, we both needed a new friend. Believe it or not, the little dog was instrumental in putting away a sadistic murderer and his accomplice. You may remember the Saffron Brooks case...but that's another story.

Sadie Mae? She came home with me. I still have her. I managed to cure her of her addiction—nicotine: she loved to chew cigarette butts—and she is now the sweetest little friend I ever had, other than Harry Starke, of course.

"But we don't talk about that, do we, Sadie Mae?" I said as I picked her up and set her on my lap.

She licked my chin and struggled to climb higher up my chest. "Okay, okay. That's enough." I put her down, scratched her behind the ears. She seemed happy with that and trotted off to a square of early evening sun shining in through one of the living room windows. She circled the chosen spot two times then flopped down, stared soulfully at me, and closed her eyes.

I was ready to do the same. I changed her drinking water, added a half-cup of kibble to her empty bowl, and headed to the bedroom. I stripped off the sweaty T-shirt and jeans, showered, and crawled into bed, naked as nature intended. I stretch luxuriously between the cold sheets and... that's the last thing I knew.

It was a little after one a.m. when I woke to find Sadie Mae curled up next to me on the bed. That was a big no-no, but I let it slide. I stroked the soft fur on her back. She grunted, rolled over, little legs sticking up, and I rubbed her tummy. I looked at the bedside clock: I'd been asleep for almost seven straight hours; good enough. I was wide awake and going to stay that way.

I showered again. I stood under the scalding water, hoping it would wash away the trauma of what happened in the Chief's office. It didn't, and much as I tried, I felt no sympathy for Henry Finkle. He pushed me to the edge, but I turned on him and tossed him over into the abyss.

Screw him. He brought it on himself. What will he do, I wonder? He's too proud to take a demotion, isn't he? I wouldn't, and if he does? What a disaster... that doesn't bear thinking about.

I got out of the shower, toweled myself off, and pulled on sweats. Then I slipped Sadie Mae's harness over her head, attached the leash, grabbed my Baby Glock and slipped it into my pants pocket. Two minutes later, we were outside and enjoying the quiet of the night. The air was cool. I could see my breath. I would have liked to run, but that was out of the question. Sadie Mae's little legs had to work hard enough as it was just to keep up when walking.

I lived in an apartment in a gated community, so it was safe enough to be out alone in the middle of the night, and besides, I had my Glock, so I was able to let it all go, relax under the stars, and think. I thought about Finkle—I couldn't help it—and I thought about the case, and how wonderful it was going to be without him breathing down my neck, and I smiled. I also thought about the two victims and wondered why I hadn't had a call from Doc Sheddon.

I didn't check my messages yet. Maybe he did call. I put my hand in my pocket, feeling for my iPhone. *Crap! I've left the damn thing at home. I'd better head back.*

As soon we were back inside, I grabbed my phone

and, sure enough, there were several messages, one of them from Doc Sheddon's number.

"Kate. It's Doc. Call me when you get this message, please."

I looked at the clock. It was two in the morning. Doc's message was timed at five after eleven that evening. I didn't hear the phone ping; must have been dead to the world.

I thought for a minute, wondering if I should call at that hour in the morning. I shook my head. If he called that late, he needed me. I dialed his number; he answered almost right away, and I felt guilty when I heard his croaky voice. I'd woken him up.

"Sorry, Doc," I said. "My sleep schedule is all off track. I thought I'd better return your call." I winced as I spoke, expecting him to grumble. I know I would have had I been awakened at that time of night.

"No, Kate. I'm glad you called. I knew I was going to have to do double duty with your homicides. Finished up with my young friend and then went home to await your call. Can you meet me at the office? Mrs. Randolph and Mrs. Dilly are waiting for us."

"I can. I'll be there in twenty."

"What about your young side-kick?" Doc asked.

"I'll let Janet sleep in," I said. "She put in a lot of hours yesterday. And I don't know how well she'd handle her first autopsy at three in the morning."

We hung up, and I headed for the bathroom. I washed my face in cold water, brushed my teeth, found a clean pair of jeans, a brand-new white blouse I didn't really want to wear, and put my hair back in a ponytail. Finally, I settled Sadie Mae down in her own bed, refilled her water bowl, left a note for my dog sitter, grabbed my Glock 17, badge, and wallet, and headed again out into the night.

15

The Hamilton County Medical Examiner's office was an unimposing, anonymous building set on Amnicola Highway just a couple of blocks from the police department. I'd lost count of the number of times I'd stood across from Doc and watched as he violated the one-time home of some poor soul sent too early to meet his, or her, maker.

I parked at the rear next to Doc's BMW. The doors were locked so I had to knock. I knocked. I rang the bell. I knocked some more.

Come on, Doc, damn it.

"Cool your jets, girl!" I heard Doc shout from inside as he came to let me in. "You'll wake my guests," he said as he opened the door.

"Sorry, Doc... Would you like to tell me why we're doing this in the middle of the night?" I asked.

He sighed. "We've got a busy night ahead of us. They brought in a student early last night, a girl, pretty young thing. Opioid overdose coupled with alcohol. Our Mrs. Randolph and Dilly will take us well into mid-morning, and I must get the young lady done as well. It's not like we haven't done this before, Kate, you and I. I think we work quite well together, don't you?" he said.

He led me back along the corridor to the examination rooms. There were just two of them: one on the left and one on the right: two autopsy tables in each room.

Doc swiped his badge in front of a black pad on the wall, a security protocol for opening the door on the left. A little light turned green, and a loud click echoed down the corridor. We entered the anteroom and suited up.

"Let's start in the order of introductions. First, Mrs. Victoria Randolph," Doc said, picking up the clipboard that dangled at the end of the autopsy table.

He pulled the sheet down to expose Victoria's dead naked body. I have to admit it: I winced when I saw the damage.

The skin was a bluish-gray color. As far as I could see, the poor woman didn't have so much as a pimple anywhere on her body, nor any cellulite.

I snapped on a pair of blue latex gloves and parked my ass on a tall metal stool on the opposite side of the table to Doc, close to Victoria's head. Since I was there merely to observe, there was no reason for me to stay on my feet.

"Female," he began, speaking for the overhead mike that was recording the procedure. "Caucasian. Age thirty-one." He used his thumb to pull open an eyelid. "Blue eyes. Blond hair." He looked down at the measure fixed to the edge of the table. "Five-feet-eight and one-half-inches tall. He glanced at the readout from the scale beneath the table. "One hundred and nineteen pounds three ounces."

He inspected the fingernails, collected scrapings and clippings, then examined the body for trace evidence of which he found none, at first.

"No tears in or around the vagina; no signs of trauma. But... hmmm..."

"What have you found?" I asked, rising to my feet as he grabbed a pair of tweezers from the tray at the side of the table.

"Maybe nothing. Victoria's husband has dark hair. But, we'll know soon enough," he said as he carefully lifted a single hair from her pubic area.

I sat down again, already bored to distraction by the droning of his voice and the slow pace of the work.

"Victoria Randolph died of blunt force trauma to the head several minutes, I should say, before she was stabbed. The stab wounds were inflicted postmortem... Six times, she was stabbed. What with I have no idea. I've not seen their like before. Anyway, they certainly aren't what killed her, although any one of them certainly would have, had they been administered before the killer deemed it fit to beat the living daylights out of her head. Such... unnecessary violence. One blow would have been quite sufficient."

Some people found Doc's morgue-ish sense of humor to be insensitive. But you only had to spend five minutes with the man, and you'd know that wasn't the case. He offered the kind of comic relief only a brother ME or a cop could understand. He didn't make light of the tragedy in front of us because he was cold-hearted; quite the opposite, in fact. So, if you can, try to imagine being in the morgue with not one, but two murder victims. A little levity can help a lot in such circumstances. I've seen strong men, Detective Tracy included, turn away and throw up at the first incision.

"I had a hunch that might be the case," I said. "There was so little blood.

"Ye-es," he mused, his face mask close to her head. "If you look here, you can see the indentation of the blunt instrument." He took a set of calipers from the tray along with a small metal ruler and set about measuring the wounds, scribbling notes as he spoke.

"I believe this to be the first blow. It came from behind and her left. It is the largest. Deepest. She didn't know what hit her, literally."

I looked carefully where Doc was pointing. It was obvious Victoria's skull had been cracked open. It was misshapen, and even I could see the indentation.

"If I had to guess she was struck with a crowbar, or possibly a nail bar, the kind roofers use. You see this arched indentation?" he said as he pointed his finger to a dark blue swirl on the side of her head. "One of her lesser injuries. It looks like the curved end of a crowbar to me." He adjusted the light from his visor to better illuminate the bruising.

"If you say so," I replied.

"The assailant hit her on the back of the head, killing

her, but as her body fell, he kept on hitting her, and continued to do so until she landed on her back. But that wasn't enough. He drove the pointed end of the crowbar, or nail bar I would think more likely, into her chest." He pointed to the multiple stab wounds.

"I count five distinct blows to the head," he continued with about as much emotion as the local weatherman. "With multiple secondary blows overlapping. No less than seven. There are six stab wounds to the chest. The good news—as if there is such a thing in a case like this— is she was already dead before she received the second blow to the head. After that, she didn't feel a thing, poor girl."

"What kind of person could do something like this, Doc?"

"Unfortunately, dear Kate, there are many, always have been, always will be.

"So the answer is," I said, smiling, "you don't know."

"Right. I don't speculate about such things because it is a futile exercise to which there is no definitive answer. Now, please allow me to continue. I don't want to be all night." He consulted the wall clock and said, "Oh dear, it seems I already have been."

I smiled and said, "You saw the crime scene, Doc. There was very little blood in that laundry room. That, I don't understand. It should have... well, it would have looked like the Dilly's living room."

"You are absolutely right, Kate. She was indeed moved after the attack. That laundry room wasn't where she died. We were able to find some trace evidence. Not a lot. I haven't gotten anything back from the lab yet. It's still too early," he said dryly.

"Time of death?" I asked.

"Sometime between the hours of ten and midnight on the sixteenth, probably closer to midnight."

"That's a pretty tight window," I said. "Could be helpful."

"It could indeed."

"I wonder if Mike Willis found anything?" I said. "Though he would have called me if he'd turned up anything significant. Still, I'd better check in with him first thing when I get to the office. What else, Doc?"

And so it went, for another ninety horrifying minutes as he delved into what once had been Victoria Randolph's vital organs

Finally, he covered her with the sheet, stepped away, and said, "Carol will close her up in the morning."

Carol Oates being his assistant.

"So," he said, rubbing his still gloved hands together. "A quick cup of coffee, I think, then on to round two, Meryl Dilly. Ready?"

"No, I don't think so, Doc. One is more than enough, unless you can't do without me."

"I understand completely, my dear." He looked again at the clock. "Carol will be in soon, in about thirty minutes in fact. Let's have some coffee, and then off you go... You know, I hate being alone in this godforsaken place."

Now that did surprise me. I looked at the clock. It

was almost seven. *My, how time flies when you're having fun.*

"Well, okay then," I said, "but I need to use the restroom first."

"Very good," he said. "I'll meet you in five."

He pulled off his gloves and tossed them into the hazmat container. I did the same and then stepped into the yellow lights in the hallway.

When I exited the ladies' room, Doc was already waiting for me at the far end of the hallway holding two large porcelain mugs.

"When I'm here at this hour, I brew the good stuff. No Folgers for us this morning, Kate. This is Dunkin' Donuts house blend," he said, handing one to me as I approached.

"Doc, if you weren't married, I'd whisk you away to paradise."

"Ah, Kate, my love, I don't think I could handle that kind of paradise, but answer me this," he said as he led the way into the tiny reception area. "Black or cream and sugar?"

"Black, of course."

"Then our love can never be. I have to have cream and sugar."

He held the door open for me. I chuckled and sat down.

16

It was almost eight o'clock that morning when Carol arrived. I stayed with Doc until she did, and then I headed home to clean up, and by that, I mean to shower and change for the fourth time in twenty-four hours. That being so, it was just before nine-thirty back at the Police Service Center when I closed my office door behind me; a fat lot of good that did. Barely had I sat down than there was a knock at the door.

"Got a minute?" Mike Willis asked as he stuck his head inside.

"I was just about to call you," I said. "Yes, come on in. Take a seat. You have good news, I hope."

"Nope, not really, but we're not finished yet," he said dejectedly. "There's a lot of trace evidence but, except for two small fibers we found in the laundry room at the Randolph scene, and four more on the section of hardwood floor at the Dilly scene, none of it is foreign to the crime scenes. Same with latents; plenty of them, but none that can't be accounted for."

I leaned forward in my chair to ask a question, but Mike answered it before I had a chance.

"And before you ask, yes, we did print the house-keeper and the two husbands to eliminate them... or not, as the case may be. We're still working both scenes, but so far, we've not found a single fingerprint that shouldn't be there, including the Randolph's housekeeper's. The blood at both scenes appears to belong to the victims; no anomalous drops or smears; that according to preliminary typing. I'll know for sure when we get the DNA results back. Sorry... By the way, I understand Doc found a pubic hair on the first victim's body. Let's hope it's not the husband's. We could do with a break."

"Yes, me too," I said. "What about the fibers, any footprints?"

"I'm thinking they're carpet fibers. But I wouldn't get your hopes up. Even if they are, they probably came from somewhere in the home, homes. I'll let you know exactly what they are when I've completed a mass spectrometry analysis. I'm having Arty Moor gather samples of the carpeting in both houses for comparisons." He paused, then continued.

"Footprints? None at the Randolph scene. The Dilly scene seems promising but, as I said, we're not yet done with either scene, so I'll let you know."

I leaned back in my chair. This wasn't what I was hoping to hear.

"So, once again, I have two major crimes, obviously

connected. Well, I won't know that for sure until I hear from Doc. And I have nothing to go on. Darn." I picked up the phone, buzzed Janet, and asked her to join me.

"Okay, Mike. Thank you. Call me if you need me."

He nodded, rose to his feet, and stepped to the door, stood for a moment, then looked at me, hesitated, then said, "What's this I hear about Chief Finkle?"

My heart skipped a beat, I looked up at him, startled. "What about him?"

"He's been demoted to captain and moved over to Narcotics. You didn't know?"

"No, I didn't know," I replied, truthfully, my stomach doing cartwheels.

"What the hell happened, I wonder?" Mike said. "He was your boss. You wouldn't happen to—"

"I've no idea," I lied, cutting him off.

I was just about to dig my hole a little deeper when Janet tapped on the door and came in.

Whew, that was a close one. Demoted? Narcotics? I can't imagine he's happy with that... Not quite what I'd hoped for, but at least he's out of my way... I hope. What the hell was he thinking taking the demotion?

"Hey, Janet," Willis said. "How are you? All good, I hope."

She nodded, held the door for him.

"Later, Kate," he said.

Janet closed the door behind him.

"Sit down, Janet," I said.

And she did, in the seat Mike Willis had just vacated.

"Well," I said, leaning back in my chair and lacing my

fingers together behind my neck, "we're off to a grand start: two friggin' murders and nothing concrete to go on."

I was interrupted by my iPhone buzzing and vibrating across the top of my desk. I grabbed it before it could fall over the edge, looked at the screen, and smiled hopefully.

"Hello, Doc," I said. "Long time no see. Hold on a sec. I'll put you on speaker so Janet can hear."

"Ah, Janet," the tiny voice said. "My very favorite detective. Well, except for you, of course, Catherine."

"That's enough schmoozing, Doc," I said. "What do you have for me?"

"Ah, but you're a cold-hearted woman, Detective. Well, first, you might be surprised to learn that Meryl Dilly was extremely fit for a woman in her late forties. You might want to check gym memberships in the city."

That was something worth looking into.

"I don't recall Victoria Randolph being particularly ripped," I said.

"Oh but she is, was, though it's not so easy to see. Mrs. Randolph was a rather... I want to say voluptuous, but she wasn't at all fat... well-endowed, shall we say."

"Yes, I assumed they were real," I said.

"They are indeed, Kate, as are Mrs. Dilly's though she is not quite so well blessed... Let's get on with it, shall we?"

"Please," I said. Making a mental note to have Janet check out the local gyms.

"I found seminal fluid in Mrs. Dilly's vagina so she engaged in intercourse within twenty-four hours of her death, which means it could very well be her husband's so let's not get too excited yet."

Or maybe not, I thought.

"As to her wounds, we have three primary blows to the head. Victoria only had one. I'd say that means the unfortunate Mrs. Dilly saw it coming. That could explain why the assailant had to use more force.

"Now we come to the wounds on her chest and torso. There are five stab wounds to the chest and abdomen. One shattered the sternum, a second fractured the fourth rib on the left side and penetrated the left lung, the third fractured ribs five and six on the right side of her chest. The two wounds to the abdomen are horrific. So much force..."

I noticed Janet going paler by the second.

"The assailant must have used both hands to drive the weapon completely through the soft tissue of the abdomen into the carpet. The entry and exit wounds are roughly one inch in diameter, consistent with a crowbar."

"That's intense," I muttered.

"Indeed," Doc said. "Rage, fury. Whoever did this to our two ladies was more than a little ticked off."

"So nothing new then?" I asked. *Stupid question!*

"Other than the seminal fluid, no."

I shivered, felt kind of lost. Then I shook the feeling off. *Get a grip, Kate. This is what you do.* I told myself. *It's just another murder case. There will be clues. There will be someone somewhere who has a hunch or was a witness to something out of the ordinary. Someone will eventually remember something. And I will find those clues, those individuals.*

At least, that's what I told myself. But there was something niggling at the back of my subconscious, something I couldn't get a grip on. There was a sinister twist to it all that I just couldn't put my finger on.

"I can tell you that the assailant was right-handed," Doc said, interrupting my thoughts. "And by the way the blows sliced across Meryl's face, the attacker got sloppy; maybe he was in a hurry," Doc said.

"You keep saying he," I said. "Could it have been a woman?"

"It's possible, I suppose, but..."

"I understand," I said. "It would have taken a lot of strength to inflict those head wounds: even more to drive what is essentially a blunt instrument through to the floor. But Meryl Dilly fought back, right?"

"She did. There are defensive bruises on her fore-arms. One of the blows shattered the radius and cracked the ulna in her left arm; she must have been trying to protect her face."

"Meryl Dilly was killed first," I said. "Her body had been there for how long?"

"Yes, about two and a half days ago, judging by the livor mortis and rigor," Doc said. "And there is already signs of insect activity. The little devils find dead meat quickly. So sometime in the late afternoon of Tuesday the sixteenth, about eight to ten hours before Mrs. Randolph."

"Little devils," I muttered, to myself.

"How's that?" Doc asked.

"Nothing. I spoke with the pastor of The Church of the Savior and, well, he had some things to say about the devil, too."

"I'll bet he did." He chuckled, but not loudly.

"DNA?"

"Just the fluid. I'll let you know what the lab says as soon as I hear from them."

"I'd appreciate that." I cleared my throat. "Mr. Dilly was away, said he left early Tuesday morning, so the semen is probably his. If it's someone else's... well, I should get so lucky. Anyway, I'll have Janet check it out." I looked at Janet and nodded.

She nodded back, scribbled a note.

I started to think out loud. "If it's his, and he left home when he said he did, he's in the clear. If not..."

"I don't envy you, my dear," Doc said.

"Neither do I, Doc. Neither do I."

"I have no doubt the same weapon was used on both women," he said. "Other than that, what the connection is, well, I'll leave that to you, the experts."

"There's no such thing as experts in this job, Doc," I said as I flipped absently through my files. "There are just people like me, too stupid to stop digging even when the dirt keeps falling back in on 'em. But you know what? We get there in the end, and I'm damned if I'll let this one beat me."

I paused, then said, "I need to let you go, Doc. You'll send me a copy of the files tomorrow? And would you please put a rush on those lab submissions?"

"Oh, of course. You know how they jump whenever I ask them to hurry."

I felt the sarcasm even over the phone.

"You're a peach, Doc. Call me when you have the results." I disconnected, set the phone down on my desk, and leaned back in my chair and closed my eyes.

Truthfully, I was disgusted. I had a lot of information, but without something to connect it to, it was useless. I sighed, checked my watch—it was almost eleven.

"Janet," I said, "I've been up since three. I need a little me time."

"Since three? Why didn't you call me?" She caught the look I was giving her and said, "Oh, okay. I'll go check out Mr. Butterworth, the airlines, and the gyms."

I waited until she'd closed the door, then transferred all of the photographs I'd taken of the two crime scenes from my iPhone to my laptop. Then I spent the next two hours going through them, sending those I thought might be useful to the printer. With the pictures in hand, and having heard from Mike and Doc, I began to set up my incident board.

The Meryl Dilly crime scene was a bloodbath. Even so, as far as I could see, there were no footprints or hand-prints. Instead, there were tracks in the blood across the carpet. Whoever did this, he made sure to smear the gory mess, and any possible footprints. I smiled.

Nice try, asshole, I thought. *Somehow, somewhere between the body and your vehicle, you left either a bloody footprint or handprint, and Mike is a genius... If you did, he'll find it.*

I gave up, went across the road to Mickey Dee's for coffee and a burger. It was while I was there, stuck away in a corner, hopefully out of sight from any other member of the department who'd had the same idea as I'd had, when thoughts of Henry Finkle popped into my head.

Narcotics? What's up with that? Why the hell didn't the Chief just get rid of him? The thorn may no longer be in my side, but it's still around, waiting for a chance to stab me in the back.

Then I had another thought, something the Chief had said: *Let's just say there's someone else in the department that's got your back... But who could that be? And why didn't he come to me?*

It was a puzzlement.

I finished up, went back to my office, worked on my board some more, handled a couple of routine tasks, returned several calls, and then headed home. It was still not quite three in the afternoon, but what the hell? My bed was calling me for a nap. Saying I was beat from my haphazard schedule the last few days would be an understatement. I needed some rest, not to mention I was more than a little frustrated at the lack of progress in the murder cases.

A long weekend of mulling over the details stretched before me. I knew I was going to drive myself crazy if I spent it at home with just the dog. So, being the resourceful problem-solver that I am, I called Lonnie Guest and invited him to dinner.

He'd been my partner on the force for years. Who better to discuss the cases with? We'd made a good team, and I missed our coffee sessions going over the details and connecting the clues. At one point we'd tried dating. Although we hadn't worked out as a couple long-term, we were comfortable together, could be ourselves and relax, and still had great physical chemistry.

As a bonus, he's a great cook and... when he left just before six the following morning, I was, in every way, feeling more like my old self again.

17

I'd been in my office no more than a couple of minutes when Janet arrived with her arms full of files, notebooks, and printouts.

"Morning, LT," she said brightly, looking fresh as always. Her red hair swept back into a ponytail added color to her freckled face. She was wearing skinny jeans, a white tee and white tennies. If it hadn't been for the Glock and badge on her belt, she'd have looked like a teenager heading to class. "Hope you had a nice weekend. Did you get some rest?"

"Good morning, Janet and yes and yes. How about you? You look happy. What have you got for me?"

"Me too, but I worked on Saturday, and I have some good news. I almost called you. Hold on a sec'."

She sat down in front of my desk, shuffled through some papers and extracted a printout from the criminal database and handed it to me. I didn't recognize the mug shot at the top left, but I did recognize the name.

"Okay," Janet said, having sorted her pile into neat little stacks. "Martin "Marty" Butterworth age thirty-nine. Seems he has quite a history," Janet said, raising her eyebrows and leaning forward slightly. "Two years in the county jail for aggravated assault in 2007. He beat up a girl who turned him down for a date. In May 2010, he was arrested for assault, but the victim refused to press charges. He hit the guy upside the head with a pool stick; they were playing eight ball, so it seems, and our Marty doesn't like to lose. And he has three drunk and disorderlies, including one resisting arrest."

"Nice. What a charmer."

"But here's the kicker," Janet said, wiggling in her seat. "Also in 2012 he killed a dog, beat it to death with an iron pipe. He told the arresting officers that it had rabies, but they could smell the booze on him and didn't buy the story." Janet leaned back in her seat.

"And he's working at the church?" I shook my head.

"To be fair, all of these charges happened six or more years ago, when he was in his twenties. Alcoholic. I could, if I were a compassionate person, say it might have been the ignorance of youth."

"And how old are you, Janet?" I asked, finding the irony in her last statement.

"I'll be twenty-five in January, but I'm not stupid," she replied defensively.

"Never said you were." I smiled. "You got an address for him."

"Yup." Janet sat up straight. "Oh, and you'll like this:

he has a connection to both Victoria Randolph and Meryl Dilly."

As you can imagine, my eyes widened, it was music to my ears.

"Oh, really. Do tell."

"Turns out that Mrs. Dilly had a couple of encounters with Butterworth. Seems he was a tad bit, let's say, inappropriate." Janet held up her thumb and forefinger about an inch. "Must have grabbed her ass or something. Anyway, it turned out that Darby Randolph was doing some pro bono work for the church, and he offered Mrs. Dilly some legal advice and Dilly filed for a restraining order against Butterworth. A temporary order was granted, and he was to stay at least one hundred feet away from Mrs. Dilly at all times. The temporary order, however, was not made permanent. Apparently, Meryl didn't turn up for the court date."

"Good work, Janet. Hmm, so we have motives for both murders then. Butterworth has an ax to grind with Randolph and Dilly. What about Connor Dilly's alibi?"

"It's good. He was on the seven-fifteen flight to Memphis out of Lovell Field on Tuesday morning."

"Did you check the gyms?"

"Yup. Both Meryl Dilly and Victoria Randolph were members of the Fit for Life gym on East Brainerd Road. I haven't been down there yet. I quit on Saturday at four-thirty, and well, I took Sunday off. I was bushed. Sorry, LT."

"Don't apologize. I don't blame you. We both needed a break. I'm surprised you worked at all. Thank you for that. At least now we have something to work with. How about we go pay Marty Butterworth a visit? Oh, and by the way: no more of those damn notebooks. Use this from now on." I handed her the iPad Pro that Jimmy had, sometime after I left on Friday afternoon, left on my desk with a note, "For Detective Toliver. User and password are..."

She took it, opened the case, looked at it, sighed and said, "I already have one, at home, but thank you. This is a better one."

It was a little after eight-thirty that morning when we headed out to Marty Butterworth's home. He lived alone in a small split-level in North Chattanooga. There were iron bars over the basement windows and the front screen door. The gravel driveway was dotted with weeds growing up through the stones, though the grass in front of the house was neatly trimmed and the house itself was freshly painted and seemed to be in good shape. The address was spray painted in white on the black mailbox, and there was a beat-up, red Chevy 1500 pick-up truck in the driveway. I pulled up behind it and shut off the engine.

"Ready?" Janet asked.

I nodded before she pounded on the bars of the security door. From inside the house, we heard some shuffling around. But for several seconds, no one came to the door. Janet knocked again.

"Marty Butterworth?" she called out. "Chattanooga police. Come on and open up."

"Ah, shit," a male voice growled.

After a little stumbling around, the sound of glasses or dishes being collected and moved, the sound of a security chain and deadbolt being unlocked, the front door opened and an unseen pall of cigarette smoke mingled with a hint of marijuana billowed out and enveloped me.

Gross, and he's living in this? It's enough to kill him.

"Yeah? What?"

Marty Butterworth struck me as a man who was not living up to his potential. He appeared to have slept in his clothes. He was maybe six feet tall, very fit and muscular, wearing a pair of khaki pants and a white T-shirt. They weren't dirty, but he did look disheveled: his hair was messy but without even a hint of gray, prominent cheekbones from good bone structure, soulful brown eyes, and he had a five o'clock shadow that might or might not have been worn intentionally.

Wow! Put this man in a suit and tie and he'd be a knockout, handsome.

"Mr. Butterworth," I said, making sure he could see the badge on my belt. "I'm Lieutenant Gazzara. This is Sergeant Toliver. We need to talk to you. Can we come in?"

"Well, I uh," he stuttered, looking over his shoulder. "The housekeeper didn't show up on her usual day."

"That's okay," I said. "We need to talk to you about your job at The Church of the Savior. A... Ms. Karen Silver suggested the we talk to you."

"Karen?" he said. He took a deep breath, smiled slightly, then nodded, stepped forward, unlocked the barred door, and held it open for us to enter.

I was surprised at how neat the inside of the house actually was. Furniture was old and worn, but good quality. The couch where Marty routinely sat had obviously seen better days, but the floor was clean and uncluttered and, aside from the cigarette butts and crumbs on the coffee table in front of the couch, all of the flat surfaces were also free of clutter and dirt. A solitary picture of Jesus adorned the wall behind the couch, and a sixty-inch TV on an antique sideboard faced it. The only anomaly was the two longnecks half hidden behind the chair next to the couch.

Janet, with her hand on her weapon, walked through to the rear of the home.

"Shall we sit down?" I asked as I took my iPad from my shoulder bag.

"What the hell is she doing?" he asked. "What's this about?"

"As I said, we need to talk to you about your job at the church."

He shrugged, muttered something I couldn't hear, nodded, waved his hand in the general direction of the couch, sat down in a recliner next to it, and grabbed a pack of cigarettes from the coffee table.

Janet joined me on the couch. I informed Marty Butterworth that I would be recording the interview and entered the usual date, time, and so on for the record, and then I began.

"Is there anyone else in the house, Mr. Butterworth?" I asked.

"No. Just me." He coughed the cough of someone who smoked... a lot.

"Mr. Butterworth, I understand that you are the handyman at The Church of the Savior. Is that correct?" I said.

"That's right. I'm also the gardener. I've been there for about six years." He took a long drag on his cigarette.

"Then you must know the people who attend the church?"

"Some of them. Some of them speak to me, say hello, that kind of stuff. Others don't. I'm not in their social league," he replied. "Look, are you going to tell what this is about or not? Because if you're not, I don't want to talk to you."

"Mr. Butterworth, we are investigating the suspicious deaths of two members of the church," I said, closely watching his eyes.

He frowned, and said, "Oh yeah, and what's that got to do with me?"

"Do you know Victoria Randolph?"

"Everyone knows her. Hell, how could you not? She's hard to miss."

He took another drag then tilted his head back and blew out a long stream of smoke. I could only imagine the dirty movie scrolling through his mind at the thought of Victoria Randolph.

"Did you know her well enough to talk to?"

"Nope. I'm way out of her league. She never speaks

to me. I'm just the hired help." He looked at me like a thirsty man eyeballing an icy cold glass of water.

"Does that upset you, make you angry?" I asked.

Marty chuckled. "Nope. I'm not her type. She likes the tall, dark, controllable types, and rich."

"What makes you say that?"

Marty rolled his eyes. "You've met her husband? That guy wouldn't wipe his ass without asking the Little Wife for permission. I heard that he almost lost his family fortune when he married her. But, you know what they say: what lies between those thighs..." He chuckled again, looked at me and said, "Why? Why the interest in Lookout Mountain's Barbie Doll?"

"She's dead, Mr. Butterworth. Murdered, last Wednesday."

"Last Wednesday? You're kiddin', right? How come there's been nothing on TV about it?"

I kept my eye on his body language and facial expressions. Did he already know?

"It's been kept out of the press, for obvious reasons." I looked directly at him, trying to keep my expression neutral, and continued, "How do you know Darby's family didn't want him to marry Victoria?"

He sucked hard on the cigarette, held it up in front of his face, contemplated it, then smiled and said, "That's the thing about a guy like me in a place like that. No one pays any attention to me. I was at the frickin' wedding. Who do you think cleaned up before and after them? Did you ever see rich people playing in someone else's yard?

They leave a mess." Another drag on the cigarette as his eyes squinted for a moment.

"Anyway, I heard the mother of the groom, Mrs. Randolph, cursing Victoria's name to anyone who'd listen. She was sure Victoria was going to drain Darby's bank account and ruin the family name. 'White trash,' she said. 'Ruin the Randolph's stellar reputation,' she said. She forgot her own father-in-law was a crook, I guess." He winked at me before taking another long drag then leaning forward and scrubbing out the cigarette in an over-filled ashtray.

I leaned forward in my seat. "What about Meryl Dilly? Did you know her?"

"Meryl Dilly's dead too?" Marty asked, quietly, his expression deadpan.

Hmm... That's not the reaction I was expecting.

I nodded. Out of the corner of my eye, I saw Janet tap something into her iPad. *Good, she caught it too.*

Marty chuckled again. "Well now, ain't that some-thing. Maybe now they'll get some decent music in that place."

"You think it's funny, Mr. Butterworth?"

"I don't know if it's funny or not, and you know what? I didn't give a rat's ass for either of 'em, but if you think I had something to do with the deaths of these women, you're barking up the wrong tree."

"It's funny you'd say that, Marty—it is okay if I call you that, right? Both women were beaten to death with some sort of blunt instrument. Didn't you, Marty, beat a dog to death with a piece of steel pipe?" I watched for the tell.

The smirk disappeared from his face. He narrowed his eyes, frowned at me, tilted his head slightly.

"That was a long time ago," he replied, so quietly I could barely hear him. "When I used to drink."

"You don't drink anymore?" I squinted back at him, quizzically. "These bottles," I leaned over the edge of the couch and picked one up. "They're not yours? Did someone plant them here?"

"So I drink a beer once in a while. So what? I barely drink at all, not since I started working for Pastor Ed."

His eyebrows nearly met in the middle casting a shadow over his eyes; it was a look of pure malevolence, and I almost shuddered.

"Wow," I said. "So you've been almost clean for six years," I needled, placing the bottle on the coffee table. "You've never fallen off the wagon, not once? You must be the hero at your AA meetings. You do go to AA? Lord grant me the serenity..."

He chewed his lower lip; I think I'd struck a nerve.

"Marty," Janet said then paused, stared at him for a couple of seconds, then continued, "There's an empty vodka bottle in your kitchen trash can. Let me guess, you had a buddy over, and it's his."

"That's right," he snapped.

"So," she said. "Let me ask you this: how much have you had to drink the past few days?"

I looked him in the eye, then at the bottle on the coffee table.

"That's none of your frickin' business. I answer to no one but Pastor Ed." He reached for the pack of cigarettes, flipped one into his mouth, his hands shaking slightly as he lit it.

"When two women at the place where you work turn up dead, beaten to a pulp, and you have a history of deadly violence, albeit just a dog, well, you can see how I might connect the dots," I said. "Were you drinking, Mr. Butterworth, during the past five days?"

"Yeah. I had a couple beers. So what? I don't drink on the job. I do my work, and I collect my check, and what I do with my money is none of your business." He took an angry drag and blew the smoke out his nostrils like a bull in a Bugs Bunny cartoon.

"You want to know what I think, Marty?" I said. "I think that on Tuesday afternoon—yes, I know you weren't at work that afternoon—I think you had 'a couple of drinks,' probably a whole lot more than a couple, got drunk, went to the Dilly's home, and you beat Mrs. Dilly to death. She had a restraining order against you, so you had motive."

He stared at me, then said, "You know what, I don't have to take this shit from you. You're fishing, Lieutenant. You've got nothing. I'm not saying any more to you. You can go get screwed," he hissed.

"Where were you that afternoon, Marty?"

"Between two o'clock and six on the afternoon of the sixteenth," Janet added.

"I was mowin' the lawns at the Craven House. I do it every week, you can check. Now, I'm not answering any more questions. You've got the wrong guy. I know it's not like the cops to actually do their job, but do a little more digging, and you might find the guy who's really responsible."

"And who would that be, Mr. Butterworth?" Janet asked without looking up from her iPad. "What else did you observe while you were roaming the church grounds unnoticed?"

"Look," he hesitated, "there are tons of people coming and going, in and out of that place all the time. Not to mention the house calls Pastor Ed makes. More than any doctor ever would."

"Is that so?" I asked. "You're insinuating that the only person who ever gave you a chance; the guy who, even though you have a police record and a history of drinking, gave you a job, is a murderer?" I looked at Janet. "Can you believe this?"

She shook her head. "He is what he is."

"Screw you, both of you. Typical shoddy police work. I got a record, so I must have done it. Like I said, screw you. Now either arrest me or get the hell off my property."

"Is that what you think?" Janet chuckled. "You watch too much television, Marty."

"Get out of my house," he said through clenched teeth.

"What about Victoria Randolph?" I asked. "Did you kill her because you couldn't have her, or because her husband helped Meryl Dilly get a restraining order against you?"

I stood up.

"You're trying to make me angry," he said, smiling. "You think I'm that frickin' stupid? That maybe I'd take a swing at you with your partner over there just waiting to make a name for herself? She looks like she's still pedaling a freakin' bike with training wheels on it," Marty hissed, but remained seated.

Janet, to her credit, didn't bite. Instead, she stood up, put her hand on her weapon, smiled, and watched Marty fidget. She remained calm, and I couldn't help but think how Lonnie would have acted in this situation. *By now,* I thought, smiling to myself, *he'd have Marty by the scruff of his neck, politely suggesting that he apologize.*

"Mr. Butterworth, can you tell me where you were four nights ago? Did you see Meryl Dilly?" I pushed.

"I ain't going to tell you again, no more freakin' questions. Now push off."

"Stop it, Marty. Just tell us where you were and we'll leave you alone," I said quietly.

"And I said, get the hell out of my house. You did say you were recording this right? That works in my favor too, right?" He leered.

He was right. It did. So I picked up my iPad from the coffee table, tapped the off button, tucked it into my bag, and headed toward the door.

"We'll be in touch, Marty," I said as I opened the door.

Janet watched him carefully but said nothing. I was glad about that. She was a smart cop for as young as she was.

"I'll look forward to it," he sneered. "Have a great day, Lieutenant. You too, Annie."

Don't do it, Janet. Don't give him the pleasure.

"Annie?" She looked puzzled. "My name's—"

"Little Orphan Annie," he finished for her.

She looked confused for a second, touched her red hair, and then rolled her eyes.

18

"Wow," Janet said as she pulled the driver's side door shut. "What a creep." She sucked in a deep breath and shook her head as I fired up the engine and backed out onto the street. "I was sure I was going to have to go all John Wick on him. He was wound as tight as anyone I've ever seen."

"Yes, I think we may have something there, but a hunch and a couple of coincidences aren't going to get us an arrest. He's slick. Did you notice how he wouldn't tell us where he was? Either he doesn't have an alibi, or he's pulling our chain. He has motive for both killings, and if you add in the alcohol factor, it becomes a whole lot more viable. We still need means and opportunity and, as yet, we can't tie him to either scene. We're going to have to dig deeper."

"Do you think there was anything to what he was saying about the pastor?" Janet asked.

"Not really. He's probably just throwing it out there. Why, do you?"

"Well, he's close to both families, perhaps too close. And he couldn't wait to go visit... Oh, I dunno."

"Come on, Janet. That's what pastors do: offer comfort and support in times of need and loss. Sounds pretty normal to me."

"Okay," she said. "So here's another thought: why did Darby Randolph get in touch with the press? Was that his idea or was it Pastor Ed's? Did he tell Wonder Woman at the church to drop Butterworth's name in front of us, hoping that if the press lit a fire under us, we'd grab the first obvious suspect, Marty, and call it case closed?"

Geez, I thought, *who did you say has been watching too much television?*

"Wow, you do have a fertile imagination, Janet. I bet you think there was more than one shooter on the grassy knoll too?" I said, smiling as I concentrated on making the turn onto Hixson Pike.

"What? What shooter? What grassy knoll?"

"Forget it, Janet. I was just teasing."

"I'm just saying," she said, "that since our evidence against Butterworth is circumstantial, and we can't put him at either of the scenes, we might want to take a look at who is pointing us in his direction. I'm not saying Pastor Ed is a criminal mastermind, but—"

"I don't think it's Pastor Ed, Janet."

"And you know this because?"

"One, it's too easy, and two, my gut tells me it isn't."

"Huh," she said as she folded her arms. "I've heard that somewhere before."

"Always trust your gut, Janet. You'll find it's your best friend when you're in need. And, for what it's worth, mine has rarely let me down... well, once or twice, maybe," I smiled as I thought about it. *You're kidding, right?*

19

I parked my car at the rear of the Police Service Center, and we entered through the back door.

"Hey, Lieutenant," Reggie Green, the duty sergeant said as we walked past his desk. "There's a reporter, Clemont Rhodes, waiting to talk to you."

"Get rid of him, Sergeant," I said.

"Er... I can't. He said he had an appointment, so I figured you'd be on your way back, and I had Trask escort him up to your office. Sorry. Oh, and when you are done with him, Chief Johnston wants to see you."

I stared at him, dumbfounded. "You did what?"

He shrugged. "He had an appointment, LT, at ten."

"He most certainly did not. Next time, you call me before you allow a stranger into the building, much less my office."

"Yes, ma'am," he said. "I—"

"Oh, forget it, Reggie. I'll handle it. Come on, Janet. Let's see what's crawled out of the newspaper."

I walked silently to my open office door. Clemont Rhodes was sitting comfortably in front of my desk, his legs crossed, checking his iPhone. I eyeballed my files and my computer, but nothing looked out of place.

"What are you doing here, and where's Officer Trask?" I said quietly.

His head spun around quickly, startled.

"I... I told him he didn't need to stay on my behalf, that I had some emails to answer while I was waiting for you."

"So help me, Rhodes, if you touched any of my files, I'll lock your ass up and throw away the key," I said through clenched teeth.

"No! No. Detective, I swear. It isn't like that." He stood, turned to face me, put up his hands, still holding his phone, and smiled that broad, blinding smile at me. "I haven't touched anything. I was waiting to talk to you. That's all."

"You lied to the duty sergeant, so get the hell out

of my office, or I'll arrest you for trespassing on government property."

"Okay, okay. Look, you've got it all wrong. Just hear me out, please?"

I didn't answer. I just stared at him.

"Okay, so have you been watching the media over the past few days?" he asked. "You saw nothing, right? Nothing... nothing about the murder of Victoria Randolph. I'm playing ball with you, Lieutenant. I've sat on it but can't for much longer. Right now it's still under lock and key, up here." He tapped the side of his head with a finger.

I walked past him, sat down, swiveled my chair, and stared up at him. He'd had a haircut, wasn't bad looking, except for that slimy sheen of self-effacing journalistic integrity he exuded.

Ah, what the hell? Can't hurt to listen to the greasy son of a...

I looked at Janet and told her to give me a few minutes, then turned to Rhodes and said, "And why would you do that?"

"Can I sit down?"

I nodded.

"Well, there are two reasons..."

I circled my hand in the air for him to hurry and get to the point.

"First, I wasn't really sure that my source was telling the truth about everything."

"Why do you say that?"

"Have you ever looked at a person and thought they were trying to get you to do their dirty work? Like you are being used?"

"Uh, yeah. All the time."

"Look," he said. "I'll admit... Okay, I was excited when I got the call and, from what I heard, I was at first convinced the CPD was screwing up this case from the get-go. But after talking further with my source, I realized I was dealing with someone who, shall we say, has more than a passing interest in the outcome and was, well, trying to use me to put pressure on the PD."

I sighed and said, "What exactly do you mean?"

"I mean, I think my source might be a little too eager

to point the finger away from him or herself. Does that make sense?"

"Mr. Rhodes—" I said.

"Please. Call me Clemont," he interrupted me.

"Mr. Rhodes, is your source a member of the Randolph family?"

"You know there's no way I can answer that. Look, I'll say this much: he was a big man yesterday, still is, even though he's retired."

"Holy shit. You're talking about Governor Randolph?" I almost whispered.

Clemont Rhodes didn't move, nor did he nod or shake his head, hell, he didn't even blink, just sat there rigid, frozen to the seat. I'd nailed it. And I was even more sure when I remember him referring to Victoria Randolph as a regular saint. Mother Theresa to be exact.

"Relax, Clement. I got it. So, what do you want for this little nugget of information? As if I don't already know."

He let out his breath and said, "What do all reporters want, Detective? Exclusive rights to the story."

He looked behind him toward my open office door, then scooted his backside forward to the edge of his seat and leaned his elbows on his knees. He couldn't get any closer to me without banging his head on the edge of my desk.

"See, here's the thing," he said quietly, conspiratori-ally. "I thought that maybe, if I was straight-up with you, we might be able to establish a foundation for future endeavors."

"Is that what you thought? And how, exactly, might that work?"

"Look, Lieutenant." He straightened up, folded his hands together, and placed them on my desk as if he was about to say a prayer. "I'm not like those others. I've got a moral compass."

I couldn't help it. I chuckled.

"I know, I know. You don't believe me." He fidgeted again. "But I know what it's like to be the outsider. Believe me when I tell you, I've got my eyes and ears on the street all the time; I know a lot of people, contacts, sources, who know... everything. You understand, right? They're none of them exactly monuments to society, if you catch my meaning, but..."

My right eyebrow shot up.

"Lieutenant, I've worked hard to develop my sources. I can be an asset to you. I can."

"And you are willing to share this fruitful world of limitless information with me for an exclusive?" I shook my head and shrugged.

"Not for just one exclusive. Look, I'll be honest with you, Lieutenant. I also write crime novels. My pen name is Jasper Crabb, and I'm pretty damn successful." He paused, looked me directly in the eye, and said, "I need more than just an exclusive; I need access to you, and the PD. I need authenticity."

Now I laughed out loud. "You've got to be kidding me. Do you think I am going to fall for a line like that? You almost had me, Rhodes. Almost. You've been watching too much TV."

Hah, where have I heard that line before? A freakin' crime novelist? Is he kidding me? Jasper fricking Crabb? I need to Google him.

"It's true," he said and sat back in the chair and folded his arms.

"I'll tell you what, Rhodes. No promises. I'll check out your lead. If it pans out, we might have a one-time deal." I stood indicating that our little chat was over.

"That's all I ask." He extended his hand, but I folded my arms in front of me and nodded toward the door.

After he left, I was wondering if I wasn't walking into some kind of trap. *Time will tell, Kate. Time will tell.*

20

There was no getting around the meeting with Chief Johnston, so I gathered up my courage and went to meet my doom. Well, that's what it felt like.

Cathy, his secretary, wasn't at her desk so I knocked on his door and waited.

"Come."

I took a deep breath, opened the door, poked my head inside, and said, "Am I interrupting?"

"No, Lieutenant. Come on in and take a seat."

Hmm, he doesn't sound too bad. Maybe...

I closed the door behind me and sat down in front of his desk, crossed my legs at the ankles, folded my arms, and waited.

"I understand you had a visitor this morning, a reporter, and this isn't the first time he's come to see you. What's going on?"

"That's right, sir. Clemont Rhodes. Someone in the

Randolph family tipped him off. I think I know who, but still, I need to do some digging."

"The Randolphs aren't your average family, Catherine. They're affluent, and well-connected, all the way up to and including the White House. Members of that family sit on every board and committee in the tri-state area. We have to be very careful how we proceed."

"I understand that, sir, and you don't have to worry. I'll handle them gently—*the hell I will*—but I will handle the investigation diligently, just as I would with any other homicide case."

He assumed his signature pose, fingers of both hands steepled together at his lips, and stared at me.

"Chief," I said, "you can rest assured that I'm doing everything I can to get to the bottom of the two homicides as quickly as possible. They are linked: same killer, same MO. Doc Sheddon is convinced of it, and so am I, and we have a person of interest." I paused, took a breath, and then continued.

"Sergeant Toliver and I have just returned from interviewing a Mr. Marty Butterworth, the groundskeeper at the Church of the Savior. Both the Randolphs and the Dillys are members of that church. Butterworth has a beef with both victims, so he has motive. It's also possible that he doesn't have an alibi, but as yet, we can't place him at either crime scene. It's not much, I know, but it's a promising lead, and I intend to follow up on it."

And there I stopped talking. By the look on the Chief's face, I could tell he wasn't going to allow me to question the one-time governor of Tennessee, not without cause anyway.

"You need to mollify the Randolph family, reassure them that you're doing all you can to close the case quickly. Keep the lines of communication open, but do what you have to do, Kate."

The Chief looked at me across the table: there was a hidden message in those eyes, and I couldn't help but feel a wave of relief wash over me. He was practically giving me permission to interview the family.

"I understand, sir, and I'll do my utmost. You have my word on it."

"Good." The stare intensified. "You'll report directly to me. No one else. Understood?"

"Absolutely. Yes, sir."

"You can go, but be careful how you handle that reporter. I want no leaks, *none*."

I stood and turned to go.

"Lieutenant... I'll call you when I have more time," he said quietly.

I turned again and looked at him. He looked back at me, nodded, and then looked at the door. Again, I got the message, and I couldn't help myself. My eyes rolled on their own. I swear they did.

I went straight back to my office. I didn't even have time to sit down when Janet entered.

"Everything okay?" she asked. "When you left, you looked awful. What did the Chief have to say?"

"Everything is fine. He just wanted an update," I said. "You up for another road trip?"

"Absolutely. Where are we going?"

"We're going to talk to former Governor Alexander Randolph," I said, "but if anyone asks, we're going to the morgue."

"Stealth mode. I got it. I'll go get my jacket."

"Don't forget your iPad," I said dryly.

21

I rolled down the car window and told the guard at the security booth that I wanted to see the governor.

"You got an appointment?" he asked.

"Chattanooga PD," I said. "I don't need one."

I offered him my badge and ID. He grabbed them, waggled his hand at Janet, took her creds too, and studied them. He checked our badges and IDs like we were about to enter the Pentagon. He looked back and forth from the photos to our faces, lingering much longer on Janet. I couldn't blame him for that. She did, after all, look more like a kid than a cop.

Finally, satisfied we were who we said we were, he reentered the guard booth. I watched as he made the call.

"He ain't here," he said, leaning around the door jamb.

"Oh, yeah? How about we go see for ourselves?" I yelled back at him.

He talked into the phone some more then exited the booth, came to the car window, leaned down, handed us our creds, and said, "Drive on, go straight to the front steps of the house where you'll be met. Do not stop along the way."

Then he stood back, pressed a button just inside the door to the booth, and the huge iron gates swung slowly open. He waved us through and, in the rearview mirror, I saw him step into the middle of the driveway and make a note of our license plate.

"Wow," Janet said. "That guy was really serious. Better safe than sorry, I suppose... Holy crap, would you just look at that."

Holy crap indeed. I'd always known that Lookout Mountain was *the* high-status area in Chattanooga, but I had no idea just how high.

We followed the perfectly paved road through the woodland for maybe a quarter mile. Every tree along the way was lush and green.

"Will you look at that fricking house?" I said as the dazzling white mansion came into view.

It stood atop a slight rise. A traditional, Antebellum structure with two-story windows, each flanked by heavy black shutters. Gigantic white colonnades guarded the front of the home, supporting the roof over a vast front porch.

Holy cow, I thought. *Talk about Gone with the Wind. All we need now is Scarlett O'Hara and Rhett Butler.*

"I feel like I should have gotten dressed up for this

one," Janet joked, looking down at her skinny jeans and white tee.

"You look fine," I said. "Ah, there's our chaperone, just like the man said."

I parked the car almost at his feet and we stepped out into the sunshine.

"Can I help you?" he said in a deep, resonant voice.

"You can." I smiled as I held up my badge and introduced us both. "We'd like to talk to Governor Randolph."

"I'm afraid Governor Randolph is not in residence." The man stood like a fricking statue.

Not in residence? What kind of talk is that?

"I take it you mean he's not in?"

"Exactly so, Lieutenant."

"Okay, then would you be so kind as to tell us where we can find him?" I said, still smiling.

"The Governor is at his club golfing. He left about two hours ago."

"Was anyone with him?" I asked.

He didn't answer.

"What's your name and function, Mister…"

"My name is Oliver, ma'am, and I'm the butler."

I stared at him, not believing what I was hearing. I looked at Janet. She didn't exactly roll her eyes, but I could tell she'd come close.

"Oliver? Okay, Oliver. We're investigating the murder of the governor's granddaughter-in-law, Victoria Randolph. Perhaps you could answer a few questions for me?"

He frowned, shook his head, then said, "I really can't."

"Oh, come on, Jeeves," I said, impatiently. "It's for the family for Pete's sake."

"The name is Oliver, ma'am and... Oh, very well then. Ask your questions."

"Can we go inside?"

"Follow me," he said, and with that, he turned and strode purposefully up a flight of stone steps too many for me to bother to count.

We followed him into the foyer and from there to a small parlor, where he invited us to sit and offered us a beverage. We sat, thanked him, but refused the offer.

"Now, ma'am. If I can be of assistance, please ask your questions. I'll answer them if I can."

"I'd like to get a little background on Victoria Randolph. What kind of person was she?"

He almost shrugged. I saw his shoulders begin to rise, but he caught himself and the shrug died almost immediately. *Interesting!*

"She was... a very attractive lady," he replied.

Very diplomatic. I can see where this is going, and it's not going to work. I need to give him a kick, jerk him out of butler mode.

I nodded. "I'm sure she was, and I understand your desire to be loyal to the family, but loyalty is not going to help me find Victoria's killer. I need to know what kind of woman she was, who liked her, who didn't, who hated her, how many people did she piss off and their names. Got it?"

He nodded, smiled, sort of, then said, "I have indeed. Victoria Randolph was a bitch, but on some levels quite likable. She had a wonderful sense of humor but didn't know when to keep her mouth shut and... well, she didn't hide her feelings. Told it like it was is the phrase, I think."

So, the house cleaner Marcie was right then.

"Did she have any enemies?" Janet asked.

"No, none that I know of. Well, none who would want to kill her. She did try to fit in and, for the most part, she did. In fact, I think she was quite popular among some of the members of the church. She worked hard at it, perhaps too hard."

"And you?" I asked. "What did you think of her?"

He thought about it, then said, "Mrs. Randolph and I didn't always see eye to eye. She... was not one to mingle with the staff."

"How about the family?" I asked, remembering what Marty Butterworth had told us. "Did she get along with them?

"Quite honestly, I don't think the Governor or his wife or anyone else with the name Randolph cared much for Victoria, with the exception of Mr. Darby, of course. He was quite besotted with her."

"Why didn't they care for her?" I asked.

This time he did shrug. "You must have heard the expression, 'You can put lipstick on a pig, but it's still a pig?'"

"Yes." I smiled. "I think I understand." I stood. So did Janet and Oliver. "I think I'll go and find the governor."

"That, Lieutenant, is not a good idea. He does not like to be disturbed when he's golfing."

"Well, never mind. We're in the neighborhood now, so we'll give it a shot."

THE VALLEY VIEW Golf and Country Club is one of the most exclusive in the Tri-State area, if not all of Tennessee. It's not a huge facility; quite small as such places go, but what it lacks in size it more than makes up for in luxury. The golf course, designed by none other than Alister MacKenzie, has nine double greens and eighteen tees. The clubhouse is low profile, but luxurious. I heard membership was by invitation only and limited to one hundred fifty of Tennessee's most influential movers and shakers. The fees were a closely held secret, but I happen to know it's presently set at one-hundred-and-thirty-thousand dollars. I know that because August Starke, Harry's famous dad, told me; he just happens to be a member.

"That was helpful," Janet said as we drove back to the highway.

"Yes, and I'm beginning to see a pattern: Victoria didn't like the hired help," I mused.

"Well, if she comes from the wrong side of the tracks, that kinda makes sense," Janet said. "She was obviously sensitive about her roots."

"I suppose," I said, and we drove the rest of the way in silence.

Once past the electronic gates at the perimeter of the club property, we had to show our IDs at two more checkpoints. When we arrived at the main entrance, a young man offered to park the car for me, but I insisted on parking it myself, as close to the entrance as I could get.

"The last thing I want is to get thrown out of the place and then have to wait for the valet," I muttered, more to myself than to Janet.

"Do you plan on getting us thrown out of here then?" she asked.

"You never know, Janet; you never know."

"I'll tell you what, LT. I'd bet my pension that there are more than a couple members here who literally have skeletons buried in their backyards. I mean real ones, skeletons, bodies. It's what rich people do."

"That's a little prejudiced, isn't it? Not to mention morbid."

"Not really. It's just the law of averages. They get away with things because they can: one law for them, another for the hoi polloi," she said as we strolled up to the entrance.

"Hoi polloi? Where the hell did that come from?" I asked as we exited the car.

"Dunno. College, I think."

I shook my head. "Janet, you never cease to amaze me."

We were met at the door by the club vice president, a Mr. Humbert, and a security guard.

"I know who you are," the VP said, nervously. "And I

must say that this is highly irregular, if not downright offensive, for you to come to a peaceful place of leisure for our members in order to harass them."

"We are not here to harass anyone, Mr. Humbert. I am pronouncing your name correctly?"

He nodded his gray head. He was a handsome older man. His tailored suit fit him perfectly, and his shoes were spit-shined. I liked him at first glance. There was something about him that made me think he was a savvy old cuss and could be trusted.

"We need to speak to Governor Randolph."

"Governor Randolph is out on the course, I'm afraid. You'll have to come back when he's finished his game."

I sighed and shook my head. "Can't do it," I said. "We're investigating a homicide. It is imperative that we speak to him... *now.*"

I didn't say any more and my hunch about Humbert proved to be true; he got it, and within seconds, he had a young man running through the clubhouse and out of sight.

"Would you and the detective sergeant care to wait in the bar?"

"That might be a little less obtrusive. Yes, thank you, Mr. Humbert."

We might have been visiting royalty the way Humbert escorted us to two seats at the bar and informed the bartender that our drinks were on the house.

"Two iced teas comin' right up."

"This is some kind of swanky," Janet said, sipping her tea and looking around.

"Isn't it just?" I replied and smiled casually at the bartender.

"I haven't seen you ladies here before."

He took my smile as an invitation to talk. *Don't they always?*

Janet held her badge up, and I introduced us.

"Is there a problem?" he asked.

"No. Not at all," I said casually. "We're just here to talk to one of the members, Governor Randolph."

I watched the bartender's reaction. He bounced his eyebrows, smirked slightly, looked down, grabbed a lime and began to slice it.

"That was a strange look," Janet said. "Do you know him?"

"Oh yeah, I know him all right. I know all of the members." He continued to slice the lime.

"Anything you'd like to tell us about him?" I watched as he grabbed another lime and started in on it.

"Are you kiddin'? You tryin' to get me fired?"

I nodded. "Gotcha. So..." I looked at his name tag. "James, how about you just answer a few yes or no questions for me? Does Governor Randolph ever come in the bar?" I took a sip of my iced tea and watched the bartender's reaction.

"Yes."

"Does he ever talk about his family?"

"Yes."

"Has he ever mentioned his grandson's wife, Victoria?"

The bartender looked up at me, then across the room

to see if anyone was paying any attention to him. He was also attractive, like his boss, Humbert, except that he was about twenty years younger. Tattoos peeked out from beneath the white cuffs of his shirt and there was a hole in his left earlobe but no earring.

"I think everyone in the clubhouse knows about Victoria. She's been here a few times," he said quietly.

"Hold on," he said. "I'll be right back."

He turned away and went to the other end of the bar to grab a bottle of something and chat for a second with one of the members. Then he was back in front of Janet and me.

"So," I said, "does he speak well of her?"

The bartender chuckled. "No."

"Really?" I asked. "Why do you say that?"

"He... She isn't exactly... Oh hell, he called her trailer trash. He even said it in front of Darby. Darby is his grandson."

I nodded, not really surprised, as he picked up another lime and began to slice it.

"What was Darby's reaction when he heard that?" I asked.

"He didn't like it, obviously, but he didn't say anything. He wouldn't, would he? The governor is a real badass, if you get my meanin'. You don't argue with him."

He topped up our glasses with more tea.

"Of course," he continued, "he never spoke like that in front of her. Uh-oh, here comes the boss."

"Excuse me, detectives," Humbert said. "Governor

Randolph is waiting for you in the sitting room. Follow me, please."

I took a twenty from my shoulder bag and tossed it on the bar with a wink to the bartender. He took the money, graciously said thank you, and dropped it in the tip jar.

We followed Humbert through the bar with all eyes on us. I didn't feel particularly out of place—I'd spent a lot of time at Harry Starke's club, and it's also upscale, and if you've seen one country club, you've seen them all —but it was obvious we didn't belong at Valley View.

There was no doubt that within minutes of our arrival half the staff and most of the members knew that two detectives were on the premises. It wouldn't take but a few more minutes for someone to deduce we were there to see Governor Alexander Randolph.

Humbert knocked on a door, opened it, and led us into a small, comfortably furnished sitting room. Governor Randolph was standing at the window, his hands clasped behind his back, looking out over the golf course.

"Lieutenant Gazzara and Sergeant Toliver, sir."

Randolph nodded but continued staring out of the window. Humbert left, closing the door behind him.

As soon as the door closed, Randolph whirled around, his eyes angry and his fists clenched.

"What the hell do you think you are doing coming to my club?" he spat.

"Hello, Governor Randolph," I said reasonably.

It felt kind of funny calling him that, considering the

old man hadn't set foot in the Governor's mansion in more than two decades.

"A little bird told me you didn't think the police were moving fast enough to catch your granddaughter-in-law's killer," I continued. "So we are doing everything we can to do just that. We have a couple of questions for you."

Janet introduced us as I got my iPad out, turned it on, and told him I'd be recording the conversation. That really pissed him off, especially when he saw Janet open her iPad too.

"I... You..." he spluttered, and then, with great effort, he seemed to get a grip on himself and slowly began to calm down. The angry, red flush on his face cooled to pale pink.

"I apologize, Lieutenant. Perhaps I was a little hasty. This... this... debacle has disrupted my entire family," he said. "Please, do sit down."

Randolph was in his early seventies, but still an imposing figure used to getting his own way. Tall, fit, strong, back straight, glittering blue eyes, aquiline nose, pure white hair receding slightly at the front... and, I'm sure, an intimidating SOB, to some, but not to me. I'd met his type before, and I'd never taken any crap from any of them; this one would be no different.

We sat in a semi-circle around a coffee table that, had it been taller, could have done duty as a small dining table: Randolph to my left, Janet to my right.

I set my iPad down, recorded the date, time, etc., and then I had a thought.

"Does playing golf clear your head?" I asked conversationally.

"Why, yes," he responded, sounding surprised, "it does. Ah, I see. You're wondering how I can play golf when my grandson's wife has just been murdered? What the hell else do you expect me to do, Detective, sit at home and mope? That's not who I am, young lady."

"I don't know, Governor," I said nodding. "I'm not sure how I'd handle such a situation myself. So, let me ask you this: how and when did you find out about Victoria's death?"

"I didn't want Victoria working at that church," he said, out of the blue. "She didn't need to work. It was just another way for her to manipulate Darby, get him to do what she wanted... He's weak, a weak man," he said quietly, almost as if to himself.

"Why do you say that?" I asked. The conversation seemed to have made a left turn, but far be it from me to interrupt the bird when it's singing.

"She wanted Darby to buy a building in Memphis, a rental property for God's sake. She had it in her head that she wanted to be a landlord; ridiculous. The girl was a complete moron, no business acumen at all. She was a gold digger, plain and simple, and no great loss to this family."

"Did you call her that, a gold digger, to her face?" Janet asked, her eyes wide with disbelief at what she was hearing.

"I did. Of course, I did. Darby is my eldest grandson. I expected great things of him. I expected... Well, unfortunately, he is, as I said, a weak man, and he fell under the spell of a pair of long legs and a pair of tits that... I'm sorry, please excuse my coarse language."

"We've heard worse, Governor. Go on," I replied.

"I told Darby he was not to buy that property. Being a landlord is a tough and thankless business. I told him to make Victoria focus on their home, and being his wife, have more children," he paused, shook his head, then continued.

"Not two days after that conversation, I get the news that Victoria is going to work at the church to earn money of her own." He nearly choked.

"Why would you disapprove of that?" Janet said. "A job, her own money, that would prove she wasn't a gold digger, wouldn't it?"

"Of course it wouldn't," the Governor spat. "That was *not* her motive. All she wanted to do was put pressure on Darby to buy her that damn rental property. Not only that, the woman was promiscuous and working at the church would have provided her with the opportunity to... well, let's just say she would have had access to the wealthiest men in the community."

"Promiscuous?" I asked. "You're saying she had an affair?"

He shrugged. "You'll have to ask Darby."

"No, Governor. You brought it up. I'm asking you. Who was she having an affair with?"

"I don't know that she was. I do know she was an outrageous flirt, and that she dressed like a damn floozy."

"That doesn't make her promiscuous, Governor," I said. "Aren't you being a little unfair?"

He sighed, then said, "Maybe I am... maybe I am. I don't know, Lieutenant. This whole business, it's unsettling. All I know is that if Darby got it into his head that she was playing around... Well, my grandson, being the weak, simple soul that he is, would capitulate and offer her the sky, moon, and stars just to keep her in line. She'd get her money pit."

"But that's your grandson's business and not yours?" Janet said.

"You're wrong," he said. "You have to understand. It was my money. Darby would have nothing if he was left to his own devices. My son, Michael, Darby's father, and my two daughters married well. They brought success and pride to the Randolph name. I have two grandsons and three granddaughters. One of the girls is married to a fine man, the son of a Texas oilman. The other is married to a doctor. My other grandson is at West Point. Darby, however, is an anomaly. He managed to find himself a piece of local trash to bring into the family."

His eyes were wide, icy blue, with not a hint of fatigue in them.

Oh yes, I thought, *he could have killed Victoria. He has motive. I bet he'd do anything to protect his family and reputation. And he's strong enough... But then there's Meryl Dilly. Why would he want to kill her?*

"I know what you're thinking," he said, jerking me back to reality.

He pulled his lips back in a sly grin. I've seen friendlier smiles on a shark.

"You think I'm a snob, a rich old man whose shit

doesn't stink. Well, you're wrong. I'm just an old man who worked for every penny I have, and I don't see anything wrong with protecting my legacy and reputation. Victoria's gone, and I feel sorry about what happened to her, but I can't say that I'm sorry... she's no longer a problem."

Wow, what a cold-hearted son of a bitch. If that's what money does to you, you can keep it. Hmm, time to change the subject, I think.

"Pastor Ed told us that he visited your grandson shortly after Victoria's body was found. Did you, by any chance, see him there?"

The Governor wrinkled his nose, and said, "That man is too involved with his flock. He should stay where he belongs, in the pulpit. I don't like his church, and I don't like the way everyone's in everyone else's business and... well, never mind; it's not natural. I, myself, do not attend."

"But everyone who is anyone on Lookout Mountain is a member of the church," Janet said. "Why would you cut yourself off like that?"

He smiled. "I'm not running for office anymore, Detective."

"You were the Governor of Tennessee, a public servant all your life," I said. "You must have made a lot of money and a lot of friends over the years... good friends, friends who owe you favors."

"That's true. I did. What? Are you implying that I... Damn it, Lieutenant, that's outrageous. I resent your insinuation."

He swallowed hard, then said, "Yes, I wanted Victoria out of my family, but I would never have harmed her. Do you have any idea how this has affected my grandson? Do you? He's suicidal. I'd give every penny I have to bring her back to him, but I can't. I can't even give him closure. Only you and your people can do that. And it seems to me that you don't know what the hell you're doing. Whatever it is, it's not much. And you sit there and accuse me... *ME!* How dare you?"

"I didn't accuse you of anything," I said, easily. "I'm just doing my job and—"

"And nothing," he interrupted me. "You're doing nothing."

I looked him in the eye, thought for a moment, then said, "You know, Governor, I can understand your frustration, but I don't believe you when you say you're not running for office anymore. You're not so old. What are you, seventy-two, seventy-three? Not even as old as the president. You're the consummate politician, Governor. You can't help yourself."

He glared at me but didn't answer, which told me all I wanted to know.

"Your call to Clemont Rhodes, your attempt to put the squeeze on the Police Department wasn't a smart idea." I leaned forward and moved my iPad a little closer to the Governor.

"What's that phrase you politicians are so fond of?" I asked. "Oh, I remember: Never let a good crisis go to waste?"

The Governor scowled, clenched his teeth, and then

said, "Is that what you think? If so, then you're mistaken. All I want is for you to find Victoria's killer."

"What do you think we are here for, Governor? A reference?" I chuckled. "I've heard that you aren't the only member of the Randolph family that disapproved of Darby's choice in women. How does your wife feel about it? Darby's father and mother? Have they asked for your help recently?"

"You obviously don't know who you are talking to. Detective Gazzara. I may no longer be governor of this great state, but I still have, as you so rightly noted, a great many influential friends. I will be calling Chief Johnston to inform him of this exchange. You really are something, Lieutenant. While a crazed lunatic is getting away with killing my granddaughter, you're wasting valuable time harassing me. What's that saying you have in law enforcement? Something about the first forty-eight hours, as I recall. I'm sure you're quite familiar with it."

He stood up. "We're finished here, I think. If you have anything else to say to me, you'll have to contact my lawyer... Oh, and one more thing," he said, taking an iPhone from his pocket. "I too recorded this interview. Good day to you both."

And with that, Governor Alexander Randolph turned and stomped out of the room, leaving Janet and me sitting there, staring at the door, then at each other. I couldn't help it, I burst out laughing.

I tapped the off icon on my iPad and sat back in my chair.

"Oh, my Lord," Janet said. "That was, like, *intense.* What do you think?"

"I think... that the chief is going to have a lot to say to me when I get back." I paused, then continued, "But, you know, I'm not convinced that the ex-governor didn't have something to do with Victoria's death. Think about it, if he is running for office, Victoria would have been one hell of a liability. Maybe he did call in a favor. But then, there's Meryl Dilly... Unless..." I scratched my head.

"Unless what?" Janet asked.

"Unless she was somehow collateral damage?" I asked as well as stated. "Or that she was killed to make it look like... Oh hell, now who's been watching too much TV? I must be losing it. That kind of crap just doesn't happen in real life." I looked at my watch and grunted.

"I guess we'll have to see ourselves out."

"LT," Janet said, "do you think he'll make good on his threat to call the Chief?"

"Oh, yes. Just as sure as I am that he's a lousy golfer and an even lousier governor. He's probably on the phone with him right now. People like Randolph never pass up an opportunity to toss their weight around."

I stood, tucked my iPad into my shoulder bag, and we walked out of the door and out of the country club.

I have to admit, I don't scare easily, but I had knots in my stomach when we walked into the PD that afternoon.

I guess he must have tasked the duty sergeant to call him when I returned, for no sooner had I entered the building when my phone rang.

"Gazzara! My office. Now!"

22

I t was six-thirty that evening when I pulled into the parking lot of my apartment building. I was wiped out, and not just from lack of sleep; two hours in front of Chief Johnston will do that to you. Governor Randolph did indeed make good on his threat and called the chief. During my session in the chief's office, however, I got the distinct impression that the call had not gone all the Governor's way; Chief Johnston managed to get him to admit that he had, indeed, called Clemont Rhodes.

I thought long and hard about that meeting with the Chief and let me tell you, it was intense. No, I'm not going to go into detail... I can't. I promised myself I'd forget it, put it behind me, and that's what I've done. Let's just say that the old tyrant gave me a hard time for what he called "stepping over the line" during my interview with the former governor, and then assured me of his unwavering support, so long as I kept him in the loop, and leave it at that. So yes, when I pulled into that parking lot that Tuesday evening, all I wanted to do was take a shower, grab a bottle of red, and hide my sorry ass.

I found a half a bottle of Cabernet gathering dust on the kitchen counter and three slices of two-day-old pizza in the fridge.

"That will have to do it," I muttered to Sadie Mae as I scratched her behind the ears.

I didn't want to think about work for the next eight hours. Sadie Mae certainly didn't want to hear about my day, I was sure, so I showered, warmed the pizza in the microwave, poured the entire half bottle of wine into a pint mug, and we settled down on the couch. I ate pizza and drank wine; Sadie Mae just ate pizza.

I turned on the TV, flipped through a hundred offerings on Netflix before deciding to binge watch Alias. I love Jennifer Garner; she kinda reminds me of me... *Hah, don't I just wish?* The series was kind of out there, more fantasy than reality, but it captured our attention enough that Sadie Mae and I nestled together under a blanket for the next four hours. It was just what I needed, to escape from the rigors of life and the job. It was wonderful. *She really does remind me of me!*

I'd dumped my gun, badge, and phone on the coffee table in front of the couch next to the pizza and mug of wine. I wanted reminders of work out of my sight, but I also wanted them close at hand: force of habit. Police work is like a freakin' drug. Once you have a taste of it, you're hooked for life, and you can never fully let it go. You can slip away for a couple hours, fall into a deep sleep in front of the TV; no bad dreams, no mutilated women, no mangled bodies on silver tables in the morgue, just blackness... but then you're jerked back to reality wondering where the hell you are and how you got there.

So, when my phone rang at just after five-thirty that following morning, my eyes snapped open and I sat upright with a jerk and put my hands to my head.

Oh shit, my head.

I looked at the empty mug, shook my head—big mistake—and let the call go to voicemail.

I sat still for a moment, took a deep breath, scratched Sadie Mae's tummy, then stood up and went to the window: the sky was just beginning to lighten a little.

I turned my head and looked at my phone. The frickin' thing was a magnet. I couldn't help myself. I went to the table, grabbed the damn thing, swiped the screen, tapped in my code and put the phone to my ear.

"Hello, Lieutenant Gazzara," the male voice sounded so tired I could barely hear it. "This is Chief Wilbur. You don't know how sorry I am to have to disturb you at this time in the morning, but you need to call me. We've got another one."

Holy shit, no!

My mouth went dry. This was not happening. I dropped back down onto the couch and, in a daze, I called him back. He started to tell me, but I stopped him; there was no point. I took down the address and told him I'd meet him there as soon as I could.

I called Janet, gave her the news, the address, and

instructions to meet me at the scene. And, for good measure, I contacted Chief Johnston.

"Thank you, Catherine," he said, not sounding the least bit sleepy. "Go to it. Be sure to keep me in the loop."

"Got it, Chief," I muttered and hung up.

I tapped the button on the coffee machine, took Sadie Mae outside for a few minutes, let her do her business, then gave her breakfast. Next, I took a two-minute cold shower, climbed into a fresh pair of jeans, tee, and leather jacket, grabbed my Glock, badge, and shoulder bag, wrote a quick note for my dog walker and dropped it onto the kitchen counter. I left my little girl sleeping comfortably on a blanket on the couch and, twenty minutes after receiving the call from Chief Wilbur, I was in my car, coffee in hand, driving west toward Lookout Mountain.

23

T he home I was headed to was on the opposite side of Lookout Mountain from where the other two bodies were found. The victim, a Lucille Benedict, was a wealthy widow just forty-two years old.

As I drove, I called Doc Sheddon and asked him to meet me at the address Chief Wilbur had given me.

"We've got to stop meeting like this, Kate," Doc said. "My wife is already beginning to wonder about us," he joked.

"Tell me about it," I replied. "I'll see you in a bit." Then I called Mike Willis.

The house on Fern Lane was beautiful, of course. A faux, rustic, farmhouse built no earlier than 2000, it must have cost its owner a mint of money. The bright blooms of red roses and petunias were a breathtaking complement to the Confederate Gray color of the house. Old Glory waved proudly above the Tennessee state flag from a tall pole in the middle of the front lawn. The front door was flanked by miner's lanterns, old tin buckets and milk pails, all filled with more red flowers.

Chief Wilbur's cruiser and a second one were there, and an officer I'd not seen before was standing guard at the entrance to the driveway. I flashed my badge and told him that my partner, the ME, and CSI were all on their way, and he waved me through.

When I arrived at the house, Wilbur was standing on the front porch talking with a man in shorts and a T-shirt. His feet were bare, but he was wearing a bizarre, incongruously large Aussie-type bush hat.

"Detective." Wilbur shook his head as he stepped down off the porch and came to greet me.

"Chief Wilbur," I said, offering him my hand. "For Pete's sake, tell me something good."

He shook his head. "The door's unlocked, but I haven't been inside yet, nobody has. I looked in through the window. From what I could see, it looks just like the others. Kyle Baker, there, found her." He turned his head to look at him.

"He's her neighbor. He was out early walking his dog when he noticed that the lights were on and decided to check on her. He knocked, got no answer so he peeked in the window, saw her lying there, and that's about it. He called us. I took the call and called you."

I heard a car approaching on the driveway. It was Janet. She parked behind my car, and I waved her over, gave her a quick run-down of what we had, and then asked her to interview Baker. The man was still standing on the porch looking like he'd just lost his best friend, which he may well have done. Wilbur and I donned Tyvek booties and latex gloves and we went inside.

The interior of the home was carefully and tastefully decorated. Every piece of furniture, every picture frame, every accent, even the covers over the heating vents, had all been chosen with care and deliberation. And there, center stage in the living room, lay the mangled body of Lucille Benedict, the right-side rear of her head caved in, cracked like a coconut, brain matter and blood pooled around her head and body. Even at first look, I could see she'd also been stabbed several times. Unlike the other victims though, her blouse was torn exposing a rather risqué black bra.

Now why, I wonder, would a widow be wearing something like that? Then again, she's not that old.

"I... er... I don't need this. I'll leave you to it, Detective," Wilbur said, backing out of the door.

I nodded absently, looked around the room, the crime scene, and was surprised that there were no photos. I shrugged, backed out of the room myself and began to wander around the house. As far as I could tell, nothing, other than the crime scene, had been disturbed. I trolled through the house until, finally, I found myself in what I assumed must have been the victim's office or den.

A large walnut desk was set against a wall under a window, upon which were several small stacks of papers, mostly bills from the likes of the electric company and the cable company, and an open checkbook. Now that did give a surprise: Lucille Benedict had just over one-hundred and two thousand dollars in her checking account.

Who has that kind of money in checking? I thought. *Motive maybe?*

"Of course, it could, but it ain't likely," I muttered to myself as I looked over the rest of her desk but found nothing else that interested me... except for a small monthly planner and a single framed photo of five people standing together with their arms around each other's shoulders, all of them very attractive, and all of them except one well known to me: Lucille Benedict, Meryl Dilly, Pastor Ed, Victoria Randolph and another young woman I didn't recognize.

Pastor Ed? Hmm, I wonder... Church function? Who's the other woman? Everyone in this town is a member of that church. It's only natural that this guy's face would pop up here and there. Nope, three out of four of those women are dead. That's no coincidence. We need to find out who that fourth woman is, and quickly.

I picked up the planner, opened it, flipped through the pages, found the one I was looking for, and saw something that made my heart leap.

Nope! That's just too frickin' easy.

I flipped slowly backwards through the pages.

Geez, Mrs. Benedict had one busy social life.

"See anything, LT?" Janet said as she walked into the room, her iPad open in the crook of her arm.

"Maybe." I looked up at her. "Probably nothing. What about you? Anything from Kyle Baker?"

"He's a nice guy, a bit of an insomniac. Lives with his

wife and mother-in-law—she's an invalid, the mother-in-law—in the house next door. He's a registered nurse, but stays home and looks after her, and he does most of the homemaking while his wife goes to work; she's an attorney."

She looked at her notes but didn't really need them.

"Anyway, as I said," she continued, "he doesn't sleep much and he's in the habit of taking his dog for long walks in the middle of the night. So that's what he was doing last night. He went out at around ten after four and he noticed her lights were on. He was gone for more than an hour, and when he came back, the lights were still on. He thought that was strange because he'd never seen them on at that time in the morning before, so he decided to check on her."

She paused, checked her notes again, and looked at me, quizzically.

"And?" I asked, a little more impatiently than I intended.

"Well, he knocked on the door, and when no one answered, he peeked in the window and saw her. Then he called the police... You think I should go talk to the mother-in-law?"

"Yes. Go ahead. I'll wait for Doc Sheddon." I looked at my watch. "But when we get done here, we'll go talk to Pastor Ed. According to an entry in the victim's day planner, he was supposed to pay Mrs. Benedict a visit yesterday... at six-thirty in the evening."

"Could it be that easy?" she asked, her eyes lighting up.

"No! It never is. But, check this out."

I showed her the photograph of the four women and Pastor Ed.

"Three of those women are dead. He sure as hell is beginning to look like a person of interest," I said.

Her mouth opened as if to speak, but she didn't. She just looked up at me in disbelief.

I smiled at her and said, "Don't get too excited, Janet. Nothing is ever what it seems. Go talk to the mother-in-law." And she did, just as Doc Sheddon had arrived.

"You look tired, Kate," he said as he ambled into the room, already dressed from head to toe in white Tyvek. "Another nasty one, I see. Let's take a quick look, then you can get out of here and go do something useful."

And so it began... again. I closed my eyes and threw back my head. I'd seen so many I'd lost count.

"No signs of a struggle; no defensive wounds on her arms or hands," he said as he rose to his feet and stepped away from the body.

"Time of death?" I asked, holding my breath.

He looked at his watch. "It's now almost seven o'clock," he said, taking a digital thermometer from his bag.

She was lying partially on her back, her right leg crossed over the left, exposing her lower back. He tugged her blouse out of her waistband and inserted the probe through the skin into her lower back.

He waited a moment then said, without any hesitation, "She's been dead about thirteen hours, so between five and seven yesterday evening."

Holy shit! Got 'im.

"You sure, Doc?" I said, biting my tongue as I caught my mistake.

He gifted me with one of his reproachful looks and said, "Yes, Catherine. I'm sure. The liver temperature is seventy-nine-point-four degrees, a loss of about nineteen degrees, give or take. The normal body temperature is ninety-eight-point-six. The body cools at a rate of about one and a half degrees per hour, so she's been dead roughly thirteen hours. I'll pinpoint it more arcuately when I do the postmortem.

"It looks like our assailant is pretty well set in his ways," he continued. "The same method of attack on each of the three victims, that we know of, and I'd say the same weapon too. They are all women of a certain age, weight, height, and they're all attractive." Doc pouted his lips as he pondered.

"What about this." I pointed to the torn blouse exposing the scandalous black bra beneath. "None of the other women had torn clothes. This rip looks like it was done on purpose."

"Yes, I'm not sure what to think about that," Doc said, looking down at the body, his left hand supporting his right elbow, right hand stroking his chin, still pondering. "But I'm almost certain the same person is responsible for all three crimes.... And the violence is escalating.

"This one didn't see it coming. I wonder why? She was attacked from behind by a right-handed assailant. See, the right rear of her skull is shattered, but look at her face. The killer tried to destroy it. Fortunately, if I can use such a word in these circumstances, she didn't feel a thing; the blow to the back of the head killed her instantly... The injuries to her face were inflicted post-mortem, as were the stab wounds: same weapon, same MO... more rage. What on earth could have caused such blind anger?"

"I'm going to catch this guy, Doc," I said in barely a whisper. "I think I know who it is, and as soon as Detective Toliver gets back, we're going to go talk to him."

"I do so hope he's your man, whomever it is," Doc said. "This is all too much. Oh, and by the way, I probably should have started our conversation by telling you that we did find something odd with the lab results. I was afraid that there might have been a mix-up so I sent them back for a redo."

"A mix-up in the lab? That's my worst nightmare, Doc," I replied and stepped closer so Doc's report wouldn't be overheard.

"Yes, mine too. They were able to identify Victoria Randolph's blood and Meryl Dilly's blood. And, as you know, there was seminal fluid present in Meryl Dilly. But the DNA to that sample doesn't match that of the husband... so either she was having an affair, or it belongs to the killer. However, that makes no sense, because there was no DNA material present inside Victoria Randolph and, by the look of her state of dress, this one wasn't raped," Doc said, scraping the tips of his fingers up and down the stubble on the right side of his chin. "And that begs the question, why Dilly and not Randolph? If I find evidence of sexual activity here...

well, we don't know yet. Do you see what I mean, Kate?"

I did.

I looked down at Lucille Benedict's body and let out a deep sigh.

"So," I said, "we have foreign DNA present in one victim and not the other. Dilly wasn't raped, so it must have been consensual... No, I have no idea what that means, Doc."

And then Janet showed up looking as discouraged as I felt.

"Hi, Doc." She gave him half a wave and half a smile.

If the two of them were to walk down the street together, they could easily be taken for grandfather and granddaughter, instead of the Chief Medical Examiner and the youngest homicide detective on the Chattanooga police force.

"Detective Toliver," he said. "How nice to see you again. I only wish it were under better circumstances. You have good news for us, I hope."

"No, not hardly." She sighed. "Kyle's mother-in-law is Shelby Winterborn. She's seventy-seven years young. She was in a diving accident about ten years ago that left her paralyzed from the neck down—such a nice woman— such a shame." She paused, shook her head, and then continued. "Anyway, since then her son-in-law has been taking care of her pretty much full-time. She's got all her faculties. His story checks out."

"Okay, well, that's good for him," I replied.

"Oh, and just as I was leaving, Kyle mentioned seeing

a car, parked here in the driveway late yesterday afternoon, around six-thirty, he thought it was. I asked him the make and color. He didn't know the make, but he thought it was an expensive model, either white or silver, he's not sure which, but he seemed to want to ere on the side of white. He didn't think to get a plate number or the make of the car since he knew that Mrs. Benedict had a lot of visitors, almost every day, in fact. It may or may not mean anything." Janet swallowed.

I sighed, nodded, patted her encouragingly on the shoulder, and said, "Good job." Then I turned to the ME and said, "Doc, I'm going to leave you to tend to Mrs. Benedict. Mike Willis should be here shortly. See you soon, I'm sure."

"Sure, Kate. Meet me at my place later. We can enjoy a quiet dinner by candlelight." He winked.

"That's the best offer I've had in months, but what would your good wife say?"

"She would welcome you with open arms, my dear. You know that. She cooks a mean lamb chop, you know. You really are welcome to join us; you too, Janet."

I laughed. "I'll think about it," I replied, but I knew I wouldn't, my nerves were jangling. I was itching to get to the Church of the Savior and talk to Pastor Ed, officially. A simple mouth swab would answer most of my questions.

I looked sideways at Janet, nudged her with my elbow, and said, "You ready to go talk to Pastor Ed?" She was.

24

J anet followed me as I drove across the top of the
mountain to the Church of the Savior and then
parked behind me just outside the entrance to
the offices. We exited the cars, but before we
approached the door, I grabbed her arm and told her
about the appointment I'd found in Lucille Benedict's
day planner.

"If Pastor Ed has an alibi for Benedict's time of
death," I said, "we're screwed, even if the DNA Doc
found in Meryl Dilly is his. It could have been inside her
for up to seventy-two hours. She was found in the early
hours of Thursday the eighteenth, so that means the
DNA could have been deposited as far back as Sunday
evening the fifteenth; it's circumstantial. Ed could have
been screwing her anytime during those three days."

"So the DNA is no good to us then?"

"Not unless we can put him at the Dilly residence
between the hours of five and seven on the day she was

killed, and even then... Well, according to her day planner, she's been seeing quite a lot of our dear Pastor, among others, over the last six months or so."

I thought for a minute, then said, "Do me a favor, Janet, go check the cars in the parking lot. White or silver is what we're looking for. Then come on in and join me."

"You don't really think he did it, do you?" she asked. "The guy is, like, as creepy and weird as all get-out... but a murderer? He's a man of God for goodness' sake."

"I hear you, but he's the only common thread that runs throughout the cases."

Janet left, and I stepped up to the door and rang the bell. Karen Silver opened the door almost immediately. This time, though, she was an entirely different person. She looked tired, harassed, and cross. She was obviously working at tasks other than secretarial because she was wearing coveralls, rubber boots and yellow rubber cleaning gloves.

"Good morning, Ms. Silver," I said breezily. "Is the pastor in? We have a few routine follow-up questions for him."

"I'm afraid Pastor Ed isn't here. He didn't come in this morning, and he didn't let me know. If you'd like to try again tomorrow you are welcome to do so," she said and began to close the door.

"One second, Ms. Silver, if you don't mind. The tip you gave us about Marty Butterfield was very helpful," I said as Janet joined me.

"Yes, well, at great risk to myself. Why haven't you arrested him yet? I haven't seen anything in the news."

"It's not quite that easy," Janet said. "We need proof. We can't just arrest him on your say so."

"Proof? He's a convicted felon. What more proof do you want? He's a nasty, nasty man with a very shady past. Furthermore, he's not shown Edward the least bit of gratitude for all the help he's given him. On the contrary, he's repaid him with scandal." Karen folded her arms and stared at me, defiantly.

I nodded. "I understand, and thanks to you," I said, ingratiatingly, "we've interviewed Mr. Butterworth and are actively investigating him as a person of interest."

She softened a little, nodded, and said, "I should think so too. So what do you intend to do about it?"

"Well, as I said, we have some questions we think only Pastor Ed can answer. Would you mind giving us his home address, please?"

"Um... er... Oh... I'm on my own here today, Detective, and very busy, as you can see." She waved a yellow-gloved hand in the air.

"I know, and I'm sorry. We can, of course, get it from the police department, but that means a phone call, choosing options, getting put on hold... You know how it is, so I was hoping that you'd help us out... please?"

She stood stock still, staring at us.

"Please?" I said again.

"Oh, very well," she said impatiently. "It's the Cloisters on Colonial Park Drive. It's about ten minutes from here. You can't miss it; there's a gravel driveway to the left. Now, if you'll excuse me. I have work to do."

The door closed with a bang.

"What's she so mad about, I wonder?" Janet asked.

"There's no telling. The pastor didn't let her know he wasn't coming in and, from the look of those coveralls and gloves, she could be cleaning the toilets, on her own. And, if the church does indeed hold fifteen hundred people, there would be a lot of them. That would piss anybody off. Let's go see if we can find Pastor Edward."

"You caught that, too?" Janet said, smiling. "By the way, there was only one car in the office parking lot," Janet whispered, "and it wasn't silver or white; it was a black Honda Civic."

"Must be hers," I said. "Okay, you have the address. Meet me there."

25

K aren Silver hadn't lied when she said the house was just about ten minutes away, but it wasn't as easy to find as she said. If I hadn't been using my dashboard mapping system, I would have driven right past the hidden driveway. It looked like nothing more than a gravel turn-around, but it was, in fact, the unmarked entrance to The Cloisters.

The driveway was little more than a well-worn dirt road through a forest of trees and dense undergrowth; it was deceiving. One hundred yards or so in, we reached a gate with an intercom.

I pulled up and pressed the intercom button, then took out my badge and identification and held them for the camera.

"Hello?"

The voice was female.

"I'm Lieutenant Gazzara, Chattanooga Police," I

said, hanging out of the car window. "I'm here to talk to Pastor Ed."

There was a buzz and the gate opened slowly. I drove on through and the driveway transformed into a gray cobblestone pathway that led up to a large, contemporary, somewhat ugly home with very few windows.

"This guy is a preacher?" Janet asked as she joined me beside my car. "He owns all of this property? Must be a couple of hundred acres of prime real estate." Her eyes wide, mouth hung open. "Man, am I ever in the wrong profession?"

"I say that to myself all the time," I replied, smiling.

She just shook her head and said, "He's a preacher, for goodness' sake."

"Yes, another huckster of holiness, I shouldn't wonder. When I was a kid, the pastor at my church lived in a two-bedroom ranch house. To live in something like this would, in his mind, have been...sinful." I smiled at the memory.

"Okay, then," I said brightly. "So this should be interesting."

Janet thumbed the doorbell and an attractive blond lady answered the door, one I'd seen before. *Holy... It's number four.* And it was; it was the fourth woman in the photograph on Lucille Benedict's desk.

"Detective Gazzara, I'm sorry you made the trip all the way up here, but my husband isn't home."

"You're Mrs. Pieczeck?" I asked.

"I am," she said, rather tight-lipped. "He's been at a retreat since yesterday."

"A retreat," I said.

"Yes. It's his monthly Shepard's Walk Men's Retreat." She swallowed. "It's to help the men of our community to remain faithful to God's calling."

"Can you tell me what time he went to the retreat?" I asked.

"He left early this morning, around seven."

"And what kind of car does he drive?" I pushed.

"An Audi S4. Why? Is he in some kind of trouble, Detective?"

"No, ma'am." I smiled. "What color is his car?"

"Metallic silver," she said frowning. "But—"

"And you, Mrs. Pieczeck? What do you drive?"

"I... have one too, but—"

"And is your car also silver?" I asked.

"Yes, but—"

Hmm. "I'm sorry to keep interrupting you, but I'm sure you've heard by now of the deaths of two members of your church."

"Yes, my husband told me about it, but I didn't know the women," she said rather quickly... too quickly.

"Really?" I said. "You didn't know them? From what Pastor Ed told us, they were both members of the church and had been for several years."

I was getting that familiar tingling sensation up my spine. This was suddenly becoming a very interesting interview.

"The church is my husband's job, Detective. I attend

on Sundays, but that is all. It is no different from having a doctor or a lawyer as a husband. I wouldn't interfere with, or insert myself in, his job. I can't do what he does. Only he can. He... is called. And he can't do what I do here at home. You see?" She smiled at me like she'd somehow successfully explained the cause and effect of the Vietnam War in less than two minutes and so the issue was resolved.

I took out my iPhone, brought up the picture of the four women and the pastor, and showed it to her.

"How do you explain this, then?"

"Oh my," she said, not looking at all surprised. "I'd completely forgotten about that. Where did you get it?"

"I'm sorry," I said. "I can't tell you that, but that's you, right there on the end, correct?"

"Yes, of course it's me. That was taken about two years ago at another of Edward's retreats. We had photos made with all of the women that attended."

Oh, yes. Sure, you did, but I bet the others, if there are others, aren't all dead.

I nodded, seemingly satisfied with her explanation, and said, "I see. So when do you expect him home?"

"He's at the retreat center until Thursday evening," she replied before looking over her shoulder into the house.

"And where is this retreat center?" I asked.

"I do hope you're not planning to go there," she snapped, frowning. "The retreats are for men only, and any disruption could have a serious effect on those in attendance."

"I'm sorry," I said sweetly, "but I'm investigating multiple homicides. I promise we'll be discrete."

Reluctantly, she gave us the address. It was more than two hours away.

"I'm not happy about this. Not one bit," she said, folding her arms across her chest and shifting from one foot to the other. "In fact, I'm going to call him... wait, I can't. He doesn't allow phones at the retreat."

I couldn't help myself, I smiled. "I understand how you feel, Mrs. Pieczeck, but—"

She interrupted me, "Why aren't you out there hunting down the killer? Why are you bothering my husband? He's a man of the Lord. He loves his flock and... and... everyone." She choked on those last words. Her eyes began to water; she wiped them with the back of her hand.

"Just one more question and I won't take up any more of your time. How often does your husband usually visit the members of his church, Mrs. Pieczeck?" I asked quietly. "Once a year, once a month, weekly... what?"

"Whenever they need him."

Again, she replied quickly, too quickly. There was something there. Something she wasn't going to share with me. I could tell by the narrowed eyes and the sudden tilt of her head to the left. I could also tell that the conversation was just about at an end. I wrapped it up quickly, thanked her for her time, and gave her one of my cards.

"If you think of anything, Mrs. Pieczeck, anything at all that might help us, please give me a call. Even if it seems unimportant. Many times families of murder victims receive closure because someone remembered something: an unimportant detail..." I watched her eyes, but they didn't waver from mine.

She took my card, looked at it, spun it around in her fingers, obviously thinking about something, but she simply nodded, stepped back inside the house, and slammed the door.

I stared at the closed door, shaking my head, then turned to Janet and said, "She is not all she would have us believe, nor did she tell us the truth about the photo, and she's hiding something."

"Yeah, I sort of got that... But why, do you think, Karen Silver didn't tell us he'd gone to a retreat and save us the trip over here?" Janet asked.

"Maybe she didn't know?" I said. "Maybe he didn't bother to mention it to her because it's below her pay grade. Maybe she did know and didn't think it was any of our damn business. Who knows?"

Janet nodded and said, "Yeah, right, but it wasn't a wasted journey, was it? We now know our man drives an expensive silver car. So what's the plan now, LT?"

"A road trip, of course," I said. "Tomorrow morning, early. Let's go back to the office. There are things I need to do."

26

I t was just after two-thirty that afternoon when we arrived back in my office. I sent Janet across the street to McDonald's to get coffee, dumped my bag on my desk, turned to look at my incident board, grabbed a dry erase marker, and began to add names and dates to it.

I hadn't been at it many minutes when I heard someone clear their throat. I turned my head, looked over my shoulder and, who should be standing there, leaning casually against the door frame, arms folded, legs crossed at the ankles, but Henry Finkle... The two stars on his collar tabs were gone, replaced by captain's bars, and he was smiling.

"You really do have a nice ass, Kate," he said quietly. "Ah, I see you're not wearing your fancy watch today."

"What do you want, Henry?" I asked, looking around for my phone. I found it and turned on the recording app, then waggled it in his face.

He actually laughed.

"There's no need for that, Lieutenant. Actually, I just stopped by to thank you for my new opportunity you made possible."

He sounded bright and cheery, but he wasn't. His eyes were chips of ice, and he was no longer smiling.

"I'd been asking the Chief for a field job for months, but he wouldn't hear of it. Now, thanks to you... Well, I really must thank you properly one of these days. I hope you have a nice rest of the day, Lieutenant." Then he stood upright, turned on his heel, and walked quickly away through the incident room.

You sneaky little SOB, I thought as I watched him go. *"I really must thank you properly one of these days." Oh yeah, Tiny, I understand. That was a threat. You intend to get me back. Well good luck, you little...*

I saw Janet exit the elevator holding two cups of coffee and stand to one side to allow Finkle to enter. He didn't stop, and he didn't look at her. She did stop. She turned and stared at him as he punched the elevator button. Even from where I was, I could see his shark-like smile as the doors closed.

"Hey, guess who I just saw?" Janet said as she placed the coffees on my desk. "*Captain* Henry Finkle... Oh, no, he didn't come to see you, did he?"

I smiled at her. "Sure did. He wanted to thank me would you believe?" And then I told her the rest of the story.

"Okay," I said. "So now you know. Let's get to work. What the—"

"Hi Lieutenant," Detective John Tracy said as he knocked on my still open door. "You got a minute, a private minute?"

I was about to tell him to get lost, but then my curiosity got the better of me. I gave Janet the nod, she nodded back, grabbed her coffee, and Tracy took a step back to let her pass. Then he stepped inside and sat down on the seat Janet had just vacated.

"I'm done with it, John," I said, grabbing my coffee. "You wanted the Barone case. I let you have it, and I've helped you all I could. That's it. I don't have time to fool with you. Now tell me what you want, then get out and let me get on with my work."

He leaned back in his seat, smiled at me, folded his arms, and said, "That ain't what I'm here for, Kate."

"Don't call me that, Sergeant. Only my friends call me that, and you're not one of them. So, what do you want?"

"Well, first I want to congratulate you. How the hell did you manage to pull it off?"

I screwed up my eyes, stared at him, then said, "Pull what off?"

"Oh, come on, K—" he started to say. "Sorry, LT. I heard Johnston is promoting you to captain, and that you're to head up the homicide division."

I almost dropped my coffee. I did let my mouth fall open, and I know my eyes almost popped out of my head.

"*Shut. Up!*" I finally managed to blurt out. "Where did you hear that? It's not true."

"Oh, I think it is. A little bird told me, a very special little bird."

I couldn't help it. I fell back in my seat and stared across my desk at him, open-mouthed.

"Get the hell out of here, John."

"No, ma'am. Not before I tell you why I came. If you're promoted to captain, and I know you will be, there will be a lieutenant's spot open in Homicide. Yours, and with you running the division, and with me up for promotion too, well, I thought that maybe you could put in a good word for me... After all, *Kate*, I did save your life. Let me know, okay?"

And before I could answer him, he stood and walked out the door, leaving me at my desk staring after him, not daring to believe what I'd just heard, but vowing to find out, and frickin' quickly.

Almost fearfully, I picked up my desk phone, punched in the Chief's extension, and waited. It rang only once.

"Chief Johnston's Office. How may I direct your call?" Cathy's voice was bright and cheerful.

"It's me, Cathy. I need a quick word with him."

"Putting you through now. Lieutenant Gazzara for you, Chief."

"Yes, Catherine. What can I do for you?"

"I just heard a rumor that you're promoting me. Is it true?"

There was a long moment of silence, and then he said, "Who told you, Kate?"

"So it's true, then?"

Again, the silence, then he said, "I told you when you left my office last Monday that I was going to call you when I had the time. This is not the time."

"Chief, you can't do this to me. How am I supposed to do my job with something like this hanging over my head? Talk to me. Tell me... something."

I heard him sigh, then he said, "Yes, Lieutenant, it's true. I do intend to promote you to captain, but not before you've cleaned up the mess on Lookout Mountain. How close are you to solving it, by the way?"

I was so taken aback I could barely get my breath, much less speak.

I... Umm. Geez, Chief, gimme a minute, will you?"

"Take your time, Lieutenant."

I took several deep breaths, shook myself mentally, *Freaking captain. Me? Holy cow. I'm not even time qualified yet.*

"Okay, Chief," I said, hoping I sounded suitably professional. "I have a person of interest. Well, he's more than that. Right now he's my prime suspect."

"And who might that be?" he asked.

"Not yet, sir. Not until I'm certain. If I'm wrong, and it gets out—"

"I understand," he said, interrupting me. "Keep me in the loop. I want to know as soon as you're prepared to make an arrest. In the meantime, I expect you to keep your pending promotion to yourself. No one is to know until I announce it. Understood?"

"Yes, Chief. Understood."

I dropped the handset into its cradle and leaned back

in my chair, grinning like an idiot. *Fricking hell. Captain Gazzara... I like the sound of that. I sure as hell do. Yay me!*

"Oh, my God," Janet said. "What on earth is that look on your face?"

"Nothing, absolutely nothing," I said, jumping to my feet and grabbing my now cold coffee. "Come on. We have work to do."

Captain frickin' Gazzara... Wow!

27

"You look chipper this morning, LT," Janet said when she walked into my office the following morning, Wednesday. Dressed in jeans, a pink blouse, and white tennies, her red hair tied back in a ponytail, if it hadn't been for the Glock 17 and badge at her waist, she would easily have passed for a high school senior on her way to school.

"Yes, well," I said, "I had a good night's sleep for a change. That's usually all it takes... That and Tiny Finkle gone from my life. I only wish it was for good." I glanced up at her from the pile of paperwork I was trying to sort through. "How about you? You ready to go beard the Lion of God in his own den?"

She laughed, then said, patting her Glock, "Locked and loaded."

"Good, give me just a few minutes to clear away this pile on my desk and then we'll go."

"You want coffee? I can run over to Mickey D's while you're doing that."

"That would be lovely, but don't take too long. It's a two-hour drive to the retreat, and I don't want to get there just as they're breaking for lunch."

DIVINE SPRINGS CAMP and Family Retreat Center was a few miles west of Spencer off Highway 285, near Telula, at the border of Fall Creek Falls State Park.

We turned off 285 and followed a narrow winding road for several miles until finally, we found the retreat tucked away on top of a bald overlooking the rolling hills of the Cumberland Plateau and Caney Creek.

I didn't count them, but there must have been at least thirty cars, SUVs, and pick-ups parked in the lot at the front of the vast log cabin style structure. I parked discreetly in the back row hoping to blend my somewhat beat-up, unmarked Crown Vic' in among the array of high-value vehicles, not one of which could have cost less than forty grand.

Yeah, Janet's right; we're in the wrong profession.

"That looks like the entrance," Janet said as she climbed out of the car and pointed to a mile-long—joking —stretch of glass doors at the front of the building.

Our arrival hadn't gone unnoticed. Even before we made it across the parking lot, much less to the glass doors, a woman, smartly dressed in a pearl gray business suit, clipboard in hand, bustled out of the building and came to greet us.

"Hello," she said, with not even a hint of a smile. "Can I help you?"

I guessed her to be in her late forties, early fifties. Her hair was natural with gray streaks, and she wore no makeup: she had the beady eyes of an eagle.

"Yes, you can," I said, looking around. "Boy, but this is a beautiful place." I showed her my badge and ID.

"My name is Lieutenant Gazzara. I'm with the Chattanooga Police Department. This is Sergeant Toliver. You are?"

"I'm Barbara Loomis, director of the Divine Springs Camp and Family Retreat Center," she said proudly. "How can I help you, Lieutenant?"

"Mrs. Loomis, we're here to talk to Pastor Edward Pieczeck," Janet said.

"It's Ms. Loomis, and I'm afraid that won't be possible," she said, drawing herself up to her full height, asserting her ample bosom. "The pastor is conducting his monthly retreat. You'll have to come back at another time," she said to Janet as if she was speaking to a smart-mouthed teenager.

It was probably something Janet was well used to. Her youthful appearance might work to her advantage with the opposite sex. But as a cop, it had to be something of a handicap... well, at times.

"It's not a request, Ms. Loomis," I said. "I'm investigating the homicides of three members of his congregation." I narrowed my eyes as I smiled. "So please tell him we're here."

"Oh, my." She put her hand to her throat. "Yes, of course. I'm sorry, I didn't know, please, follow me."

She turned quickly and led us into the building where we were greeted by the heady scent of sandalwood, the pleasant sound of trickling water, and the haunting tones of bamboo flutes. I was reminded of the music used for relaxation at spas, yoga studios, and new age shops—and I wanted to stay and soak it up.

"Please wait here. I'll return directly," Loomis said, waving a hand at several of what I knew to be zero gravity chairs, and then she hurried away across the lobby and disappeared down a hallway.

"How would you like to spend a couple days here every month?" Janet asked.

"Uh, I'd love it. Wouldn't you?"

"Yeah, but I don't get it. When did church become such a cushy lifestyle?"

"When they took God out of it," I muttered.

"Do you believe Pastor Ed is some kind of flimflam artist?" Janet asked.

"Flimflam artist? You've been watching those old gangster movies again, with Humphrey Bogart and James Cagney, haven't you?"

Janet blushed and shook her head. "Maybe."

"You know," I said thoughtfully. "I read a book once, some time ago, about a televangelist and his wife —can't remember their names—who made millions of dollars from their TV show. People were sending them their life savings, hoping it would help them get into heaven. That televangelist lived like royalty; didn't steal a dime. His congregation gave it all to him."

I shrugged and then continued, "But he still went to jail for it, and his wife divorced him. That was a long time ago. He's dead now, so is his wife, I think, but there are more just like him, many more: smarter, savvier, and a whole lot more careful than he was, but hucksters just the same. Beats me just how gullible the public can be."

"Yeah, I know," Janet said. "You think this is the same kind of scam then?"

"Doesn't matter if it is. We're here investigating three murders, not Pastor Ed to find out if he's using the church collections to furnish his summer home."

"I don't know. I find it all a little creepy," Janet said. "Jesus didn't say 'follow me and get filthy-stinkin' rich,' did he? It was something like, 'Give up thy worldly goods and...' Oh, I don't know. Maybe I'm just too old-school," Janet said.

I chuckled. "You're old-school? At the age of twenty-four?"

"Will I get in trouble if I tell my Lieutenant to shut up?" Janet asked.

"No, Old School. Not this time anyway." I laughed.

Before she could say anything more, Loomis reappeared with Pastor Ed following behind, and he didn't look happy.

"Detective Gazzara, this is quite a surprise," he snapped.

"I know, and I'm sorry. I hate to bother you, Pastor

Ed. Is there somewhere where we can talk privately?" I said looking at Loomis.

"Of course," she said.

She kneaded her hands as she looked to Pastor Ed for direction. I had the impression he'd scolded her for interrupting his ministry.

She led us down another hallway and opened the door to a small conference room, with a round table in the center surrounded by four chairs. The exterior wall was wall-to-wall, floor-to-ceiling windows that overlooked a vast panorama of lush gardens, tall grass, wildflowers, and old-growth trees.

Loomis left us alone, closing the door behind her.

"Please sit down, Pastor," I said as I took my iPad from my shoulder bag.

He did so, and I informed him I was going to record the interview.

"Am I under arrest?" he asked as he slowly sat down.

"Should you be?" I asked.

"Good Lord, no."

I smiled at him. "No, sir. You're not under arrest, but I do have some follow-up questions. I'm sure Ms. Loomis informed you that we've found another body, Mrs. Lucille Benedict," I said slowly as I watched the pastor's reaction.

"Lucille?" he gasped. "Oh God, no. Loomis didn't tell me... But I just saw her."

Wow, give the man an Oscar!

"When was that?" I asked.

"Just yesterday, around five-thirty in the afternoon.

She asked me to stop by. I... I can't believe it," he stuttered.

"Why did she ask you to stop by?"

"She knew I was going to be gone for a couple days with the retreat. She just wanted... to talk and to visit... ohhhh."

"Just to visit and talk? What about?" I arched my eyebrows.

"What transpires between a pastor and a member of his congregation is private. I can assure you that it was harmless." He cleared his throat and fidgeted in his seat.

"What are you talking about? You mean confession?" Janet asked. "That's a Catholic thing, not a Baptist thing."

"No, I'm talking about the conversation we had together. It was between Lucille and I. There was nothing insidious about it," he stuttered. "I feel insulted that you would insinuate that I would be improper. In fact, I don't think I want to discuss it with you anymore. I'm extremely busy with the retreat. If I'm not under arrest, I'm not going to answer any more of your questions."

Pastor Ed folded his arms, just as his wife had done, and pressed his lips together.

"Pastor, Lucille Benedict is dead. Victoria Randolph and Meryl Dilly are dead. They were all beaten and stabbed. They were members of your church. I have to find the killer. Your feelings don't come into it. I need answers, and I need them now."

I watched as his gaze flitted here and there, everywhere but in my direction. He pressed his lips tighter together.

"Even our dear Lord suffered wrongful accusations," he said finally, quietly.

"Our dear Lord wasn't the last person to see three women who were bludgeoned to death," I snapped.

He looked balefully at me, then said, "I really can't do this now. I need to get back to the members."

"Very well," I said, "we'll continue this in Chattanooga. Before you go, however, I need a DNA swab from you."

"What?" he shouted.

"The medical examiner found seminal fluid and blood on the victims. I need a sample so that we can eliminate you as a suspect." I smiled sweetly at him.

"No... No, I... don't have time for this. You... you need a court order. Please leave now."

"No time for a simple swab? My, you are a busy man, aren't you, Edward? You're right, if you won't cooperate, I do need a court order. I'll have one waiting when you return."

I picked up my iPad and shut it off. Janet got up and walked to the door. She opened it and stepped outside. Pastor Ed also stood and followed me to the door.

"Tell you what, Pastor," I said, turning and staring him in the eye. "How about you come down to the police department when you return to Chattanooga? We can wait a couple of days. The victims aren't going anywhere."

I could see his body start to tremble. So I upped the heat even more.

"Oh, and by the way, that's not a request. I'll call you."

The hell I will. I'll drag your sorry ass down there in handcuffs.

Without another word, he stomped out of the conference room and disappeared in the opposite direction from where we'd come. I joined Janet in the hallway.

"That's it then," Janet said as we walked toward the exit. "He won't cooperate. We're screwed. Why didn't you arrest him?"

I sighed. "Come on, Janet. You know why: no probable cause. Just because the man drives a silver Audi and was probably screwing one of the victims, doesn't mean he killed them. We can't ride roughshod over his rights."

"But he admitted he was with Benedict the evening she was killed."

"So he did, and that means what?" I asked.

She thought for a minute, then said, "It means we can place him at the scene and that he had opportunity."

"Good one, Janet, but what else do we need?"

She sighed. "Motive and the murder weapon."

"And physical proof," I said. "Fingerprints on the weapon would be ideal. What we have right now isn't much, and it's circumstantial. I told you before, the DNA, even if it's his, doesn't mean very much. The silver Audi, his admission to being at the scene during the window of opportunity... It doesn't mean a whole lot either.

"His refusal to give us a sample though, that's something else. Why would he do that?" I pondered. "He knows we'll get a court order and that he'll have to comply, eventually. Nope, we need more, much more, and I think I know how to get it. Come on. Let's get out of here."

"So what's the plan now, LT?"

"I need to make a phone call."

28

"A stakeout?" Chief Johnston asked. "Surveillance? Of one of the wealthiest, most popular pastors in the entire city? You'd better be sure of what you're doing, Lieutenant."

"Chief, I know, and I am. I've got a feeling that Pastor Ed is hiding something, and his wife is privy to it."

I swallowed hard. "Victoria Randolph is the only victim who was killed somewhere else. I need to find that crime scene. The pastor is my prime suspect, for several reasons I can't go into over the phone. If he did it, sir, and I'm thinking he did, he and his wife are hiding something, and it's not that they're dipping their fingers into the collection plate. I just want to watch their comings and goings for twenty-four hours. Forty-eight at the most."

"Forty-eight at the most? Hmm. I'm not entirely opposed to it, Lieutenant, but I can't spare the manpower. If you do it, you must do it by yourself. Do *not* involve Detective Toliver. Understood?"

I sighed, promotion or not, Finkle or not, things hadn't changed a whole lot.

"Yes, Chief. I understand."

I had him on speaker. I looked at Janet in the seat beside me; she'd heard it all. She just shrugged and looked as if someone had stolen her last piece of candy.

I DROPPED Janet off at the PD then went home, showered, changed clothes, took Sadie Mae out for a few minutes, and then called Lonnie and asked him to come get the dog and look after her for a couple of nights. Next, I grabbed a few bottles of water and headed back to the retreat center, only this time I didn't park in the lot. I found a secluded spot among the trees, parked there, checked the time—it was almost five-thirty in the afternoon—grabbed my binoculars from the glove box, got out of the car, locked it, and headed west about a hundred yards to the tree line. There I settled down to watch... and then the first mosquito found me.

Damn! I forgot to bring bug spray.

As it happened, it didn't matter... well, not much. I hadn't been there more than thirty minutes when I spotted Pastor Ed hurrying out the front doors of the retreat center, dragging a roll-on suitcase, shuffling clumsily toward a silver Audi S4. It was spotless, shiny, and rather sporty for a guy with a wife at home. He flung the suitcase into the trunk, almost ran around to the driver's side doors, jumped in, and peeled out of the parking lot as if the devil himself were chasing him. Little did he know it wasn't the devil. It was me.

What the hell's going on? I thought. *The retreat doesn't finish until tomorrow night. What's he up to? Oh shit. He's running... but where to?*

I figured it would be one of two destinations: the Chattanooga Metropolitan Airport or Texas and the Mexican border.

He drove like a freaking maniac: sixty, seventy, even as high as eighty on those narrow back roads, forcing me to do the same, risking my life to keep up with the crazy SOB. Luckily, my Interceptor had more than enough oomph in her to keep up.

The silver Audi turned south on Route 111 and increased speed, which could mean trouble, for both of us. I considered radioing a request for mutual aid, but didn't; I wanted to know what he was doing, not arrest the stupid SOB for speeding.

He turned south again onto US 127 and scorched through Soddy-Daisy and then inexplicably slowed as he entered Red Bank.

Sheesh, he's not running, he's headed home. So why the urgency? Talk to his wife about me showing up at his retreat? And risk your damn life? That's frickin' crazy. What the hell is wrong with you?

But that wasn't it, not at all. I continued to follow him into Red Bank and from there into a secluded new subdivision of mid-level bungalows. He then drove straight to a corner unit and pulled onto the short driveway.

Things were about to get tricky. If he spotted me, I'd ruin my chance of finding out what he was up to. I parked on the street two houses back, and I waited, watching.

He sat in his car for almost fifteen minutes; I couldn't figure it out. I could see through my binoculars that he wasn't on the phone. He was just sitting there.

He's waiting for someone? Oh well, time to check out the neighborhood.

I didn't need to get out of the car, just a quick glance around told me the development wasn't quite as new as I first thought it was. The houses had that lived-in look, the one Ed was parked outside more so than most of the others.

Surveillance can be one of the most rewarding police tactics, but you have to have patience, and that I had aplenty. So, I pushed my seat back as far as it would go and reclined it so my head was barely visible, and I continued to watch.

The minutes ticked by, but Pastor Ed stayed right where he was until finally, I say him put his phone to his ear. He talked for only a few seconds before throwing his phone onto the passenger seat. He sat for a moment more, his hands to his forehead—thinking or crying, I couldn't tell. Then he exited the car and stomped —*angrily,* I thought—to the front door of the home, pulled keys from his pocket, unlocked the door, stepped inside and slammed it shut behind him.

Oh, now that's interesting, I thought. *A man with a*

house in Lookout Mountain has a second home just twenty-five minutes away. There's something weird going on. It's more likely they'd have a cottage in the Berkshires or maybe a condo in Miami. Not a crappy bungalow on the other side of town.

I settled down to wait again. *It looks like I could be here all freakin' night. Oh well...* And then I was struck by a truly demoralizing thought. I had no coffee. *Oh dear Lord, this is going to be the longest and most miserable stakeout ev-er. What is he doing in there, I wonder?*

Fortunately, I didn't have long to wait at all. Some twenty minutes later, the pastor stepped out onto the front porch, looked warily around, then walked unsteadily to his car and drove away, leaving me there looking at the house and wondering what to do next: chase him some more or...

"No search warrant, Kate," I muttered as I contemplated the question. "Ah, screw it. What've I got to lose?"

Your frickin' promotion, and possibly your job, stupid!

It was almost eight-thirty and growing dark when I exited the car. I looked up and down the street. It was deserted, so I took a deep breath and walked up the front steps and looked around. Where the doorbell was supposed to be was just an empty hole in the doorframe. I knocked; no answer. I tried to look in through the windows. It wasn't happening: the curtains were heavy, drawn tightly closed.

Damn it!

I scratched my head and decided to check around back.

The ground was dry. The grass, primarily the crab variety intermingled with weeds, hadn't been cut for at least a couple of weeks.

If I stood on tiptoe, I could've seen over the sills of the side windows, but I could see the thick curtains would've blocked any view I might have had of the inside there, too.

Maybe he's decided to go into real estate and this is a piece of property he bought to flip. Yeah, right, that would make perfect sense, I thought sarcastically. *Would a guy like Pastor Ed with the world and Heaven at his feet, really dirty his hands on a place like this? Not hardly, I think.*

I stepped up to the back porch and gently pulled on the screen door handle and was thrilled when it opened. I went inside the screened-in porch and tried the back door; it was locked. I went to one of the windows. It was covered only by a lace curtain, dirty but transparent enough for me to see through it into a kitchen that looked like it had never been used. There were no dishes, no tea towels, none of the niceties you'd expect to find in any kitchen.

I knocked on the door: nothing. I knocked again, harder, pressed my ear to the doorframe, listening for anything that might indicate someone was inside, but I heard nothing.

It was an impossible long shot, but I felt along the top of the door frame for a key anyway. My fingers encountered nothing but dust and dead bugs. *Ew!* I flipped the doormat and...

Holy shit, a freakin' key. Who does this anymore? I should buy a lottery ticket. It must be my lucky day.

The key slid smoothly into the doorknob, and with a gentle twist, I pushed the door open. I held my breath and listened, pulled my Glock, and stepped inside.

The light in the kitchen was enough to look around, but down the hallway, toward the front of the house, it was nearly pitch black.

I took a deep breath, said a quick prayer, hoped that no one was home, and stepped forward into the dark nether world that was the hallway and, at the same time, I also stepped way over the line. Internal Affairs would salivate over this one, if ever they found out.

The floor creaked as I made my way slowly along the hallway. I paused, took out my iPhone, turned on the flashlight, and the darkness became a weird, shadowy half-light; not great, but at least I could see that there were four doors, two on either side, all of them closed but one.

Again, I listened for movement, but heard nothing but my own heartbeat pounding in my ears.

The entire house smelled of cheap incense, the sort you could pick up at a gas station, fifty sticks for two bucks.

The open door gave entrance to a bathroom. The glass window was frosted, a dark rectangle faintly illuminated by the orange light of a nearby streetlamp. I stepped inside. There was a medicine cabinet over the vanity. I opened it, shone my flashlight into it, and stared at the contents.

Wow, would you just look at that?

I counted six boxes of condoms—one of them open—and a half-dozen tubes of a well-known lubricant. I smiled as I picked up a bottle of those famous little blue pills and read the label: the prescription was for... *Edward freakin' Pieczeck! Holy cow!*

I replaced the bottle exactly as I'd found it, closed the cabinet door, stepped back into the hallway and listened: nothing. By then, I was sure there was no one in the house but me. Yeah, that; I was alone, but that didn't make what I was doing any the less nerve-racking. I opened the door to one of the other rooms and looked inside. It was as bare as a baboon's butt, no furniture, nothing, unused. The same with the next one.

I closed that door and opened the last one. The beam of light from my phone cut through the darkness and... I'd prepared myself for another body, or a naked prisoner bound and gagged, so I kind of giggled to myself when the reality of what I did find sank in.

I felt along the wall for the light switch and flipped it on. *Geez!* I shook my head in amusement. Four red fluorescent lights set high on each of the four walls flickered then popped on, bathing the room in an eerie red glow.

There was a bed set against the far wall. Next to it, on a cheap nightstand, were a variety of sex toys, some of them so bizarre I didn't know what they were. On the walls, belts and straps of different sizes and thicknesses, chains, handcuffs, and shackles dangled from hooks.

Holy shit! Is that a fricking sex swing? Hahaha, our dear pastor is Lord of the Swings?

To top it all off, a high-end digital video camera was positioned on a tripod in the corner of the room.

I stepped into the room, turned it on, and hit the play button... pushed rewind, then play again... and there I found the answers to several of my questions... sort of.

29

"Y ou did what?" Lonnie asked.

"Well I had to see what was going on inside the house, now didn't I?" I asked as I drove to his house.

Lonnie and I had been through a lot together, and I could talk to him like I could no one else... except Harry Starke, and that wasn't an option, not with Amanda the way she was... but that's another story. And Lonnie watched Sadie Mae for me when I had to put in long hours. That little dog absolutely loved him. He had a yard for her to run around in, which I didn't, and Lonnie took her to his barber shop where she got more attention than a newborn baby. Little minx.

"I can't believe you did that, Kate. It was a huge risk. What if you'd gotten caught? You'd have lost your freakin' badge."

"Yeah, but now at least I have some answers, something to squeeze him with. The pastor of the wealthiest church in the Tri-State area, on film, doing the nasty... and a whole lot of weird kinky stuff with a member of his church, now dead, murdered, beaten to death... Hey, I'm pulling in your driveway now."

I heard Lonnie shut off his phone as I drove up the short gravel driveway and stopped in front of the garage.

The front door opened and Lonnie appeared with a beer in his hand, and Sadie Mae galloped out between his legs. I gathered her up, and she covered my face in kisses.

I really don't like beer that much, but what the hell. I was parched, so I set the dog down and happily accepted the beer.

I stretched out in my usual spot on the corner of the couch. Lonnie, mineral water in hand, dropped into his throne, a worn-out leather recliner. Sadie Mae leaped up into his lap, flopped down and stared sleepy-eyed and content at me.

Lonnie glared at me over the top of his bottle.

"Don't even say it," I said. "I had to do it; you would have done it too... You know you would. So would Harry. He wouldn't even have thought about it; Bob Ryan would have kicked the damn door in. I had to go into the house, right? I know he did it, the pastor, but I can't prove it, not even with this." I showed him the memory card from the video camera.

"You sure as hell can't now that you stole the frickin' thing. Why did you do that? You could have gotten a warrant. That thing is not admissible now. More than that, it could get you arrested."

I shook my head. "You don't understand, Lonnie. He

was acting suspiciously. He could have been in there destroying evidence. And anyway, I can still get a warrant to search the place. I'll make a copy of the card and put it back where I found it." I was looking for his approval, but all I got was a shrug.

"So now you have this information, but you can't use it, and if IA finds out you committed a B&E, you're screwed. Unless..." Lonnie looked down at the dog and stroked her head.

"Unless what?" I smirked. "And it wasn't B&E. I used a key."

"Unlawful entry, then. Come on, Kate," Lonnie said, frustrated. "You're a senior police officer. You know you can't do that: unlawful search and seizure. It's cop school 101. Yeah, you've got to put it back where you got it, but first, maybe, just maybe, you can put the screws to the pastor and get him to admit to... I dunno, something... He sure as hell isn't going to confess to murder; kinky sex, maybe, but not murder," Lonnie replied like he was apologizing for standing me up on a date.

I took a long, deep gulp of my beer. It tasted good. The bitter flavor brought back memories of hot summers, hotter nights, and a more carefree time when... At least for me, it was.

"Yeah. I know. And I've got to get to it sooner rather than later."

I gulped down the last of my beer, put the bottle on the side table, and mentally prepared myself to get up and go. I would have given just about anything to stay there and talk strategies, but I was bushed. I needed sleep, in the worst way, because, as Scarlett O'Hara said, tomorrow is another day.

And then, wouldn't you know it? My phone rang.

"Gazzara," I answered.

"Kate. It's Doc. You busy?"

"No, Doc." I looked at my watch. It was almost eleven-thirty. "I was just about to call you," I said, a little more sarcastically than I intended, but he didn't seem to notice.

"Yes, well that's good, because I just finished with my swimming accident postmortem, and my wife has gone to visit her sister in Atlanta, so I thought I'd get started on Lucille Benedict. But that's not what I'm calling about. I received the reports back from the lab. This is a second round, remember?"

"Yes, I remember."

"We have the same result. They identified the victim's blood, but there are two other unidentified DNA profiles: the seminal fluid and the blood.

"So, I could be looking for two killers, not one."

My heart sank to the pit of my stomach. The pastor was my only viable lead, and I was ready to bet my job that the semen would be a match for his DNA profile.

Then, I lightened up and snapped my fingers. "That's great news, Doc." I looked at Lonnie and winked.

"I'm glad you think so," Doc replied.

Oh yeah, I bet you do, I thought, *and there goes any thoughts I had of sleep.*

"I'll be there in a jiffy. You can tell me all about it."

I said goodbye and hung up.

"Sorry, partner," I said to Lonnie. "Duty calls. I have a date with Doctor Death, so I'll take a rain check on the next round, if you don't mind."

I stood. Lonnie was about to do the same, but I stopped him.

"You'll disturb the baby," I said, nodding at the sleeping dog. "Thanks again for watching her. You're a good egg, Lonnie."

"Good egg? You've been watching too many old movies," Lonnie replied as I kissed the top of his head.

"Very funny," I said, remembering I'd said almost the same thing to Janet. "I'll let you know when I can pick up the dog."

"Take your time, Detective. You know where to find us," Lonnie called out as I shut the screen door behind me and hurried to my car.

I missed having Lonnie as a partner. But, it was how things usually worked at the Chattanooga Police Department, and probably everywhere else. Give it a couple more months and who knows, maybe Janet would be gone too.

I reversed out onto the street, turned on my emergency lights and siren, and hit the gas; I didn't intend to waste time driving to Doc's lair.

30

This time Doc was waiting for me. The door opened as I walked across the parking lot.

"You hungry?" he asked as he pulled the door closed behind me and snapped the deadbolt in place. "I have some goulash left; I made it yesterday."

"Sounds great," I said, not really that sure that it did... sound great.

I couldn't remember the last time I'd eaten, but left-over goulash? *I dunno!*

"I worked up an appetite on the way over here," I lied.

"Fine. Let me get the files and we'll take them into the kitchen," Doc said.

The kitchen was a sterile, much smaller clone of his autopsy room: all stainless steel and white plastic. A large pot was simmering on the stove. He opened a cabinet, grabbed two stainless steel bowls, and spooned the hot food into them: chunks of beef, potatoes, carrots, and speckles of fresh parsley sprinkled throughout.

"This smells fantastic," I said, "but steel bowls and plastic spoons?" I smiled. "Doggy bowls, Doc?"

"Not exactly, my dear, but they're all I have. Ah me... if only I had some red wine," he said, opening the refrigerator door and extracting a three-liter bottle of Orange Crush. "Then we'd really be in business."

Orange Crush? Gross!

We ate in silence for several minutes, then we put our bowls aside, and Doc spread the three files across the table and opened them.

Each file contained photographs of the crime scene, the bodies, the stages of the autopsy procedures, and copies of his reports.

"Here you go, my dear," Doc said as he handed me three sets of reports each stapled together. "I printed these out for you, and I emailed the photographs."

"Just give me the Reader's Digest version, Doc," I said, setting them aside.

"I spoke to Mike Willis earlier this afternoon. As I mentioned earlier, he was following up on a semen sample, pubic hairs, and blood samples. The semen sample on Meryl Dilly is not her husband's," he said. "Neither are the two pubic hairs."

He looked at me and raised his eyebrows.

"I'm not surprised," I said.

He continued, "It appears the attack on her was so violent that the assailant cut himself, thus providing us with an additional DNA profile. Several of the blood spots Mike found on her clothing didn't match Mrs. Dilly's profile, nor that of Connor Dilly, or that of the seminal fluid, I'm sorry to say."

Doc paused and took a sip of his soda.

"So, one must conclude that Mrs. Dilly had sexual intercourse with someone other than her husband, and then after that, either someone else killed her on their own, or there were two people present when she was killed, one of them the person she had sex with."

"How about the semen and the hairs?" I asked. "Are they a match?"

"They are indeed."

"Well, that's something, I guess."

I stared at the crime scene photos, lost in thought. *Wow, that's not good. So if the pastor was screwing her, and I'm sure he was... But if he wasn't, and someone else was... That means there's a third person out there somewhere with whom she was having an affair... So who the hell does the blood belong to? Geez... geez... geez.*

"I dunno, Doc. I checked Connor Dilly's hands at the scene, Darby Randolph's too. Neither one had any cuts or scratches on their hands." *And neither did Pastor Ed.*

I thought about Pastor Ed's video. Unfortunately, due to the camera angle, and the fact that the woman was blindfolded, I couldn't be absolutely positive that it was Meryl Dilly he was doing disgusting things to, and never once did I see him actually penetrate her. He could have, but again the camera angle made it difficult to see.

"Are you ready to get started?" Doc asked, breaking into my thoughts.

I looked at my watch. It was just after midnight. I looked at him and said, "No, not really, but let's do it." And we did.

Back under the lights, I took my seat on the opposite side of the table and watched Doc work his magic.

There was little difference between the state of poor Lucille's body and those of the other two victims. The cause of death was a single blow to the left side of her head that split her parietal bone almost in half—*another single killing blow*—indicating a right-handed assailant. Her face had been beaten almost to a pulp. From the shape of the wounds, Doc surmised the killer had used the same weapon as was used to kill Victoria Randolph and Meryl Dilly, probably a crowbar. And, just like the other two victims, she'd also been stabbed… twelve times, three of them through and through.

No, I thought. *I can't do this, not now. I need to get out of here and catch the SOB when he's not expecting it.*

"Doc," I said, "it's been one hell of a long day. I'm about to fall over. Do you mind if I head out?"

"No, no, of course I don't, my dear. Run along home. I'll call you when and if I find something."

"Thanks," I said. "You know, I feel like we are on the edge. Just one stiff breeze and we might be able to topple it over."

He nodded, the plastic face shield banging his chest, and gave me a casual wave with his bloody, purple-latex-covered gloved hand, scalpel glistening with blood in the artificial light.

"Until next time, my dear. Be careful out there."

31

It was well past midnight, and I was bone tired. It really had been a long day, but I wasn't ready to quit, not yet. I hit the gas and headed to Pastor Ed's home on Lookout Mountain.

I know it probably makes me sound like a real jerk, but the idea of busting into his house at that hour of the night gave me a thrill.

I drove up to the gate with my bright lights on and the grill-mounted blue and red emergency lights flashing, just to make my point.

I pressed the intercom button, and pressed again and again, like I was tapping out a message in Morse code.

"Who is it? Do you have any idea what time it is?" Pastor Ed shouted, his voice crackling with distortion through the speaker.

"It's Lieutenant Gazzara. Open the gate. I need to speak to you, *now*."

"Uh, er, I'm sorry, Lieutenant, but my wife and I

have retired for the evening. I'll meet you at the Police Service Center tomorrow morning."

"I said, open the gate, Pastor. If I have to call for backup, you'll be headed down there tonight, in handcuffs, and I know you don't want that. So do as I ask and open the gate."

Several minutes went by, but the gate didn't open, and I was beginning to get nervous. Sometimes when suspects realize they're cornered, they react in a bad way. I pressed the intercom again.

"Pastor Ed? Can you hear me?"

Nothing.

"Pastor Ed? Mrs. Pieczeck?"

I continued pressing the button. The last thing any cop wants is some kind of standoff or a murder-suicide. Hell, for all I knew, he and his wife could have been card-carrying members of the NRA with an arsenal of firearms in there.

I pressed the buzzer again.

Finally, after what felt like an eternity, the lock on the gate clicked and it slowly began to open. I let out a deep sigh of relief, licked my lips with my dry tongue, and rolled slowly through the gate.

As I drove to the house under the canopy of the trees, with the window rolled down, I was sure I could smell rain in the air. The crickets were having a grand time making their sweet music for each other.

Pastor Ed was waiting for me at the front door. He was wearing a robe tied at his waist. It revealed the top of a hairy chest, well-defined pectoral muscles, sculpted calves, and bare feet. The man was in great shape for a pastor.

"What's this all about, Lieutenant?" he hissed as I exited the car.

"It has been a really long day, Pastor. Mind if I come in? My backside could use a break from the rough seat of my car." I smiled. I wasn't joking: police Interceptors are not built for comfort.

He took a deep breath and when he exhaled, his whole body slumped. He stepped aside for me to enter. I did and was immediately taken aback by the breathtaking beauty of the interior.

It was a truly amazing home. As I stepped inside, just to the right of the foyer was a life-sized wooden cross. There was no Savior nailed to it. No symbol of the risen Lord. It was just a big cross.

He motioned for me to step into the living room, a vast chamber with high ceilings, white walls, and gold trim. The furniture, the picture frames, the knick-knacks all were white, some with gold trim. The room was absolutely spotless.

"Please, sit," he said distractedly.

I took a seat on the white sofa, opened my iPad, tapped the record icon, crossed my legs and leaned back, and informed him I would be recording the interview.

"Do I need my attorney present?"

"I don't know. Do you?"

He didn't answer. He just stood there staring down at me. I probably should have been wary that he might attack me, but for some reason, I wasn't.

"Oh, this is nice," I said, rubbing the smooth white fabric. "What is this? Silk?"

"Please," he said plaintively. "What is this all about, Detective?"

"Oh, right, we're hurrying this right along. By the way, will your wife be joining us?"

"No. She's asleep."

I nodded. "Yes. Well, why don't you tell me about your little... shall we call it, retreat, in Red Bank. And please, tell me the truth. It kinda hurts my feelings when someone tries to bullshit me."

The man's face didn't just pale, it turned ashen. It was as if he died standing up but couldn't quit breathing. I have to admit, I felt kind of sorry for him. "Maybe you should sit down before you fall down, Pastor," I said firmly.

He looked over his shoulder toward the open hallway. The lights were off, and it was dark and, as far as I could tell, Mrs. Pieczeck wasn't out there listening.

Pastor Ed nodded, sat down opposite me, and wiped his top lip with the back of his hand.

"She... she can't know about that," he stuttered, his voice hushed.

"I really don't care what your wife does or doesn't know," I said. "What I want to know is why you didn't tell me about it?" I folded my arms and stared at him.

The pastor chuckled nervously, his lip twitching on the right side. He didn't answer.

"Let me ask you this, how do you think Mrs. Pieczeck will react when she finds out that you have a secret hideaway where you take the lady members of your church for kinky sex games?" I tilted my head to the right, opened my eyes wide, and smiled at him.

His demeanor changed. "I don't know what you're talking about," he said defiantly.

I took the memory card from my jacket pocket and held it up between finger and thumb for him to see. "This isn't you in the video? It sure looks like you..."

His lip twitched again.

"Yes," I said, teasing him. "It is you, and oh, my Lord if that isn't Meryl Dilly swinging there while you... well, you know, don't you, *Pastor?*"

I sat still and watched him. It was like watching a building collapsing in slow motion.

"I didn't kill her," he said finally. He closed his eyes and let his chin drop to his chest.

"I didn't... kill her. We had a mutual arrangement." His eyes started to glisten. "Oh God. Oh God."

"Oh God is right, but He can't help you. Only you can do that. You, Pastor Edward Pieczeck, are my prime suspect for the murders of Victoria Randolph, Meryl Dilly, and Lucille Benedict. What have you got to say for yourself?"

"Oh God! No. You can't be serious. It was nothing like that. She was home alone, Meryl. She said her husband was preoccupied with his business. She was lonely. She came to me for help, and things just happened." He stood up and started to pace.

"What about Victoria Randolph? Did you make videos of her, too?"

"No. We were only alone together once, and we didn't have sex. There was a lot of heavy petting, but she never let it get any further than that," he confessed.

"Is that why she was working for you? So you could push the issue with her, too? She was very beautiful, very sexy."

Pastor Ed swallowed hard, almost as if he was remembering. He looked toward the hallway and then back at me. He ran his hand through his hair, sat down again and leaned toward me, his elbows on his knees, kneading his hands.

"Yes, I wanted her, but she was a tease, Victoria. She liked to play the game but wasn't ready to go all in." He looked down at his hands.

"Is that why you killed her?"

"I didn't kill her. I wanted her, yes. I wanted to share my visions with her. We were getting closer, and I knew she'd soon see how I felt about her," he stuttered. "But I didn't kill her."

"Your visions? What are those, exactly?"

He cleared his throat as his eyes darted all around the room.

"I enjoy domination. Every woman I've ever been with understands that and has willingly accepted the submissive role. Every one of them. They all agreed to being videotaped in addition to... everything else, except for Victoria." He pointed to the floor for dramatic effect.

Holy cow. The man's a raving perv. Fricking hell, who would have thought it? He's freakin' nuts.

"So, what happened with Meryl, Pastor? Did something go wrong? Perhaps you didn't catch her safety word? Things got a little out of hand and oops... Goodnight Meryl." I shrugged. "So you covered it up by beating her almost beyond recognition."

And then something just popped into my head. "Or did your wife do that? She couldn't let word get out that her pastor husband is a pervert, now could she?" *Oh, wow, that could be it. Why didn't I think of it before? She drives a silver car too, a twin to Ed's.*

"No. That didn't happen; none of it. I'm telling you the truth. As God is my witness, I did not—"

"I hate to think of what God witnessed in that house on Baker Avenue. What about Lucille Benedict? Was she one of your willing participants, too?"

"Yes, yes. She was. Unbelievable... Oh, God. I'm sick. Do you hear me? I'm sick. I need help, I've got a beautiful wife who adores me, and I've strayed from the paths of righteousness."

He stood, threw his head back, folded his hands in front of his chest, and looked pitifully up at the ceiling.

"Please, dear God, forgive me."

"Stop praying, Pastor. You'll have plenty of time for that later. Look at me."

He did, his arms still crossed over his chest.

"You were the last person to see Meryl Dilly alive.

You were the last person to see Lucille Benedict alive, right?" I shook my head. I was almost becoming as overwhelmed by it all as he was.

"Lucille was leaving to visit her son in Atlanta," he whispered. "She wanted to see me before she left. I went to her house. We had sex, sweet, sweet sex, and then I left." He sat down again, panting, as if he'd just run a marathon. "Oh, God. Please forgive me."

"Unprotected sex?" I asked.

He nodded.

"Out loud, please, Pastor.

"Yes, unprotected."

So that could account for the semen in Meryl Dilly.

"And then you killed her?" I asked quietly.

"I didn't kill anyone!" he wailed quietly, his eyes rimmed with red, his teeth clenched. "I swear to you. It was only sex. I didn't kill these women."

"You know what I think, Eddy? I think you're a team, you and Mrs. Pieczeck. Oh, look at you! I just don't believe that she doesn't know, about the house, the deviant sex... Does she participate? Maybe we should get her in here."

He stared at me in horror. "You... you can't. She doesn't know about the house. She doesn't know about what I do. Please, please, don't tell her."

I sat there looking at him for a full minute before I decided it was time to go. I had what I'd come for, in part. No murder confession, but boy would Clemont Rhodes like to get his hands on what I had?

Thankfully, getting the pastor to admit to the house,

the videos, and withholding information made things a little easier for me. How I'd gone about getting him to admit his sins wasn't ethical, not by any means. But then, when dealing with multiple homicides, lines tend to become blurry, sometimes almost invisible.

"Pastor Ed, I need to look inside the Red Bank house. I have what I need to get a search warrant, but if you want to keep it quiet, and I'm not promising I can, I need your permission." I stood up. "Let's see if we can avoid unnecessary publicity, shall we? Do I have your permission to enter the home at 221 Baker Avenue in Red Bank, and will you agree to accompany me?"

He nodded, looked miserable, then shrugged.

"Out loud for the recording, please, Pastor."

"Yes, you have my permission. You can do that. I will do that." Pastor Ed nodded slowly. "Just please, don't tell my wife. That's all I ask."

"I won't say a word unless I absolutely have to. That I promise, but I can't promise that the story won't get out, develop a life of its own." I put my hands on my hips.

"Can we please go to the house tomorrow?" he pleaded. "That way, my wife won't become suspicious?"

"Does she know I'm here now?"

He shook his head. "No, we have separate bedrooms."

"I understand. I'll meet you there at ten tomorrow morning, not a minute before, not a minute after. Understood?"

"Yes, I understand," he mumbled.

"I should warn you that the house is being watched,"

I said sternly. "So don't get any ideas about cleaning the place up before I get there. If you tamper, I'll arrest you on the spot for obstruction of justice. Do you understand, Pastor Pieczeck?"

Pastor Ed swallowed hard and nodded.

I turned and walked to the door.

"Ten o'clock, Pastor. Not a minute later." And then I turned back again. "Just one more thing before I go. I need that swab, please."

This time there was no argument. He simply opened his mouth and let me take it.

I let myself out and was happy to be out of the house. It was a beautiful home, but after hearing all that I had from the pastor, it had become little more than a mirage, all a huge fake, and I wanted to get away from it. His sex bungalow in Red Bank was more real than his expensive monument to modern architecture. It was seedy, sickening, true. But it was real, and I could deal with real. The smoke and mirrors that was the home of the Pieczecks I could deal with if I had to, but... I'd said it before, and I was right. Pastor Ed Pieczeck was just another huckster of holiness.

Sheesh, and this guy is supposed to be helping people.

I got in my car and drove home. It was almost two o'clock in the morning. I texted Janet and told her to call me at six-thirty in the morning, then I set the alarm for six o'clock, stripped off my clothes, and fell naked into bed.

32

The following morning, I left my apartment fresh, enthusiastic, and ready to do battle on behalf of my three murder victims. I drove to Red Bank, stopping at Hardee's along the way to get coffee and two sausage and egg biscuits to go. Thus, it was just after eight o'clock when I arrived at the subdivision and parked on the street directly in front of Pastor Ed's hidey-hole.

Janet had called earlier as I'd requested, and I'd given her the address and told her to meet me there at nine-thirty, thirty minutes before the pastor was supposed to meet me. She agreed.

So why was I there so early? I was just covering the bases. If our erstwhile pastor arrived early, I wanted to be there.

I took a couple sips of the steaming hot coffee, unwrapped a biscuit, rolled down the window, reclined the seat slightly, and settled down to watch the house.

The ninety minutes passed uneventfully. Janet arrived at nine-thirty. She parked behind me and then clambered into the passenger seat of my car with two large coffees and a dozen donuts.

A dozen? Are you kidding me? It would take me two weeks to burn off the extra calories.

True to his word, Pastor Ed arrived at ten o'clock sharp. The black bags beneath his eyes were telling: the guy probably hadn't slept all night. I so wanted to ask him if and what he'd told his wife, but I bit my tongue. It wasn't important. It wasn't my business, and it wasn't relevant to the case.

"Here, put these on," I said, handing Janet latex gloves and Tyvek booties.

"Good morning," he muttered, without looking at us as we joined him on the front porch. He unlocked the front door, pushed it open, and stepped aside for Janet and me to enter.

I asked him to stay out on the front porch while we cleared the house. In the harsh light of day, with the drapes not open, it was beyond depressing.

My first stop was pastor Ed's inner sanctum. I stood for a moment, looked around, then I looked sideways at Janet. She was wide-eyed, smiling. She looked at me and rolled her eyes. I smiled, shook my head and went to the camera, pretended to look through it, and slipped the memory card back into its socket, smiling as I did at the thought that I'd made a copy of it before I left home that morning.

The other bedrooms were also unfurnished and

unused except for a spider that had taken up residence in the corner of the ceiling. The kitchen, the last stop on the tour, was also bare, except for a half-dozen bottles of water in the fridge. I turned to go back to Ed on the front porch when I noticed a door partially hidden by the open kitchen door.

No wonder I missed it last night.

I opened the door to find a rickety flight of wooden steps that led down into almost total darkness. I flipped the light switch on the wall and descended the steps into a windowless basement. But for a couple of ancient dining chairs and a rickety kitchen table, it was bare, unused... At least that's what I thought at first glance, but then I spotted a large, discolored patch in the otherwise uniform gray color of the concrete floor. And then I noticed another patch on the back wall. Above that, and on the ceiling, I could see what I was sure was blood spatter. I'd found what I believed to be my crime scene, where Victoria Randolph had spent the last few terrifying minutes of life.

Oh, my Lord...

"Janet, come down here," I called up the stairs.

"Look at this," I said when she arrived, pointing to the patch on the floor. "And this, and this. Look at the ceiling."

"It's blood, isn't it?" she asked. "Someone's tried to clean it up, but it's blood. Is this where Mrs. Randolph was killed, do you think?"

"I don't know," I said despondently. "Not for sure,

but probably. Go get the field kit from my car and test it. I'm going to go talk to that frickin' freak of a pastor. Let me know the results as soon as you know."

She ran up the stairs. I followed and went out onto the porch to talk to Pastor Ed. He was sitting on the steps with his head in his hands, crying.

"Pastor Ed," I said gently. "Does anyone else have a key to this place?"

"I have a key, and I leave another under the mat on the back porch." His breath hitched in his throat. "It's sometimes necessary for some of the games we play. That's it, just the two keys."

"Who knows about the key under the mat?"

"Just my... friends."

Oh geez, what a creep.

"What about the basement?" I asked, watching for the tell. "What do you use it for?"

He frowned, shrugged, then said, "Nothing. I've only been down there once..." and then he shuddered.

It could have been one of those involuntary things that happens every now and then—we all know about those, right? Or it could have been that he was reliving the demise of Victoria Randolph.

Janet appeared in the doorway, her face white. She looked like she was about to throw up.

"Do you have a minute, LT?"

I nodded and stepped back inside.

"You're right; it turned pink. There's blood all over the place, everywhere. Oh, that poor woman. Someone tried to clean it up. We should call Mike Willis, ASAP. If we had a Luma-lite, I think the basement would light up like a Christmas tree."

I nodded. "Call him, now. Tell him what we found and to get here ASAP."

And she did.

I ran my tongue over my lips, turned and looked toward the front door, then pulled my cuffs from my belt and walked back out onto the porch.

"Edward Pieczeck," I said. "I need you to stand up for me please."

He turned his head to the right, attempting to look over this shoulder.

"Excuse me?"

"I need you to stand up and put your hands behind your back."

"What for?" he asked as he slowly started to stand.

Janet was now behind me, her hand on her weapon.

"I'm arresting you for the murder of Victoria Randolph," I replied.

"But I didn't kill her. I swear to you." He started to back off the porch with his hands up.

"Don't try it, Ed," I said quietly. "Don't make me take you down. Just turn around, put your hands behind your back, and we'll get you to Detective Toliver's car and then to the PD as quietly as possible."

"Quietly? Are you out of your mind? My wife is going to find out. She's going to find out about everything. She's going to think I'm a murderer." He began to sob.

"Please. Don't do this. I swear by the Almighty God that I didn't kill anyone!"

"You have the right to remain silent," I began.

I carefully took hold of his right hand and drew it gently behind his back. The man was as limp as a piece of tissue paper left out in the rain.

I continued with the Miranda Rights up to the point where I had to ask, "Edward Pieczeck, do you understand these rights as I've just read them to you?"

"No. I don't understand them. I don't understand anything. Why are you doing this to me? I've done nothing wrong."

He cried, his cheeks wet with tears, his eyes wide and wild, as the cuffs tightened around his wrists. He began to twist in my hands, as if, even with the handcuffs on, he could somehow get away from me and take off running.

"Please, stay calm, sir," Janet ordered as she walked to her car and opened the back door.

I helped him into the back seat of the car... and stood for a minute, and then closed the car door. I would have stayed with him and left the door open if he hadn't started to cry and shake like a baby. It was too much for me to handle. I hated to see a grown man cry even under the most tolerable of circumstances: His mom dies. His dog dies. But this... It was pathetic, and God knows he had money enough for the best attorneys.

Hell, if anyone should be crying, it should be me. I'm the one who has to make a case out of the mess. I just arrested a man for murder and, as yet, I'm not even sure he did it. I don't know whose blood is in the basement; I'm betting it's Victoria's, but it could be anybody's.

I watched as Janet stretched the yellow tape across the front of the driveway, and then I heard the sound of sirens wailing off in the distance. Minutes later, there were blue and white cruisers lined up along the street and more on the way: Baker Avenue was about to become a very active place.

"Janet," I said, "get the pastor out of here. Have one of the uniforms take him to Amnicola and make sure he understands that he's to put the pastor in an interview room, *not* the tank."

"I understand, LT. An interview room; not the tank."

I posted two officers at the entrance to the driveway, one with a visitor log, and went back inside the house. It's always the same. You make the call and everybody and his uncle arrives on the scene. *Talk about overkill.*

As I mounted the porch steps, I heard one of the neighbors, a black woman, talking to one of the cops I just posted at the driveway.

"It's about time," I heard her say.

I turned and joined her at the roadside, interrupting her discourse with the officer.

"Excuse me?" I said, "I'm Lieutenant Gazzara. Can I help you?"

I looked hard at the woman. She was an older lady, heavy-set, thin red hair, and she wore a lot of makeup. She looked like a tough one. I could tell she was not only not intimidated by me, but eager to talk to someone.

"Help me? I was just..." she said, drawing herself up to full height.

I had to smile, tongue in cheek.

"Yes, I heard you," I said. "What did you mean, 'it's about time'?"

"Well, it is. Look at the place, girl. It's a disgrace to the neighborhood, and I gotta live next door to it. And the comin's and goin's... It's disgraceful. Why are you here? What have they been doin' in there?"

"Care to tell me about it?" I asked, ignoring her question and handing her one of my business cards.

"I've seen that man you just put in the back of the police car. He's been bringin' women here, different women, two or three days a week. They stay an hour or two, and then they leave. I seen 'em. Pretty women," she replied. "Otherwise, the place is like it's vacant, the grass never mowed, weeds growin' everywhere... Is it a crack house I got next to mine? I'm retired. I'm not movin' until they plant my fat ass in the ground at St. Josephine's Cemetery over on Lincoln. The last thing I want is problems with the neighbors."

"What is your name, ma'am?" I asked, taking out my iPad and opening the Note app.

"My name is Lorretta Friedman. I've lived here for more'n ten years. I was happy when they finally sold this house." She pointed a bony finger at Pastor Ed's place. "I thought they'd fix it up." She shook her head and frowned. "But they didn't, did they? So what's been goin' on in there?"

"I'm going to ask you to make an official statement,

Miss Friedman. I'll record it and have it printed out, then you can read it and sign it. Can you do that for me, please?"

"Well, I suppose," she huffed and folded her arms.

I took her up onto the porch and we sat down, side by side, on the steps. I turned on the recording app, entered the relevant details, and then guided her through what she's already told me.

"So what else can you tell me?" I asked.

"Well," she said earnestly. "Sometimes there's no one in the house for days and days. And then suddenly, at around eleven or twelve o'clock at night, you hear people goin' in there. An' it's just the voices I hear. Then there are... the other things." She wrinkled her nose as if the thought of it caused an insufferable smell.

"What other things, Miss Friedman?" I prompted her.

She moved closer to me. "The whippin' sounds. The groaning. The yellin'. It was disgustin'. I may be old, but I'm not dead. I know what those sounds were. They was doin' the nasty, an' a whole lot more, if you ask me. And that man they just took away... he was always here when it was going on."

"So you could hear people having sex inside the house?" I asked.

She chuckled, then said, "It weren't the kind of sex I know about, but yes, I guess it was. How his wife could go along with this, I have no idea."

"His wife?" I asked as a cold shiver ran down my back.

So she is in on it. Lying little SOB. He was so desperate that his wife must not find out about his deviant second life. Did he lie to protect her? Was she part of this scene, too?

"I'm assumin' it was his wife. I saw her come to the house without him sometimes, and sometimes they came together. I just thought that maybe she came to clean the place, or check on it. I don't know... You know, I think there's a family of raccoons taken up residence up there in the attic." She pointed at a couple of torn shingles on the roof.

"Can you describe her for me?" I asked.

"I don't really remember much about her. She usually came in the evening. She was dressed nice, like. She had hair to her shoulders. More of a healthy athletic build than one of those too-skinny types. But I never got a close look at her face."

"You didn't happen to see what kind of car she was driving, did you?"

She nodded. "Not the model, but it was silver. That's all I know." She pointed to a nearby streetlamp. "And the only reason I know it was silver is because one time she parked under that light."

Out of the corner of my eye, I saw Mike Willis's CSI Command Unit pull up two houses back. He couldn't get closer because of the police cars; the count was up to nine, along with two fire trucks and an ambulance.

"Thank you, Miss Friedman. I'll get all this transcribed and then have you read and sign it, okay?"

"I suppose," she said.

"And I may be back to ask you a few more questions, would that be okay? I'll call you first, of course."

She shrugged. "Okay," she said as she pulled her sweater tighter around her.

I thanked her, told her goodbye, then went to meet Mike.

33

"**F**rea-ky," Mike said when he looked inside the pastor's bondage room. He was dressed from head to toe in white Tyvek complete with a face mask and latex gloves.

He was right, it was freakish. I know a lot of people will say live-and-let-live and who am I to judge and all that mumbo-jumbo. But we do judge, don't we? And the playroom at 221 Baker Avenue was, by any standards, just plain weird.

You know, I've seen some horrible things during my years as a homicide detective, and maybe it's because of that, the idea of bringing it home and into my kitchen or the bedroom is beyond me. I can't wrap my head around it.

I thought back to those first couple of days after they made me Harry's partner. I remember he showed me some crime scene photos. This is what? Ten years ago...

Anyway, there was this old couple, both in their mid-seventies. What he did to piss her off, I've no idea, but she beat him to death with a ball-peen hammer. She hit him with that thing so many times, well, they had to stop counting at eighty-one. The rest of the blows were unidentifiable, so was the old guy; it was hard to tell he was even a human. Can you image? I can still see those photographs. Terrible... but it's what I do, right?

"This stuff can wait, or maybe you can put your techs on it," I said, taking Mike's arm and pulling him away from the torture chamber. "Where I need you is downstairs."

I pointed him toward the basement and then followed him down the rickety steps.

"Oh boy," he said, placing his case on the floor at the bottom of the steps. "Someone's been hard at work."

"What's that?" I asked as we descended the steps into the basement.

"Don't you smell it? Bleach."

It hadn't registered with me since so many homes have washing machines in the basement. When I came down the first time, I didn't even think about it. Why wouldn't the basement smell like bleach or any other cleaning fluid? But as I looked around, I was ashamed to admit I didn't even notice that there was no washing machine or dryer... And, it was a frickin' big basement.

"No problem, though," Mike said. "Turn off the lights will you please, Lieutenant."

He popped open his box of goodies... Well, I thought it was a forensic kit, but it wasn't. It was a Foster+Freeman Crime-lite. He removed the device from its case along with two sets of what looked like one-piece welding goggles; one of which he handed to me. I remembered the department had ordered him one from the UK, but I'd never seen it. Now I got to do so up close and personal.

We donned the goggles, and he turned on the Crime-lite and integrated video camera. The entire south side of the room was illuminated, almost from our feet to a point on the ceiling just in front of us. I'd never seen anything like it...

And oh, my, God! There was no doubt now of what happened in that basement. It had been a blood bath. It was everywhere— all over the south wall and floor and what do you know: there were footprints, one full, the other a partial.

"I'll take it from here, Kate," Willis said thoughtfully. "I'll gather samples and get them to the lab immediately. The photographer will get the footprints. Have you any idea what happened, or to who?"

"Oh, I have ideas... I'm thinking that this is where Victoria Randolph died. She was the only one not killed at home," I replied, shaking my head. "And I think I know who killed her, but the footprints don't look right."

The partial was smaller than I would have expected. Pastor Ed was tall and worked out. I hadn't checked his shoe size. He could, I suppose, have small feet. I took my iPhone from my pocket and snapped a couple of quick photos of the glowing footprints for myself.

Two people? Could he and his wife... She's looking more and more like a person of interest.

"Okay, Mike," I sighed. "I'm out of here. I have a suspect to question. Keep me up to speed, will you please?"

"You got it, Kate. Take care."

As I ascended the steps, I felt a weird twisting in my gut. It wasn't the delicious nervous state of anticipation I usually experienced when I was about to interview a suspected killer. Nope. This was something else. A piece of the puzzle wasn't fitting, and no matter how hard I tried to force it, it wasn't going to.

Janet was waiting for me outside. She'd already stripped off her gloves and booties; I did the same.

Pastor Ed had been transferred to a blue and white and was already on his way to the station.

"What's the matter, LT?" Janet asked.

"Something isn't right. Mike's magic light revealed a blood bath and a couple of footprints. So someone walked in the blood, possibly two people... or not. I dunno. We'll have to wait and see,

"Maybe they're Victoria's footprints," Janet said.

"Well, that's a thought. I don't think so. What the hell was she doing down there in the first place?"

"Well," Janet said, "the footprints could only belong to one of three people, right? The victim, the killer, or an accomplice, or both, and I'm liking Pastor Ed. You should have seen him when I transferred him to the blue and white. It won't take much for him to crack and spill his guts. Especially when he finds out we're going to call his wife."

"Did you tell him that?"

"Not yet... Hey, there were originally sixty blue pills in that prescription. Is that for just one month, do you think? One a day, two, three? Who has that kind of stamina?"

I had to smile to myself when I thought about that. I did actually know someone... *Hmm, those were the days. And he didn't need any frickin' pills to keep him going.*

"Hey, LT, what are you smiling at?"

I didn't know I was, smiling.

"No one can," I said. "That's why they take the little blue pills," I muttered. "Come on. I'll meet you at the station. You want to play bad cop?"

"Ooh yeah. Don't I always?" Janet nodded enthusiastically.

I had to laugh because she looked like a sweet young kid, but she did have a knack for the bad cop routine. Though I didn't mind; it made a change for me to be the good cop, kind of refreshing.

34

For some reason traffic was light that day, and we made it to Amnicola quite quickly.

The first thing I did when we arrived was send Janet to check on Pastor Ed. He was secured in interrogation room C. A and B were occupied by a woman who'd been caught shoplifting at a convenience store and a guy Traffic had picked up walking on the hard shoulder of I-75 in torn jeans, a ratty shirt and with more than three-thousand dollars in his pocket along with a bag of heroin. It takes all sorts.

The second thing I did was call the Chief.

"I hear you've made an arrest, Lieutenant, Pastor Edward Pieczeck. That makes me very nervous. I hope you have it locked down tight."

Sheesh, so do I, I thought, and that thought made me nervous too.

I quickly brought the Chief up to speed, and then continued, "He never told us about the house. Mike

Willis and his team are there now. Someone died in that basement, Chief and I'm convinced it was Victoria Randolph. He owns the house, and he's lied to us consistently. I have his DNA, but we still have to send it to the lab for processing. He's admitted a lot, but not to the homicides. I'm going to interrogate him now. I don't think it will take much to get him to talk."

"I hope you're right, Catherine; I hope you're right."

So do I, Chief, so do I.

"There are some anomalies, though, Chief. Lieutenant Willis found some bloody footprints at the scene, and I'm thinking there's something not quite right about them. It could be that Pieczeck had an accomplice. We'll have to wait and see on that."

"Are you going for a confession?"

"I think I have to. There's plenty of evidence to suggest that the pastor is the perp, but it's all circumstantial and fairly easily explained away. A good attorney would him have out of here in minutes, but the guy is a wreck. If might be able to get him to cop a plea."

"I'm afraid a plea will not be good enough, Catherine. I have half the movers and shakers on the Mountain breathing down my neck, especially Governor Randolph. You need a confession, free and clear."

"I'll do my best. He may be a wreck, but he's got everything to lose."

"Well, get in there. Let's see if you can work your magic. Good luck, Kate." And he hung up.

Again, as I headed down to the interview room, I

could feel that twisting feeling churning away in my stomach.

I stood for a couple minutes with Janet, watching Pastor Ed through the one-way glass. She'd already gotten him a bottle of water. It stood unopened on the table next to his right hand. He was still wearing the cuffs, his hands clasped together on the tabletop; his eyes were red, puffed, his hair mussed.

"Has he said anything?" I asked, finally.

"No. He just cries and then stops and then cries some more." Janet shook her head. "It's pitiful," she added, taking a sip of coffee then looking down at her watch.

"Janet, you want to start?" I asked.

"No. Lieutenant, you start," Chief Johnston said, almost making me leap out of my skin.

I hadn't heard him come in and neither had Janet.

"Geez, Chief," I said. "Don't do that. You'll give me a heart attack."

He smiled, a rare occurrence in itself, then said, "You're only going to get one shot at this, Catherine. If he lawyers up... You did Mirandize him, I assume?"

"That I did, Chief, and I recorded it, just to be sure."

He nodded and smiled again.

Wow, two in a row.

"Okay, Janet," I said. "Let me have the file, please."

She handed me not one file, but three. I laid them on the table, opened the Randolph file and flipped through the images, again noting the minimal amount of blood found around the body. I nodded to myself, gathered my thoughts, and then the three files, stepped into the small room and sat down opposite the pastor.

He looked up at me. His eyes were wet, his bottom lip trembling; it was freaking pitiful.

"Detective, this is all a mistake. I didn't kill anyone—"

"Stop," I said, interrupting him.

He looked startled.

"Edward Pieczeck," I said quietly. "I must inform you that this interview is being recorded. Do you understand?"

He nodded, then whispered, "Yes, I understand."

I then read the date, time, etc., for the record and, read him his rights again, and asked him if he wanted his attorney present. He hesitated, then declined, and I had to wonder why. He was in more trouble than he knew. I glanced up at the one-way glass and shrugged.

"So you think this is all a mistake?" I said.

He nodded vigorously, then said, "I had extra-marital affairs, yes. To that sin I humbly confess. I did, but that's not a crime. As God is my witness, I did not commit murder. I should not be here, like this." He held up his cuffed wrists.

I stood, took them off him, then sat down again.

He was drenched in sweat. His shirt, a pink button-down, once stiff with starch, was a wrinkled rag. Dark circles of sweat had formed under his armpits.

"Do you own the property at 221 Baker Avenue in Red Bank?" I asked.

"Yes. Yes. I bought it when the neighborhood was starting to change. It was a foreclosure. I got a real deal on it and was able to pay cash. I just wanted a place to get away... and..." he stuttered.

"You wanted a place where you could play your games, and... kill?"

"*No!*" he yelled. "I'm telling you I didn't kill anyone!" He looked down at his hands.

"Pastor," I said, "we found blood evidence in your basement. Someone died horribly down there."

I opened the file and laid out the pictures of Victoria, Meryl Dilly, and Lucille Benedict.

"Oh, my God," Pastor Ed muttered.

"These women had families, Pastor. Friends. Neighbors and people who cared about them. Now they are gone. They must have suffered terribly, all of them. How did you feel, Pastor, as you smashed their heads and faces, over and over and—"

"*I didn't hit anyone!*" he shouted, rising to his feet, his hands curled into fists on the tabletop, supporting his weight. "I didn't do this! I could never do this!"

He stood upright, then leaned forward over the table. I didn't move, not an inch. His hands were trembling as he pushed the pictures away, and then he sat down again, looked down at the table, took several deep breaths then looked up at me.

"I was having an affair with Meryl, yes," he said quietly. "It had been going on for almost two years."

He paused then continued, "Lucille, may God bless and keep her, we had the same tastes, the same desires. Both of them were willing participants. They signed their contracts. It was just sex. That was all."

Contracts? I thought. *What the hell is that about?*

But I didn't interrupt him. Now that the door was open, even if was only a crack, I wanted to keep him talking.

"And what about Victoria?" I said. "That's her blood in your basement, isn't it?" I took a deep breath and folded my hands in front of me.

"No, it can't be. She hadn't signed a contract," he stuttered.

"Contract?" I leaned forward.

"A dominant-submissive contract. All my partners signed a contract. It was part of the game. Part of the role-playing. Victoria hadn't signed hers yet. She wanted something in exchange, and I was working on it," he blubbered. "Oh, God."

"What was that? What did she want?"

"She wanted to buy a piece of property in Memphis. I told her I'd front her the money, but then she'd owe me. We were negotiating the terms." His cheeks burned red.

"Is that what you were doing when you killed her?" I asked. "Negotiating the terms?"

He sighed, his shoulders drooped, his chin dropped to his chest, and he whispered, "No. I didn't kill her. You've got to believe me."

"I'm sorry, Pastor, but that's not going to happen. You see, we have your video camera and the memory card. There are recordings on it of you engaging in sexual acts with Meryl Dilly in your house at 221 Baker Avenue. One is time-stamped between twelve-twenty-three and two-twelve on Tuesday afternoon. She died less than two hours later. Her husband was away on business. You were the last person to see her alive. What do you have to say about that, Pastor?"

He just shook his head and said, "I didn't kill her. I didn't kill anyone."

"By your own admission, you were also the last person to see Lucille Benedict alive. Look, Pastor Ed," I said gently, pleading with him. "Just tell me what happened. If the sex got too rough and there was an accident, we can work it out. Believe me, it wouldn't be the first time that something like that has happened. You got excited; she tried to stop you, but... If it was an accident, it's better to admit it now, while you still can."

Holy cow. What am I thinking? How the hell can you accidentally beat three people to death with a crowbar? Oh well, it was worth a shot... And where the hell is that crowbar?

"*No, no no!*" he yelled, interrupting the thought.

"Fine," I snapped. "So, you beat them to death to cover up a sexual act gone wrong."

"*NO!*" He began to sob.

"Then if you didn't kill them, who did? Who else has access to that house, Pastor? Who else could have lured Victoria there and then killed her?"

I watched his expression change. The man was a chameleon. He sat a little more upright, put his shoulders back, wiped his eyes on his shirt sleeves, narrowed them, thought for a minute.

"No one. I told you, I have the only key, except for the one under the mat." His voice was quiet, controlled.

It was then I had a sudden thought, one I should have had much earlier.

"What about Martin Butterworth? Did he know about the house?"

"Well, yes. He did some work on it when I purchased it, but—"

"Did he know about the key?" I asked.

"I... I don't think so. I don't know how he could."

"Did he know why you purchased the house?"

He slowly shook his head, then said, "No, I kept that to myself, but..."

"But what, Pastor?"

"He could have followed me, I suppose."

That, I would have to look into. I changed course.

"So who is the woman your neighbor saw coming and going late at night?" I asked.

He looked up at me and shrugged.

"I don't know." His demeanor changed yet again. He began to cry and howl, "I don't know, I don't know," over and over again.

"Pastor, if you are covering for your wife, we'll find out. You have to tell us, and it would be better for you if you did so now. You're not helping anybody by covering for her."

Another change, he became self-righteous. "Shelly knows nothing about it. I made sure of that," he snapped.

It was like he expected some kind of approval for keeping his kinky affairs secret from his wife.

"How many women from your church *have* you been sleeping with?" I was almost afraid to hear the answer.

"Over the past few years, just the women you..."

"Just the women who are dead?" I said. "I don't believe you."

"And... Karen Silver," he muttered.

Now, I had to admit, I didn't see that one coming.

His chin was on his chest again. I turned and looked toward the mirror, my eyebrows raised in surprise.

"Karen Silver? And how long has that been going on?"

"Years, five, six, a long time." He looked at the palms of his hands. His breath hitched in his throat as he choked the sobs back. "I think I want my lawyer now, please."

I knew what was happening to him. I'd seen it so many times before. The initial shock was wearing off, and he'd just realized he was out of his depth and in it for the long haul. It had suddenly come home to Pastor Edward Pieczeck that he was in big trouble and he wasn't equipped to handle it. This was real. He could pray and make deals with the Almighty all he wanted, but that wasn't going to help him one bit here in the real world. He needed a good attorney.

"All right, Pastor," I said, rising to my feet. "You get one phone call." I grabbed the files and left the room.

I entered the observation room to find Janet staring at me with her mouth wide open.

"Close that," I said, "before something nasty flies in."

"Oh, my God," she said, drawing out the words. "Karen Silver? I wouldn't have guessed that.""That's exactly what I thought. I think we need to go talk to her again. She was very insistent that we focus on Marty Butterworth. She obviously knows more than she's letting on..." and suddenly, an image of those two bloody footprints popped into my head.

What size did Mike say they were? Nine-and-a-half? I tried to remember what size shoes Karen Silver had been wearing when we interviewed her, but I hadn't taken that much notice. *Still, judging by the size of her, that sounds about right.*

I looked at Chief Johnston and raised my eyebrows quizzically.

"Fine," he said. "You can hold Pieczeck for forty-eight hours, and then you have to charge him with something or let him go. Do what you have to, but I need a result, and quickly." He turned to go, then changed his mind, turned again and said, "Before you go, Lieutenant, I need to talk to you. In my office, in say, ten minutes."

It was said in a casual manner, but I thought there might be an underlying menace rippling away beneath it.

35

"What is it, Chief?" I asked warily as I took my seat in front of his desk

"That reporter, Clemont Rhodes showed up again. He was asking for you, but I had him brought here, to my office," he said as he steepled his forefingers and placed them on the tip of his chin.

"I haven't spoken to him or anyone else," I said firmly.

"I didn't say you did. But he told me something very disturbing. Did you know he's been following your every move for the last week? No, I can tell by the look on your face that you didn't. Be that as it may, he observed you entering the house on Baker Avenue on Wednesday evening, illegally. He's insisting that he gets an exclusive or he's going to run with the story... Catherine, we can't have that."

"Sir, I had probable cause."

"You didn't have probable cause until after you went into his house."

"It was a house he failed to mention when I initially interviewed him," I said. "I had him under surveillance, as we agreed. He led me to the house. I thought it must be the Randolph crime scene. I was also concerned that he might be holding someone hostage in there, another victim. So I entered the property. I was right, the basement was a bloodbath and probably where Victoria Randolph died."

I thought it sounded like a solid defense. But I knew I didn't have a damn leg to stand on; if the Chief decided to throw the book at me, well, I'd be screwed.He put the forefingers to his lips and looked at me, contemplating me and the situation, I was sure.

"Hmm... That's extremely thin, Catherine. Still, it seems you were right so, as I've said before, I'll back your play. Talk to that reporter. Tell him you'll give him what he wants. Now get out of here. Go catch me a killer. I really don't think it's the pastor, do you?"

Inwardly, I shook my head. *The old bastard really does have my back. Wow!*

"Perhaps not," I said. "Thank you, sir. I will."

He smiled at me—it was kind of scary; he never smiles, ever—and said, "I know you will."

So, in a daze, and with a mental sigh of relief, I thanked him for his support and left his office, and almost ran to my own.

I buzzed Janet and asked her to join me.

"You okay, LT?" she asked as she came into my office.

"Yes, why, what's up?"

"Pastor Ed called his lawyer. They took him to holding. He'll have a few hours to sit and stew there," Janet replied.

"He'll have exactly forty-eight hours, unless we can gather enough evidence to charge him with something... He didn't call his wife?"

"NOPE." She shook her head. "What did the Chief want? Anything I can help with?"

"He just wanted an update, and yes, there is something you can do: find out all you can about Karen Silver. That relationship is one hell of a poke in the ribs. I *wasn't* expecting it. Maybe I should have seen it, but I didn't."

I pulled my hair back from my face. "And get the property info on Pastor Ed's love shack. I'm going to head home for the day. My body has run out of gas. I need to sleep. We'll talk to Ms. Silver in the morning when we know a little more about her."

"You got it. I'll have everything on your desk first thing tomorrow." She nodded. "Anything else?"

"Yes, actually. Find out what you can about a local reporter named Clemont Rhodes, but keep it under your hat. Okay?" I winked. "Oh, and if he should show up here, or calls, tell him I'll talk to him tomorrow... On second thought, let's head him off at the pass. Here's his card." I dug in my desk drawer, found it, and handed it to her. "Give him a call now and tell him I'll be in touch and that I'll have something for him soon."

"Sure thing," Janet said with a devilish glint in her eyes.

"Thank you, Janet. You're doing a great job," I said. And I meant it.

She blushed. "Thanks, LT. I appreciate it." And she left.

I stayed at my desk for a few more minutes, then shut everything down and left my office, taking with me a short list of phone calls I could make once I got home. I pulled into my parking space in front of my apartment, got out of the car, and then, via my peripheral vision, I spotted a silver Kia sitting in a fire zone in front of a store at the Minnie Mall just across the greenway on East Brainerd Road, and my paranoia kicked in. I could see there was a woman behind the wheel, and it looked like she was talking on the phone.

I shook my head.

Silver cars. I'm seeing them everywhere. Pastor Ed drives a silver Audi. His wife, Shelly, drives its twin. Some unknown woman, maybe the pastor's wife, or maybe Karen Silver, has been visiting the playhouse in a silver car. No, Ms. Silver's car is a black Honda... or is it? And now there's a woman parked in a towaway zone in a silver car across the street.

I looked around my own parking lot and noticed there was a silver Jeep, a silver Honda CRV, a silver E-class Mercedes, and a gray Volkswagen.

"Geez, Kate," I muttered as I inserted the key in my front door, "get over it... Gray doesn't count."

I opened the door and stepped inside, slipped the key ring over my finger, and closed the door. I set the dead-bolt and the security chain, then I dropped my shoulder bag on the kitchen table, took my badge and Glock from my belt and laid them down next to it, poured myself a glass of wine, eased down on the couch, and began to mull over the events of the day... and then I fell asleep, glass in hand; fortunately, it was already empty.

IT WAS JUST after ten o'clock that night when Doc called.

"Damn it, Doc. If I were married, my husband would think we were having an affair. Can't you ever call during normal business hours?" I grumbled.

"What are those?" he asked with a chuckle. "Look, I don't have time to talk endlessly, but your hunch was right. The blood spatter in the basement does indeed belong to Victoria Randolph. She was killed at the pastor's house." He cleared his throat. "We need a swab from him to match it with the DNA found on Meryl Dilly, as soon as you can please, Kate."

"Damn it, Doc. I forgot. I already have one. It's in my bag. I'll drop it by on my way into the office in the morning. How did you get the DNA report back so quickly? It's only been a few hours."

"I didn't. I matched her blood type. She's A-negative. It's rare, but it's not definitive; it's close enough, though, and would have been enough to convict back in the good old days before DNA. I'll have the profiles expedited, which means they should be available... when they are available." He chuckled.

"Pastor Ed already confessed to having affairs with

Meryl and Lucille," I said. "He hadn't gotten around to Victoria yet, not sexually, anyway, but he was working on it." I yawned.

Doc continued, "We need a match for the foreign blood on Meryl Dilly. If it isn't his, the killer is still out there."

"True," I said, "and maybe not just one killer."

I told him about the bloody footprints.

"I think I have enough to get a warrant," I said. "I'll grab his personal and work computers. These sexual predators like to share their experiences online. Maybe Mike's people will find something there."

"Good luck, Detective. We'll talk again soon."

"Good night, Doc. I'll not forget to drop off the swab."

I checked my watch. It was just after ten-thirty, way too late to request a warrant. Even I wouldn't dare call a judge at that time of night, not even my good friend, Henry Strange. It would have to wait until morning, even if it was a Saturday.

36

The following morning I woke up before the sun, slipped into a pair of sweats, tied my hair back in a ponytail, grabbed my keys and my pocket mace and headed out for a run, a big no-no, and I'd made the mistake before, much to my regret. I was supposed to go armed, always, but the damn Glock weighed a ton. The mace would have to do, not that I expected to have to use it.

I checked the towaway zone. The silver car was no longer there, not that I really expected it to be, but paranoia is a strange bedfellow and one I never chose to ignore.

Without Sadie Mae to slow me down, I was able to push myself a little harder than usual, and it felt good to feel my lungs burning, my thighs tightening with each stride. I was hot and sweaty by the time I got back to my apartment.

The sun was up, just over the horizon when I caught

sight of a cardinal flitting through the trees. My mom always said if you saw a cardinal, it meant there were angels close by. Whether it was the angels that made me turn and check the towaway zone once more, or just blind luck, I can't say, but the silver car was back.

I didn't hesitate; I leaped over the fence and ran flat out across the greenway... and she saw me. I heard her start the engine and then she reversed out of the parking spot and peeled away.

I swear I broke the record for the sixty-yard dash. I knew there was no way I could catch her, but I wanted her plate number. Fortunately, the early morning traffic on East Brainerd Road was heavier than usual, and she had to wait for a gap. I ran across the parking lot and was just in time to catch a glimpse of the plate. Unfortunately, I managed to get only the first three digits of the number before she disappeared at high speed heading toward Gunbarrel Road.

The three digits were LS8.

THE FIRST THING I did when I arrived at the PD that Saturday morning was buzz Janet and ask her to do a DMV search for a silver Kia with LS8 as the first three digits of the registration. Then I called Chief Johnston.

"Chief, I just wanted to let you know I'm going to get a warrant for the Pieczecks' computers. His wife has access to both. Guys like Pastor Ed like to share their experiences, and I suspect that she might be involved somehow, and she might pull a Hillary on us and BleachBit the drives."

"That's what I like about you, Catherine," he said. "You think of everything."

"Err, not hardly," I said, thinking about the damn swab I still hadn't dropped off at the forensic center.

"What else do you need, Lieutenant?"

"Nothing, sir, that I can think of right now."

"Good. Call me when you have something."

He hung up the phone, and I made the call to Judge Isaac Walker, whom I knew was on duty that weekend, and asked for search warrants for the Pieczeck home and the Church of the Savior. Probable cause wasn't a problem as we already had the pastor in custody. The judge told me he'd prepare the warrants, and I could pick them up whenever I was ready. I told him I'd be by within the hour.

37

"**G**ood morning, LT," Janet said, bright and breezy as she bopped into my office, her red hair was pulled back in a ponytail, two large Mickey D's coffees in hand.

Wow, did I ever have that kind of energy, and if I did, where the hell did it go?

"You're not going to believe what I have to tell you," she said, with a giggle, as she set the coffees down on the desk and sat down.

"I probably should have called you, but I knew you were tired, and I didn't want to disturb you. Anyway, about twenty minutes after you left yesterday, Mrs. Pieczeck arrived downstairs. She asked to talk to her husband, so I escorted her to an interview room, and she and the good Pastor had a long talk."

Janet looked down for a moment before lifting her head and meeting my eyes. "I... well, I couldn't help myself. I watched, and I recorded the conversation... Yes,

I know we can't use it, but I thought maybe you'd like to see it. He, like, spilled his guts, LT. He told her everything, about his affairs, his perversions, the little house in Red Bank, everything, but he insisted he didn't kill anyone. He cried, too... like, a lot."

Oh, how I would have liked to have watched it with her.

"So," I said. "What did she say?"

"Just what you might expect?" She smirked and raised her eyebrows. "She told him goodbye."

I sat back in my chair, sipped my coffee, thinking, then said, "You know, Janet, you did good, recording that conversation. I'll look at it later, but right now, I'm thinking that if she didn't know about the pastor's secret life, it rules her out as the killer's accomplice."

"Killer?" she asked. "So you don't think it's the pastor?"

I shook my head.

"Wow! If it's not him, then who is it?"

"I have an idea who it might be, but I'm not quite sure."

She smiled, looked slyly at me, and said, "Yes, you are, and I think I know who it is."

"Oh, you think so? Do tell."

"Karen Silver! It has to be."

"Go on," I said, smiling indulgently at her.

"It might take a while."

"We have time."

"Well, you had me run a background on her," she

said, flipping through the screens on her iPad. "The lady has quite a past."

She glanced up at me. I sipped my coffee, said nothing.

"Karen Lyn Silver," she continued. "She's forty-two years old. Divorced. Graduated from Columbia College in Chicago with a degree in Communications. Got a job with the Diocese of Chicago where she worked for almost ten years... until she was let go."

Janet looked at me, smiling. "She was having an affair with the spiritual director at the diocese home office, a guy named Marcus Burkowski. Seems they both were members at the same gym and worked out a lot... together."

She paused, looked at me, sipped her coffee, then continued.

"Anyway, they had an affair and it went bad. He dumped her, and she must have gotten totally pissed off, wouldn't accept it, because she was served with not just one, but two restraining orders by Burkowski and the Diocese of Chicago. Apparently, she began stalking him, kept showing up outside his home, at the gym, at the church on Sunday. She even threw a rock through his office window."

"So she's got a temper, then?" I felt a knot growing in the pit of my stomach.

"Uh, yeah, but I'm not done yet."

"Curiouser and curiouser," I said. "Please continue, my little mouse."

"*What?*" she screwed up her whole face as if totally confused.

"Nothing," I said. "I was just quoting *Alice in Wonderland.* Go on. Tell me more."

"Well," she said, a little less enthusiastically, "she moved to Chattanooga about ten years ago and got the job at the Church of the Savior. Since then she's been a good girl: her record is clean... Oh, but you're gonna love this: she owns a silver Kia, registration number LS8 6RP."

I nodded grimly. "She's stalking me," I said thoughtfully.

"*What?*"

"That car was parked near my apartment last night, and again this morning. I ran after it, but she was too quick, but I did get those first three digits. That's why I had you do the search. I didn't know it was her, but now I'm not surprised," I said. "Seeing as how she has a history of obsessive behavior. And I have, after all, taken Karen Silver's lover away from her."

"But you didn't say anything about it?" she said.

I shrugged. "There was nothing to say, not until we knew. Look, Pastor Ed admitted to having an affair with her, and Meryl Dilly and Lucille Benedict—"

"But not with Victoria," Janet interrupted me.

"No, but he was working on it," I said, thinking out loud. "And the more lovers Pastor Ed added to his harem, the less time he'd have for Karen, right? She wouldn't like that, would she? And if she has OCD— obsessive compulsive disorder—and we know she does, I wonder if she decided to remedy the situation?"

Janet nodded enthusiastically. "Yeah, that, and plus, she works out, a lot, as does Pastor Ed. They are both members of the Fit for Life gym. How convenient it must have been for them to meet up there, get sweaty, and then slip on over to the little playhouse on Baker Avenue for some S&M... G-ross!"

"So—" I didn't get the rest of the thought out because she interrupted me.

"Oh, my God," she yelled. "They were all members of Fit for Life: Ed, Karen, Meryl Dilly, Lucille Benedict, and Victoria Randolph."

I already knew that, but now it took on a much greater significance.

"She killed those three women," I said thoughtfully. "But the question is, did she kill them because Pastor Ed told her to, or did she do it of her own volition?"

And then I had another thought. "But if she killed Victoria Randolph in that basement, who helped her move the body? Fit and strong she might be, but she sure as hell didn't move that body on her own."

"C'mon." I stood up, grabbed my iPad and car keys, and headed out the door.

Janet, taken totally by surprise, jumped up, flipped the cover of her iPad closed, and followed me.

"Hey," she said, hurrying to keep up with me. "What's the hurry? Where are we going?"

"First to drop off a swab. Then to get the warrants

and then to the church. Call Chief Wilbur and have him meet us there with backup."

"You're going to arrest her?" she asked, dumb-founded. "Do we have enough?"

"We will when I'm done with her," I said, a little more confidently than I felt.

38

Chief Wilbur arrived at the Church of the Savior just a minute or two before we did. I drove around back and... the parking lot was empty: no other cars, either in the front or the back. Nada.

I sat for a moment, thinking, *Where the hell is she? She must know by now that we've arrested the pastor. Where would she run to... She wouldn't. She'd want to finish the job... If there was another... And if he's in custody... Then he couldn't... But who?*

I closed my eyes, mentally scanned through the crime scene photos... *Oh, my God! Got it: number four.*

I hopped out of the car and briefed Chief Wilbur on what I planned to do. I had a warrant for the Pieczeck home. So that would be my first option.

The second part of my plan was for Wilbur to find Karen Silver.

It was all a bit of a Hail Mary, but what the hell. If I was right, we were dealing with an extremely dangerous woman and, somehow, we had to get her out of circulation before she killed again... because I had the creepiest feeling that I was next on her list... after Shelly Pieczeck, that is.

"I'm not liking this one bit, Chief," I said. "Janet and I will head on over to the Pieczeck home and serve the warrant. In the meantime, you need to try to locate Karen Silver. I'm thinking her house, the gym, or she's still stalking me and watching us right now."

Janet and Wilbur involuntarily glanced over their shoulders.

"Chief, if and when you or your men find her, you're to sit tight and call me. Do *not* approach her, is that understood?"

Wilbur nodded. "I'm to call you if I find her. Good enough, Lieutenant."

We talked for several more minutes then Wilbur went to meet with his crew, gave them their instructions, then got into his car and drove away, presumably to Silver's home.

Janet and I headed to the Pieczeck home where I hoped to find Shelly Pieczeck still in one piece... and alive, hiding out, ashamed to show her face in public after her husband's arrest.

Or throwing his things in the trash, more likely, I thought.

I turned the cruiser off the highway, through the unmarked entrance to The Cloisters, onto the gravel driveway, and then on to the electronic gate... It was open, smashed, hanging askew. One of the hinges had been torn out of the brick post on the right side, and there were chunks of brickwork scattered on the driveway. As we drove past the gate, I glanced at Janet. Her face was white, a stark contrast against her red hair.

"This isn't good, LT," she said, shaking her head.

"Not good at all, Sergeant. Be prepared, okay? Check your weapon."

She did.

The cruiser's tires sang a tune on the cobblestone pathway as we continued driving toward the house. We rounded the corner and approached the ugly, bock-shaped home from the east. At the south side, a silver Kia Optima with a badly damaged front end was parked out front next to a beat-up, red Chevy pick-up truck.

I parked at the west side of the house, in front of the garage, out of sight of the front door.

"I think we have ourselves a situation, Janet," I said as I looked sideways at her. "You okay?"

She gulped. "You don't think we should wait for backup, LT?"

I shook my me head. "No. If Karen Silver's inside, Shelly Pieczeck's in big trouble. She's number four in that photo with Pastor Ed, remember?"

She nodded.

I grabbed my phone and called Wilbur. "She's here, at the Pieczeck home. We're going in. Come as quick as you can, Chief." And I hung up.

"Vests," I said.

We exited the vehicle and donned our body armor. I set my iPhone to record, stuffed it into one of my vest pockets, and then we drew our weapons and headed to the front door. I placed my hand on the hood of the Kia. *Still warm; maybe we aren't too late.*

Believing a crime to be in progress, I didn't bother to ring the doorbell. This wasn't a social visit.

Janet and I stood on either side of the door, backs to the wall, weapons drawn. I looked at her, took two steps forward, turned and nodded. She grabbed the knob, turned it, and I slammed the door open with a well-placed kick.

We burst into the room... Shelly Pieczeck was sitting on the center of the couch, her face ashen, her hands clasped in her lap as if praying. Karen Silver was sitting next to her.

"Lieutenant," Shelly Pieczeck said, half rising to her feet. "Oh, thank God you're here. I've been trying to convince Karen here that it's over between me and Edward, that I know all about what's been going on and that I've already instructed my attorney to file for divorce, but she doesn't believe me."

Karen Silver reached over and grabbed Shelly Pieczeck's wrist. "Shut up and sit still, bitch. I'll do the talking. Lieutenant, why don't you put those nasty guns away. You're scaring my friend."

Karen was a mess, dark bags under her eyes, hair unkempt, and she had several nasty-looking cuts on both hands.

I nodded to Janet, and we holstered our weapons. We had to try and get Karen away from Pieczeck before we could make a move.

I wonder where the hell Marty Butterworth is, and where the hell is Wilbur and his men; they'd better get here and damn soon.

"Karen, we'd like to talk to you," I said calmly.

Her eyes were glazed over. "Screw you, bitch... and your little girly friend. You think I don't know what you're here for? Not to talk, that's for sure. You're here to arrest me." Her voice was calm, her demeanor relaxed, her eyes mere slits that glinted in the artificial light.

I had a sudden feeling it was all about to go sideways. I shifted my weight onto my left foot and hooked my thumb in my belt, an inch in front of my Glock.

"No, Karen," I lied. "Why would you say that?"

It was now obvious to me that either she was on something or her mind had slipped and her brain was on the dark side of nowhere. *This isn't going to end well.*

"*You took him away from me,*" she screeched, so suddenly and so loudly I just about jumped out of my skin. "And now..." she said, all calm and serene again, "you've come for me too. You want to keep us apart, but you can't because I'm going to be his bride. It's destiny, don't you see?" she said dreamily. "You just have to understand, that's all, and then you'll see... you'll understand God's plan for Edward and me, *and it doesn't include you, you slut,*" she screamed in Shelly Pieczeck's ear.

"Understand what, Karen?"

"It's part of my job," she continued in the sing-song voice.

"Part of your job?" I asked gently. "What job? Was it your job to kill those women? Did Pastor Ed ask you to kill them?"

Shelly Pieczeck gasped.

Karen's eyes seemed to clear a little. She blinked rapidly. It was like she'd been daydreaming, but when she heard the word "kill," it was a trigger and brought her out of it.

"No, he didn't ask me to kill them. He had nothing to do with it. How could he? He's a man of God. It was just... something I had to do."

"Why, Karen? What had they done to you?" I asked.

I glanced at Janet. She was standing rigid, transfixed by what she was hearing. I looked at Shelly Pieczeck; she was trembling.

Karen's eyes flickered rapidly, gazed here, there around the room, at me, at Janet, Shelly, as if she were searching for something. *Maybe she's looking for Marty.*

"I don't expect you to understand," she snarled. "I love him, you see. And loves me too. He said he was my protector, my master, my God. And like our heavenly father, he would create me anew."

Holy cow. Are you serious?

"God tells us to love our enemies, as we love our friends," she said. "And I did, for a while; all of them, with all my heart, until I realized that they were just using him, taking advantage of him."

"Karen," I said ever so gently, trying not to spook her. "What happened to your hands? How did you get those cuts?"

She held her free hand out in front of her and admired it.

I'd known other detectives who talked about seeing the face of a killer shifting, darkening, transforming from a normal person into something abnormal like they were possessed. I'd never seen it myself. Not until that moment.

"Those women didn't have a real desire to serve Edward. We were his servants, his handmaidens. He was the master. We followed his commands inside the fortress and out. It was the way it had to be but… they weren't… doing… that," she said. Her eyes narrowed and she licked her lips.

Oh, my God. A forty-three-year-old handmaiden. It can't get any better than that.

"The fortress?"

"The house on Baker Avenue. You know what I'm talking about. I saw you there yesterday, talking to that nosey old skank next door. And you took Edward away from me," she said snarling.

Fortress? That nasty little two-bedroom property? Yuck!

"I had to, Karen. You know that, don't you? That house is where Victoria Randolph died, isn't it? Would you like to tell me about that?"

"Yes. Yes, yessss," she shouted, standing up and waving her arms like the sails on a windmill. "I killed her.

Killed Meryl Dilly too, and Lucille. Meryl wanted Edward all for herself. That was against the rules. But then she started seeing Edward by herself. I saw the videos. Who did she think she was?"

"How did you see the videos?"

"I have a key. When I couldn't find Edward, when he wasn't answering his phone, I'd go to the fortress. No one was supposed to enter without his permission, but I did. I couldn't help myself. I'd park outside the house if I saw his car and wait for him and Meryl or Lucille to leave."

"Lucille went to the fortress, too?"

Karen looked at me as if I was stupid. "Edward would call, and we would come. It was the way of things."

"How come you had a key? Did Edward give it to you?"

"I..." she drew the word out, swept her arms out in front of her, "am his principle handmaiden. I know everything about him. I know where he is... always, every day and every night. I know his schedule, his finances, his likes and dislikes. I am the gatekeeper. I was the first one, the first of his handmaidens and... And I made a copy of the key under the mat, you silly bitch." She dropped her chin to her chest, her arms spread wide, "He was ready to replace me with... one of *them*."

She began to cry.

"It's okay, Karen," I said. "I'm here to help. You can tell me everything."

"I didn't mean for him to get the blame. He didn't know," she said as if I wasn't there. "I didn't think anyone would ever figure out what happened. I went to talk to

Meryl at her home to try to convince her to stop seeing Edward. She was married, you know. She was committing adultery—a terrible sin—willingly and without remorse."

And killing her isn't? I tried not to let any negative emotion show on my face.

Karen continued, "I thought if I appealed to her woman to woman that she'd see what I was trying to say. She had a husband. I didn't. But she wouldn't listen to me. She laughed at me. She laughed while I cried."

"What did you hit her with, Karen?"

"I had a crowbar in my car." She smiled. "That was lucky. She told me to leave, that she was going to tell Edward. I almost did, leave. But the Lord intervened, spoke to me, showed me the way and the awesome power of his will." She said it with her eyes closed, arms held out slightly from her sides, palms out, like Christ welcoming his children, as if she was reliving a dream.

Her eyes snapped open. "I went to my car, took the crowbar from the trunk, and returned to the house. She hadn't bothered to lock the door. I walked right back in and..." She shrugged.

It was as if she had gotten caught stealing a second slice of chocolate cake when she was supposed to be on a diet. My mouth fell open.

"What about Victoria Randolph?" I asked her again. I had to force the words out.

Shelly Pieczeck tried to wiggle away, but Karen pointed at her and said, "Don't move. I'm not done with you yet."

Shelly whimpered.

Karen's face became serious and angry. "Victoria Randolph," her voice changed to a flinty rasp, "was not one of the chosen. She spurned Edward. For even the smallest shred of attention, Edward would gush over her. He became weak, gave her a job in the office so he could watch me suffer her barbs. He said jealousy is a sin, and that I was being punished for it, and that I needed to learn humility. So he planted that tease in front of me so I'd have to look at her."

She looked down at her hands, began to nervously pick at her fingers. She chewed her bottom lip as she stepped slightly away from the couch. I raised my hands so she would see I was not going to make any sudden moves.

"I was being punished for loving him. She was being rewarded for using him. I saw he had a contract drawn up for her that included the exchange of certain favors. He would give her money to buy an apartment building in Memphis or somewhere, and she would sit at his feet for an hour. Can you believe that? And he was willing to go for it. To have a woman like a Jezebel, sitting at his feet." Tears flooded her eyes. "He never did that for me. The things I did for him, the horrors I endured for him."

I didn't dare speak for fear of ending her rant.

"I told Victoria," she continued, "that Edward wanted her to meet him at the fortress. I told her that he had some paperwork for her to sign, that he was closing on a piece of property. Ha, the silly bitch ate it up. Poor

Victoria, she had no clue what it was like to be told no. She found out soon enough."

"How did you get her to go down to the basement?"

"It was easy. I just left the lights on down there and the door open. The radio was on playing some nice music. Of course, she thought it was for her. And it was, in a way, but not in the way she thought... Oh, don't be so shocked, Detective."

Karen Silver rolled her eyes and then continued, "Victoria was willing to cheat on her husband. It was early in the morning, just after midnight. She crept out while Darby was still asleep—you see, I knew they slept in separate rooms. She told me so. She was always sitting at her desk," she said and waved a hand at an imaginary desk, "bragging to me about how she didn't have to screw Darby anymore, and how she didn't have to work, but couldn't say no to Edward when he offered her the position. She didn't think I knew about their plan. Bitch! She didn't know I was the gatekeeper and everything that Edward did had to go through me first."

"How did you get the body out of the basement, Karen?"

"Marty Butterworth helped me, naturally. Edward was the only person ever to do anything for him. He worshipped Edward. He would do anything to help Edward, to keep his secret from getting out... And, of course, for his reward." She put back her shoulders, pushed her ample bosom forward, and slid her hands down the curve of her hips.

I felt exhausted, from the endless tension, but I

couldn't let my guard down. She began to pace back and forth, babbling on about her undying love for Edward and how she didn't mean for him to get hurt, be blamed for what she had to do.

"I'd never wanted anything bad to happen to him. He is my master, and I'm here to do his will."

That was when I saw it for what it really was. I couldn't help it; I rolled my eyes as I listened to her confess her undying love for a man who enjoyed abusing her, tormenting her not just physically but also mentally.

"Karen? Karen, you didn't tell me anything about Lucille Benedict. What happened to her?"

"Lucille? Oh, that little cheater. She was screwing Edward, too. I actually liked her," Karen admitted reluctantly. "But she was *so* needy."

"What?" I said, trying to control my sarcasm. "She was needy?"

"Yes. You see, she was always trying to change the rules. She succeeded in persuading Edward to go to her house. That was a strict no-no."

"Why is that?" I asked. I really didn't care, but I had to keep her talking.

"Because we were only supposed to be with Edward at the fortress. If it was at anyone's home, it was they who were in control, not the master."

Good grief, this woman has some screws loose.

"I followed Edward, you know," she said, distantly, staring down at some doodad on the side table. "I always followed him. One night he led me right to Lucille's doorstep *knowing* that they were breaking the rules, *his rules,*" she snapped. "If the rules don't apply to all, then you have anarchy, don't you? She screwed him, many times, right there in her own house. I know she did. I could hear them. It made me so mad. I almost burst in on both of them and... Well, all I can say is that she deserved to die for her transgressions... and, she did." The woman actually smiled at me.

"So why are you here, Karen?" I asked. "Why his house?"

"To finish what I started, of course. When my master Edward gets out of jail—he didn't do anything wrong you know—he's going to need me, going to marry me. And his bitch wife here is in the way... of our happiness."

I'd heard enough. I turned my head, looked at Janet, and nodded. She drew her weapon.

"Karen Silver," I said, "I'm placing you under arrest. Please put your hands up where I can see them."

"Oh, no! Wait! You can't. You don't understand!" She began to sob as she backed up next to a side table. She had her hands up, but she wasn't complying. She was stalling.

"Karen, I'm not going to ask you again," I said gently. "We have the place surrounded. You won't get out of here."

"That's okay," Karen said.

Not a good sign.

"Turn around and put your hands behind your back. Now!" I shouted, taking my cuffs from my belt.

Karen looked at me, then at Janet, then at Mrs. Pieczeck, and then she turned slowly around to face the side table. But instead of putting her hands behind her back, she bent down and grabbed something on the floor beside the couch and spun around, grabbing Shelly's arm and yanking her up off the couch.

Karen was now standing behind Shelly holding one of the biggest crowbars I'd ever seen; it had to have been at least three feet long.

The murder weapon?

"Don't come near me!" she screamed, holding Shelly by the collar with one hand, and waving the crowbar over her head with the other. Her face contorted, her eyelids flickering wildly.

Shelly Pieczeck struggled frantically to get away.

"Karen, stop this!" I said, loudly. "We can work this out if you'll just put the crowbar down."

"You'll have to kill me." She was defiant.

"You don't want that any more than we do, Karen..." I hesitated for a second, then tried to mollify her.

"Look," I said, "love makes us do stupid things. You think you are the first woman to kill for her man?" I shook my head. "Do you think you're the first woman who had a man who didn't appreciate her love?"

She blinked, stopped waving the crowbar in the air, and stood still with it suspended over her head.

"Look, I've been there, too," I continued. "I had a guy, once. I was crazy about him. But I wasn't enough. He cheated on me."

"What did you do to her. How did you *punish* her?" Karen asked as her eyes filled with tears.

"I didn't do anything to her. It wasn't her fault." I

took a deep breath. "Even if it had been her fault, what good would it have done? Then I'd look like the bad guy when I wasn't the one who cheated."

"But how else was she going to learn?"

She was on the edge, teetering. She'd lowered the crowbar a little, listening to my story. Just a few more seconds and this could all end peacefully.

"What about him? Did you punish him?" she asked.

"I broke up with him."

"You broke up with him? Then you didn't really love him. Not like I love my Edward." She shook her head. "When you love someone, you'll do anything to be with them," she said with fire in her eyes.

She let go of Shelly, grasped the crowbar in both hands, raised it over her head, and directed it at the back of Shelly Pieczeck's head.

I didn't see it coming. There was a flash of blue and white as Janet streaked by me, leaped into the air, and landed on top of Karen Silver. And then they were on the ground, struggling. Karen was without a doubt the stronger of the two, but Janet was the more limber. She managed to get her fingers onto Karen's carotid artery and apply pressure, and in seconds, it was over. The crowbar fell from her nerveless fingers, and she lapsed into unconsciousness.

I swooped in with my cuffs, snapped them onto her wrists, and just a few seconds later, she was awake again, groggy and submissive.

Shelly had retreated to a corner of the room, slid

down to the floor, and sat there, her head in her hands, shaking and crying.

And then Chief Wilbur and his officers burst into the room, weapons drawn.

"Oh, I see," he said, holstering the gun. "You don't need me then? Shame. How about him?" he asked, gesturing toward one of his officers who was holding Marty Butterworth by his arm; Butterworth's hands were cuffed behind his back.

"My men found him downstairs, in the basement," Wilbur said.

What is it with these people and basements? I wondered.

"He was waiting at the bottom of the stairs with a tarp and rubber gloves."

"Geez, she *was* going to do her in then? Good job, Chief."

"Thank you, ma'am. I think Governor Randolph will be grateful..."

"Ha," I said and laughed. I wouldn't count on it, but I wish you well anyway," I said with a wink and shook his hand. "You want to bring them to the PD on Amnicola so we can formally charge them both?"

He nodded. "You got it!"

"Thanks... and you might want to call for the EMTs. Mrs. Pieczeck looks like hell."

I shook his hand again and then walked with Janet back to my cruiser.

"Great work, Janet," I said as she opened the

passenger side door. "That was one hell of a takedown. I was about to shoot the bitch."

"Thanks. It *was*, like, intense," she said. "Hey, was that true what you were telling her about a guy? It was Harry Starke, wasn't it?"

"No," I lied. "I made it up. Let's get out of here... rookie."

39

J anet put the call in to Amnicola about the arrest of Karen Silver and Martin Butterworth, and we arrived there just in time to see a very disheveled and wrinkled Pastor Edward Pieczeck being escorted out of the holding cells. He was carrying his tie, belt, and a large brown envelope containing his personal effects.

"Pastor Ed!" I shouted. "Don't go on any long vacations, and don't leave the country. I haven't finished with you yet."

He scowled at me, then saw Karen Silver and Marty Butterworth being escorted into the holding area, in handcuffs, by two Lookout Mountain officers.

Karen saw him and for a second, their eyes locked, the pastor looked away.

"I didn't mean for it to happen!" Karen shouted. "You know I love you and that I'd never do anything to hurt you!"

He glanced back at her, his face deadpan, and then he did the worst thing he possibly could to a woman like Karen. He ignored her. He looked past her as if she wasn't there. She wilted, and I couldn't help but feel a little sorry for her.

She did love him, in her own twisted way, and so did he love her, maybe, but she was a victim, too. Not like Meryl Dilly or Lucille Benedict or the beautiful and manipulative Victoria Randolph, but Karen Silver was a victim. Pastor Edward Pieczeck was a sexual predator of the worst kind.

Oh, I know what you're thinking. You're thinking that she made her own choices, and you're right. She did, and they were bad choices, the worst, but that didn't make what had happened to her any the less sad. You think I'm soft, right? It's true. I do have a softer side, but I try to keep it well hidden.

I was just finishing my paperwork when Janet knocked on my office door and peered at me through the glass window. I waved her in.

"Hey, LT," she said. "You okay?"

"Yes, of course. Why wouldn't I be?"

"Just checking, I guess. Look, I didn't get a chance to tell you about that other guy you asked me to look into, the reporter, Clemont Rhodes," she said as she gingerly sat down on the edge of the seat in front of my desk.

"Oh, shit. I forgot all about him. What did you find out?" I sat back, stretched my arms up over my head as I yawned.

She took a piece of paper from her pocket.

"He does work for the Bugle but only as a sort of stringer. He's focused on the crime beat. And really blasts the CPD for not doing their job in his stories. Seems to me like he's trying to get the paper to hire him as a regular. I think he's looking to make a name for himself."

"Really?" I said. "Too bad I have to be the one to make it for him. I have to give him an exclusive, per Chief Johnston."

"Um, I hate to have to tell you this but," she said, hesitated, then took a deep breath and continued, "Clemont Rhodes is Captain Henry Finkle's brother-in-law." She winced as she said it.

I sat there staring at her for a moment, then said, "Okay, so you just made my frickin' day. That's just about the worst news I've had this frickin' year. Definitely the worst…"

Does Chief Johnston know that, I wonder? I bet he does: the old goat knows everything. I chewed my bottom lip. *That sneaky bastard Finkle set me up.*

I could feel my rage begin to bubble up deep in my gut. Thoughts of revenge whirled around inside my head. I was beginning to feel light-headed.

"Are you okay, LT?"

I snapped out of it, smiled at her, and nodded. "Yeah, I feel just great," I said sarcastically. "But do me a favor and keep it under your hat. I don't want Finkle to know I know, and I certainly don't want anyone to know that you know. Let's just forget we ever looked into it, okay? I'll give Rhodes a call and tell him to drop in for his exclusive on Monday. Go on home, Janet. Get some rest."

"Okay, that sounds fine, LT."

"Great," I said, smiling at her. "Look, you did an amazing job on this case. You should be proud of yourself. So, what are you going to do tonight to celebrate?"

"Well, I hadn't given it much thought, you know. I—"

"Sergeant Toliver!" Finkle shouted from my open doorway. "I just dropped by to congratulate you on your amazing work on the Randolph case. A couple of us are going out for a drink. You must come with us. We'll celebrate. You'll be the guest of honor."

"Well, Lieutenant Gazzara was the lead investigator," she said hesitantly.

"We all know what Lieutenant Gazzara's role was. But I don't think she'd deny that it couldn't have turned out the way it did if it wasn't for your contribution. Isn't that right, Gazzara?"

Finkle was loving this. He was no longer my boss, but he hadn't given up.

"That's right, *Captain*." I looked at Janet. "Go on, Janet. Go and have a good time, you deserve it. Just make sure he keeps his hands to himself."

"What do you mean by that, Gazzara?" he snapped.

"Not a thing, Chief, whoops, I mean *Captain*."

Finkle's posture stiffened.

"I know these cheapskates, Janet," I said. "You'd better grab the free drinks while you can because they won't buy you another round until you reach retirement."

Janet laughed out loud. "Okay, I will. Are you coming too?"

"Ohhhh, no." I shook my head. "I've got more work to

get done. Then I'm calling it a night. You have fun... Oh, and by the way, there's a great place called the Sorbonne, a really fun joint. Maybe you should ask Henry to take you there. It's one of your favorites, isn't that right, Captain?"

The expression on his face was a joy to behold, a mixture of surprise, anger, and embarrassment.

"I think we'll stick a little closer to home," he growled.

"See you tomorrow, then, LT," Janet said.

"Nope. Tomorrow's Sunday, and I'm going to church."

I waited until they'd all left. Then I picked up the phone and dialed a number I knew by heart. Maybe it wasn't the best idea I'd ever had, but what the hell. What did I have to lose?

"Hello?"

"Case is closed. I'd like to get my dog back."

"Aww," Lonnie said. "And we just got comfortable in the recliner. Hey, there's a COPS marathon on TV. Come on over. There's plenty of room for you on the couch."

"You got a couple of cold ones for me?" I asked, unable to hide the smile in my voice.

"Sure do. I even have a nice bottle of Merlot. I bought it just for you."

"You did? Great. Give me an hour. I need to go home, take a shower, and change clothes."

"No rush, darlin'. Take your time. We'll be here when you're ready."

I disconnected the call.

Wait... did he just call me darlin'? What was that about... Oh no, that's not happenin', I thought as I headed to the shower. *No, no, no, I'm way too busy for that kind of... any kind of serious relationship...*

Hmm, Captain Gazzara... I like the sound of that...

*****

Thank you:

I hope you enjoyed reading Victoria as much as I enjoyed writing it. If you did, I really would appreciate it if you would take just a minute to write a brief review on Amazon (just a sentence will do).

Reviews are so very important. I don't have the backing of a major New York publisher. I can't take out ads in newspapers or on TV, but you can help get the word out. I would be very grateful if you would spend just a couple of minutes and leave a review.

If you have comments or questions, you can contact me by e-mail at blair@blairhoward.com, and you can visit my website http://www.blairhoward.com.

Made in United States
North Haven, CT
17 February 2023

32751308R00189